"You don't have any say in what I do, Justin," she said softly.

"Don't I," he frowned. "If I wished, I could simply reveal your identity to the room. No one would touch you if they knew you were my wife. They wouldn't dare."

"No. You won't do that."

He chuckled, challenge in his expression and posture. "And why wouldn't I?"

"Because doing that would hurt you far more than it would hurt me."

His brow wrinkled. "And how would it possibly hurt me for the world to know my wife is the most sought after woman in the country?"

"Because I'm not just the most sought after woman in the country. I'm the most sought after *courtesan* in the country. And the reason so many men want Ria is that she was taught exotic sensual arts by a long string of talented lovers. None of which was you, husband."

Other AVON ROMANCES

AT THE BRIDE HUNT BALL *by Olivia Parker*
HIS DARK AND DANGEROUS WAYS *by Edith Layton*
JEWEL *by Beverly Jenkins*
LET THE NIGHT BEGIN *by Kathryn Smith*
SEDUCED BY SIN *by Kimberly Logan*
TEMPTATION OF THE WARRIOR *by Margo Maguire*
THREE NIGHTS OF SIN *by Anne Mallory*

Coming Soon

SURRENDER TO ME *by Sophie Jordan*
TOO DANGEROUS TO DESIRE *by Alexandra Benedict*

And Don't Miss These
ROMANTIC TREASURES
from Avon Books

IN BED WITH THE DEVIL *by Lorraine Heath*
A NOTORIOUS PROPOSITION *by Adele Ashworth*
UNDER YOUR SPELL *by Lois Greiman*

Lessons from a Courtesan

Jenna Petersen

AVON
An Imprint of HarperCollins*Publishers*

This is a work of fiction. Names, characters, places, and incidents are drawn from the author's imagination or are used fictitiously and are not to be construed as real. Any resemblance to actual events, locales, organizations, or persons, living or dead, is entirely coincidental.

AVON BOOKS
An Imprint of HarperCollins*Publishers*
10 East 53rd Street
New York, New York 10022-5299

ISBN 978-0-06-113814-0
www.avonromance.com

First Avon Books paperback printing: July 2008

Printed in the U.S.A.

10 9 8 7 6 5 4 3 2 1

For Kate, who always knows when to comfort me and also knows when to tell me to get over myself. Thanks for reading it!

For Michael. Even if we can never go back to Arizona. I love you, babe!

Lessons from a Courtesan

Prologue

1812

By tomorrow morning, she would no longer be a virgin. Victoria Reed—no—Victoria *Talbot* stared at herself in the mirror. How could she be unchanged when in a span of little more than hours, her whole world had been altered completely?

She had a new name and a new home. She even had a title. Lady Baybary. The Countess of Baybary.

It didn't sound right. It *wasn't* right.

Victoria covered her face with her hands. Just a month ago, she had been living her normal life. Yes, she had to endure her father's drunken tirades and suspicious ramblings, but she was accustomed to those things.

And then, seemingly out of nowhere, her father had come to her with the news that he'd arranged a marriage for her with Justin Talbot, Earl of Baybary and the son of her father's former best friend. A man he now despised and cursed regularly. When she dared inquire how and why he had picked that match, she'd gotten a harsh slap and no further answers.

And now here she was, sitting in the master chamber of her new husband's sprawling country estate, looking at herself in the mirror. And wondering what in the world her father had gotten her into.

Loud voices outside the door intruded upon her troubled reverie. She shot to her feet and took a step forward. Though she couldn't make out the words being said, she recognized the sound of her father's slurred cadence. He was drunk again.

His companion was also shockingly familiar. It was her new husband. Though they'd conversed all of a dozen times in the last month, his voice was already one she knew in an instant. Dark and husky, a low rumble that came from deep within his chest.

The voices went up in volume. They were arguing. Victoria moved toward the door and leaned closer. She could make out only the angry tone and occasional words like *drunk, annulment, wife,* and *secret,* which pierced the barrier occasionally. She winced at each one.

Justin Talbot had been surprisingly quiet on the subject of their marriage, keeping to polite, empty exchanges when they were alone. She had assumed this marriage was some kind of business arrangement, but now she wondered . . . was he being forced into the union as much as she had been?

And if that were the case, how would he treat her? She had been unable to determine her fiancé's true character so far.

Before she could ponder that troubling thought any further, the door she was leaning against opened and Victoria stumbled forward. Strong arms caught her as her forehead came to rest against a broad, warm chest. Well, there was no denying she'd been eavesdropping on Justin and her father now.

Slowly, she looked up and met her new husband's eyes. Dear heavens, he was a handsome devil with his harshly defined features, strong jaw, and sensual lips.

If she had to describe him in one word, it would have been *dark*. Dark hair, dark eyes that hid his emotions handily, and a dark aura that seemed to swirl around him. With just a look, even an innocent could see he was a man of secrets, of vices, of everything his reputation spoke of and more.

She pulled from his hold and staggered back a few steps. He said nothing, simply stared at her . . . waiting.

"I—I heard voices," she stammered, hating the heat that flooded her cheeks. She didn't want to show him that weakness. "I was not trying to pry."

"Weren't you?" he asked, his tone measured. There was no indication if he was amused or angry or affronted. "And what did you hear?"

She shook her head. "Nothing."

He watched her for a long moment, as if judging the truth of that statement. Then he stepped into the chamber and shut the door behind him. He stared at her, his gaze roving over her body with a lazy possessiveness that made her spine stiffen. He was *appraising* her, as someone would do with a cow or a horse!

Worse, as angry as that thought made her, she wondered how she came up in his estimation. He, a man rumored to be a voracious lover; she, a woman in a white cotton night rail.

"You needn't look at me like I'm going to strangle you in your bed," he said quietly. "I have no intention of harming you. The voices you heard were mine and your father's." His dark gaze grew even darker. "Mr. Reed was simply wishing us well before he departed for the inn."

Now it was her eyes that narrowed, but in disbelief. "What you are describing doesn't sound like something my father would do, Lord Baybary.

And you two were clearly not having a warm good-bye. You were arguing."

His gaze, which had been fixed on the bottle of whiskey across the room, flitted to her face, and his expression was one of surprise. Again, Victoria's stomach tightened with anxiety. She had been impertinent. Who knew what punishment that would garner her?

But he didn't roar or strike her. Instead, Justin tilted back his head and let out a chuckle. "I've always appreciated spirit in a woman."

Victoria pursed her lips. "I don't find the situation amusing, my lord. If you were somehow forced into marrying me, I demand the truth."

His laughter faded, and he looked at her again. Again, the gaze was appraising, but this time it wasn't her body he was making an account of. It was something deeper. Her intent, perhaps. Her character. But he gave no outward indication about his conclusions.

"First, you should call me Justin," he said. "We are married, the pretense of titles seems foolish. Secondly, it doesn't really matter how or why we came to this 'union.' We are here now, legally wed. Well, almost legally. One thing remains to be done to make the marriage a binding one."

Victoria stared at him and watched as his gaze slipped pointedly to the big bed along the back wall of the large chamber. His eyebrow arched, and he stood silent as she stared at it. His bed. How many other women had shared it before her?

How many would share it after?

"Yes," she finally said, clearing her throat so her voice wouldn't crack. It still did. "There is that. I, er, my father and my maid told me a little about what I'm to experience tonight. I realize it is my duty, and I assure you I will do my best to bear it."

Justin's eyebrow arched even higher, and he took a step toward her. Slowly he reached out and cupped her chin. Instantly a shot of hot awareness sliced through Victoria, taking her aback and making her jolt a little at the touch.

"You know, you are quite lovely," he said absently, as if he had never noticed it before. His thumb swirled gentle circles against her cheek. "You should forget whatever nonsense you were told, Victoria."

She jolted as her name passed his lips. He had always called her Miss Reed in the past. There was something undeniably sensual about his gravelly voice purring her given name.

"Should I?" she squeaked.

He nodded, and his fingers slid into her hair. He threaded her locks loose until the pale blue ribbon she'd used to tie them back fluttered to the floor.

"I cannot imagine what your father would tell you about tonight," he said. "But whatever else has happened, whatever else is true, when you are with me, it won't be an experience you'll be forced to 'bear.' You shall be a most willing participant."

She opened her mouth to protest that arrogant statement, but he didn't allow a retort. He silenced her with a sudden kiss. Not a sweet kiss. Not a nice kiss. Not the kiss of a man courting her. A kiss of a man about to take her. Claim her.

His mouth burned against hers and then his tongue was inside, swirling around her own, sucking her in, demanding she respond. And though new sensations crashed over her, confused her, she *did*, almost as if she couldn't control what she was doing. As if she were forced to lift her hands to his chest and cling to the loose woolen fabric of his lapels.

Just as suddenly as he had begun the kiss, Justin pulled back. He stared at her, and through blurred vision, she saw him frown.

Was he disappointed? No, that wasn't it. He looked . . . confused, but only for a brief moment. Then he shook off the emotion and let his fingers trail down the front of her white cotton robe.

It was shocking to be touched like this by a man she hardly knew. And it was also thrilling. Victoria couldn't help but gasp as his fingers stroked over the layers of fabric covering her.

With a few quick movements, the cotton fell away in a pile by her feet, leaving her in an equally drab nightgown.

He looked her up and down, dark eyes dilating with every gaze, then shook his head. "Not a very pretty wrapping for such a pretty body."

She was too dizzy and off-kilter for a response, not that he seemed to expect one. He was already looping his fingers beneath the flimsy straps of her gown and pulling it down.

Victoria swallowed. Hard. She was now naked in front of a man who was no more than a stranger. Emotions bombarded her. Shame at having her body exposed when she had been taught to cover herself by every maid, governess, and aunt she encountered. Anxiety that Justin would be unhappy with what he saw.

And low in her belly, something else. A tiny tingle of what could only be described as desire.

"A very pretty body, indeed," he all but purred.

She shivered at the compliment.

He cupped her shoulders and met her gaze. "Don't be afraid. I will bring you pleasure, Victoria. I swear it."

She nodded, mute, unable to do anything else. In a few short moments, this man had woven a potent spell over her. He had overpowered her senses and her reason, leaving only the looming presence of *him*. As his head dipped, she briefly thought of what a dangerous thing that was, to lose herself so completely with just a few touches.

Then his mouth brushed her throat, and her mind emptied of all thoughts except sensation. His lips trailed down her flesh, and tingles followed in their wake. When his mouth closed around one nipple, her knees buckled.

He caught her, supporting her bare backside, drawing her against him fully as he suckled her breast. Pleasure coiled from the point of contact, forcing her to lift her hips against him in search of . . . something. She didn't know what, except that it was as if she'd been sleeping until now.

In a smooth motion, he lifted her and deposited her against the soft coverlet. Justin drew back and stared for a long moment before he shed his jacket and made quick work of the cravat, shirtwaist, and crisp linen shirt beneath. Victoria leaned up on her elbows as he began to work on his trousers. She hadn't ever seen a man divest himself before. It was fascinating to watch him unfasten his clothing, to reveal what seemed like endless planes of hard muscle and smooth flesh.

It again occurred to her that they were hardly better than strangers. They didn't know each other, they certainly didn't care for one another, and yet they were about to join in the most intimate way possible. She was about to see . . .

Her breath caught and her mouth went dry as he kicked his discarded trousers away.

That. That hard thrust of muscle that jutted between his thighs was what she saw.

"Your eyes are like saucers," he said with a wry smile as he took a place beside her on the bed. "*This* is why I've avoided virgins."

She shot him a look as heat flushed her cheeks. His words were a reminder that where she was innocent, he was oh-so-very experienced.

"I—I wish I knew what you wanted," she said, her breath coming short. "But I don't."

He lifted two fingers to her lips. "Did you like it when I kissed you?"

Hot blood warmed her cheeks, and she turned her face away in embarrassment. Slowly, she nodded.

"And when I touched you"—he cupped one breast, strumming a thumb over the sensitive, distended tip—"here?"

"Yes," she managed to groan out.

"Then do not worry about what will come next. Trust me."

She stared into his eyes. So dark they were hardly brown, almost black. They were beautiful eyes, but not kind ones.

"How can I trust you when I hardly know you?" she murmured.

His smile pinched. "There is little choice for

either of us now. This must be done, we might as well take pleasure in it."

He leaned forward and blew a gust of warm breath over her nipple. Feverish want built in her with every grazing touch. His mouth closed over her a second time, and she fell back against the pillows with a helpless sigh.

The pleasure peaked, pulsing in time between her legs. As he continued to lick and tease her breasts, his hand dipped down, first resting against her belly, then lower to her hip, her thigh.

Through her haze, she barely felt the shifts, just the ricochets of new sensation that followed. It was actually a surprise when he finally cupped her mound gently.

"Justin," she gasped, eyes flying open.

When he touched her there the deep ache multiplied, its level rising to a terrifying and out-of-control height.

"Shhh, just feel," he reminded her, nuzzling the underside of one breast even as his fingers lazily parted her slick folds, opening her in the most private, intimate ways.

His rough hands aroused her, stroking, and finally, after he'd teased and played and driven her mad, filled her. One long finger dipped into her clenching, wet channel, and she let out a moan that seemed to echo around her.

He gently thrust, using his thumb to massage the bundle of nerves hidden within. Pleasure arced, building at a blinding speed, rolling over her in waves until she was overcome. Her back arched and she cried out, shaking as he dragged her through the pleasure mercilessly until she was weak against the pillows.

As Victoria's vision cleared, she let her gaze slowly move to him. Justin stared at her, expression unreadable except for the hungry want in his eyes.

He withdrew his fingers from her still clenching body, but she wasn't bereft for long. He slung one long, muscular leg over hers and moved to cover her with that hard, hot body. He bracketed her head with his hands and brought his mouth down against hers. She arched against him reflexively and didn't fight when he parted her legs with his thighs.

She gasped when the hard, heavy tip of him nudged her entrance, but the sound was lost in his mouth. He drove his kiss deeper, shutting down her defenses and keeping her fears at bay. He held her against him and drove forward.

A slash of pain shattered the pleasure, and she yelped in surprise. He drew back and gazed down at her.

"I'm sorry," he whispered, and his tone was genuine. "There was no getting around that."

She nodded, though she was shocked by his apology. Her maid had told tales of the pain that would accompany the loss of her virtue. And also how callous men could be when it came to that moment. But the pain Victoria felt was mild, and fading with every moment Justin held still inside her, watching her, waiting for her to acclimate to the new sensations.

She shifted experimentally, squeezing around him, lifting her hips ever so slightly. To her surprise, Justin's eyes shut, and he let out a feral, dangerous moan.

"Careful now," he panted. "I'm trying to wait for you."

She met his gaze, losing herself in the wanton pleasure of being naked beneath him, joined with him, *his*.

"Justin," she whispered. "Don't wait."

He let out a lewd curse beneath his breath, but didn't argue. He drew back and slid forward again. The second thrust didn't hurt as much as the first. The third didn't hurt at all. And the rest were pure pleasure.

Victoria dug her fingers into his back, thrashing beneath him as he drove into her, circled his hips to pleasure her. She lifted to meet every stroke, going on pure instinct. It was shocking that an act she had been told was so wicked could feel so *good*.

The pleasure she'd experienced beneath Justin's fingertips roared back with a deeper intensity than before. She felt the edge coming, but this time she didn't wonder at it. She embraced it, shaking and quivering against him, bucking her hips wildly until he roared out a sound of untamed pleasure and his seed moved within her.

For a long time they lay entangled in each other, Justin's body covering hers with delicious, erotic weight, their breath merging into one shared rhythm. She marveled at her feelings in the aftermath. Weightless and satiated. But had she given him the same kind of pleasure?

Her eyes came open, and she looked up to find him staring, focused, at her face. But when their gazes met, he rolled away, leaving her cold as he reached for his discarded trousers.

"Did I hurt you?" he murmured without looking at her.

She sat up a little, watching with disappointment as the fine muscular curve of his buttocks disappeared into his trousers.

"No. Not after the first." She blushed. "It was lovely."

He stopped and looked at her over his shoulder. "Good. I'm glad of that fact." He cleared his throat as if he were uncomfortable. "Victoria, tomorrow morning at first light, I'm going to London."

She blinked in confusion. Her father had

brought her all the way to Baybary, she had assumed that she and Justin would spend a few weeks here before they ventured to Town. But if he intended a return so quickly, why had her things been unpacked?

"We are?" she asked.

He flinched ever so slightly before he shook his head. "No, *I* am. You will stay here."

Victoria caught her breath, but was too taken aback to respond. When she didn't fill the silence, Justin did.

"The estate is fully staffed, and I will see to it that you have funds. You'll have the freedom to run my holdings here as you see fit, within reason. Everything has been arranged."

The heat of a blush burned at her cheeks when he turned a blank stare in her direction. She grabbed for the blankets to cover herself. When he looked at her with such emptiness, her nudity was shameful again.

"I don't understand," she said, as calmly as she could.

He frowned as he crossed the room and grabbed for the whiskey bottle he'd been casting glances at all night. He poured himself a hefty swig and downed it.

"You already knew this marriage was one of convenience, nothing more. You said yourself that we are strangers, with no bond between us other than a scrap of legal document and one night together." He met her gaze with a cool one.

Her lips thinned as understanding fully dawned. "I see. You have made the marriage legal, and now you will cast me aside and return to your life without further thought of the vows we took this afternoon."

His mouth turned down. "Those vows were meaningless."

She bit back a gasp. "Perhaps to you, they were."

He shook his head. "Your life here cannot be worse than at your father's house. You will have money and the respect that comes with being a countess. I am certain you will easily make new friends and be very comfortable."

"I just will be a wife in name only," she said, proud she could keep her voice flat when she was so humiliated.

"I'm afraid that is the best I can do, Victoria." Justin set the empty whiskey glass aside and shrugged. "You may hate me if you like. But I *am* going to London tomorrow."

She nodded, hardening her heart so she wouldn't feel the disappointment that now threatened to overcome her. "If that is what you must do, then I wouldn't dare stand in your way. If you are finished here, then I wish you a good evening, my lord."

He opened his mouth as if he wanted to say something else, but then closed it. Instead he executed an apologetic bow and stepped from the room, leaving Victoria alone.

And for the first time in her life, she truly felt alone in every way.

Chapter 1

Lesson 1: Every man loves a mystery.

Three Years Later, 1815

Justin Talbot, Earl of Baybary, entered the packed ballroom with a wide grin. He looked over the rowdy crowd and felt a sense of welcoming, of home. After months abroad, sampling the many French pleasures long denied by war and strife, it was good to be back in London.

"Look who has made his way back to British soil!"

Justin turned at the familiar voice booming behind him. He couldn't help but grin as he watched his good friend, Russell Shaw, come toward him with long, sure steps.

"How *did* you manage to tear yourself away from the French lovelies, old friend?"

Justin laughed as Shaw pounded him on the back in greeting. "Caleb told me you'd be here tonight."

Shaw smiled as he looked off into the crowd. "And just where is your younger brother?"

Justin nodded in the direction Caleb had headed. "Fetching the drinks, of course."

"Ah." Shaw nodded knowingly. "But you must be exhausted. You only just returned, yes?"

Justin shrugged. "I've been back for all of a day, and I unfortunately spent part of it in the company of my mother, father, and sister."

Shaw pulled a face. Everyone in Justin's acquaintance knew he was not close to anyone in his family beyond Caleb. His friends made assumptions for the cause of the breach, but no one had ever come close to the truth. Not even Caleb, who continued to strive for their family's approval and fall short in equal measure.

"But despite a pounding headache, Caleb insisted on dragging me here tonight," Justin continued. "He told me there would be something I wouldn't want to miss. It was all very cryptic, I don't suppose you want to share. What have I missed while on the Continent?"

Shaw's bright blue eyes lit up with humor. "Where should I begin? While you were gone there were fisticuffs, more than a few drunken routs, oh, and old Middlemach finally discovered his wife was diddling with Franklin."

"Well, that was bound to happen," Justin said absently. "Adelaide was never discreet about her affairs. That's why I broke it off with her."

Shaw nodded, "Same with me. Didn't she dally with your brother as well?"

Justin gave half a sheepish smile. "She's dallied with the lot of us, I'm afraid. But what else? None of what you've told me warrants the mystery Caleb wove around this party."

Shaw pursed his lips in thought for a moment before realization dawned in his eyes. "Ah, I think I know what your brother is cackling about. The mystery must revolve around Ria. She's the only other thing you've missed that is of any consequence or interest."

"Ria?" Justin repeated as he looked over the milling crowd of gentlemen and the women who came to these events.

Although it was being held in a respectable home and there was an orchestra playing music for a stream of dancing couples, this wasn't the normal boring London rout. There were no simpering virgins or clawing mamas in attendance. This was a gentleman's diversion, filled with courtesans and mistresses and opera singers, all of whom were more than willing to warm a man's bed.

Lovely.

"Shaw, you ruin everything!" Justin's brother, Caleb, laughed as he strode up to the two men with drinks in hand. He handed Justin a tumbler of whiskey and continued, "*I* wanted to reveal Ria to my brother. I consider her a homecoming gift."

Justin shook his head with a wry chuckle. Trust Caleb to be wrapped up in a woman. Women, drink, and cards had been his brother's downfall since he was out of short pants. Likely Justin would be called upon to sort out the newest trouble before their father uncovered it and had an apoplexy.

"Opera singer or dance hall girl?" Justin asked, taking a sip of his drink.

Caleb shrugged. "That's the beauty. No one knows for certain."

Justin tilted his head, intrigued. "What do you mean?"

"No one ever heard of the young lady until a month ago, when the whispers began. People said she had been sequestered away in the countryside with some soldier who taught her all the wicked ways of foreign sex practices." His brother's eyes lit up. "Then men started claiming they knew others who had been with her, that she was the best courtesan in all of England. When she showed up in town a fortnight or so ago, she was the instant rage. Word has it she's looking for a new protector.

Someone with a bit more influence than a randy soldier who read some naughty books while stationed in India."

"Sounds like a bunch of rot to me," Shaw snorted. "But I do admit, the woman is a beauty. Lush, like a ripe peach ready to be plucked. If she knows half the sexual secrets the gossip says she does, I would certainly have no trouble overlooking the colorful nature of her past."

Justin smiled. The new lady *did* sound interesting, and it had been quite some time since he'd had a mistress. Lovers, certainly. He'd rarely been without someone in his bed. But never anyone who lasted more than a couple of tumbles. Not since—

He cut the thought off.

"So what about you, Justin?" Caleb asked. "Do you want to throw in on the lady? Should we make a wager about which of us will claim her for his bed first?"

"Yes, Baybary." Shaw laughed. "Care to make it interesting?"

Justin shook his head. "I have no idea why you two like to throw away your money. If this Ria is the best, as you claim she is, then I'll certainly win her. I always do."

Shaw snorted out a sound of derision. "Cocky bastard."

Caleb motioned behind Justin. "Before we

make ourselves a wager, let's allow my brother to see exactly what he is claiming. There is the lovely Ria now."

Justin turned toward the door to watch a young woman sweep into the ballroom. A crowd rushed to greet her, so Justin could see only dark hair and the flash of a sinfully low-cut, scarlet red gown. Finally the men parted in her wake and revealed a clear look at her.

The empty glass in Justin's hand hit the floor, crystal shattering at his feet. Ria *was* the most beautiful woman he'd ever seen. But she was no stranger. She was the woman who had haunted his dreams since he last saw her three years ago, naked and delectable in his bed.

She was his wife.

Victoria drew a surreptitious gasp of breath and hoped it might calm her. As had been the case since her arrival in London a fortnight ago, every time she entered one of these scandalous gatherings, she was terrified someone would discover she was a fraud. Or worse, that she would do something utterly out of place and reveal *herself* to the group of circling men who had been enticed by tales of her supposed sexual prowess.

She straightened her spine and gave the nearest gentleman a teasing smile, another an audacious wink. She couldn't afford to fail or reveal herself.

She couldn't afford to give in to her fears. Her true purpose for traveling to London was far more important than all that.

Her gaze moved over the room subtly as she attempted to determine if one or more of the many men she had an interest in was attending this evening. She paused for more smiles and hellos to her copious admirers. Good heavens, it was easy to make men want you. If only she'd known that years ago.

Pushing those thoughts away, Victoria continued her sweep of the room, making a mental note of the gentlemen she had to especially garner the attention of. It seemed like an overwhelming list, and she wasn't certain she was up to the task of tempting the most sought-after men of the Upper Ten Thousand.

But that was just rot. Silly doubts brought on by memories of the last man who had turned away from her. She clenched her fists tightly. She would *not* allow thoughts of Justin Talbot to enter her mind and make her question her success.

The man wasn't even in England to bother her. Her sources said that he was on a tour of the Continent. No doubt taking his pleasure with anything that walked and had a pretty smile. Bitterness flooded her mouth at the thought.

"My dear, are you quite well?"

Victoria started at the voice that was suddenly

at her elbow. She turned to find Mortimer St. James at her side. The older gentleman was the host of this particular party. One of the many men who desired her pretty face to decorate his gallery and show that age hadn't affected his prowess. He placed an ungloved hand on her arm, and Victoria fought the urge to flinch away.

"Yes, I'm quite well, Mr. St. James," she said with a false smile. "It's very crowded tonight, is it not?"

He nodded as he looked out over the milling groups of people and launched into a self-important speech about the numerous influential attendees. Victoria did her best to ignore his droning voice.

God, how tedious this all was. Not one man she had met since her arrival as "Ria" had held her interest for more than a moment's time. They were all pretentious idiots who wanted to impress her into their beds. A thought that made her shudder. If her true purpose were to find a lover, she never would have found one here with this lot. Thank God it wasn't.

"So, since I *am* so prominent, who may I introduce you to?" St. James pressed. He leaned a bit closer and squeezed her arm. "Unless you have taken a fancy to me, of course."

Victoria swallowed back a gag and gently extricated herself from his clammy grip. "Oh, Mr.

St. James, I fear I could easily fall in love with you, and that is dangerous in my profession. Perhaps it is best if you *do* introduce me to someone who would be less of a temptation to my fragile heart."

She could have choked on the insincere words, but St. James was nodding along like his neck was on a hinge. This was the perfect opportunity to make a move on one of her true targets.

"Name the gentleman," St. James said.

"Well, sir—" she began, but before she could finish, her host's eyes lit up.

"Ah, here comes one of the most powerful men in all of London. Surely you will want to make his acquaintance."

Victoria forced a smile. She was in no position to demand anything from this man. All she could do was go along with his suggestions and hope that the person who was now approaching was one of the men she wanted to meet.

Slowly, she turned to face the intruder. But instead of finding another leering stranger, what faced her was a far greater danger. Her legs began to shake and her heart rate doubled. It was—it was—

"My dear, may I present the Earl of Baybary, Justin Talbot. And Baybary, this is—"

"Oh, I know who she is," Justin said with a smile that chilled Victoria to the bone with its falseness. It didn't even come close to reaching his dark eyes.

He meant to reveal her. She would have bet every cent in her reticule that was true. His mouth, which had drawn her attention the moment she recognized him, damn her weakness, had a cruel twist to it. A righteous anger that rankled her to her soul.

He had no right to feel *any* emotion when it came to her, but especially possessiveness or anger. He had thrown those rights away with all his other husbandly duties.

"Ria," he said, so soft and yet with so much power. "You are the courtesan of the hour. The woman who every gentleman wants to . . ." He trailed off with a suggestive wave of his hands that made her so utterly aware of them. "Meet," he finished, his tone dry as aged firewood.

She expelled a breath of relief that he didn't call her out immediately, although she doubted he did so for her benefit. Justin always had a selfish motive for everything he did. He was either protecting his own reputation or waiting to torment her at a more convenient time.

St. James leaned between them and began to chatter at Justin, but her husband's stare never left her, even as he engaged in a tedious conversation with the little man. St. James couldn't seem to stop his mouth even when the tension in the air was so thick that she could have cut it with the knife she had stuffed in her boot just in case.

But for once, she welcomed his stream of chatter. It forced a distance between her and Justin and gave her a blessed moment to regroup now that the shock of his approach was beginning to pass. She stared at him, taking in every detail.

By God, but he was handsome. Time had changed her, she knew that. In the three years since they last spoke, she had experienced crushing heartache and survived. Certainly that had made her into a different woman than the girl he had seduced. But *he* had been left the same.

He was taller than most of his contemporaries, and his long, muscled limbs and broad shoulders forced her to remember the way his big body felt when he pressed his naked flesh to hers. His hair was a bit longer than it had been on their wedding night, longer than fashion dictated. It fell into his eyes with a lazy elegance.

No, he had not changed. He was still arrogant and mysterious, with an aura of sinful promise that swirled around him. With just one glance, she felt all the memories she'd tried to suppress coming back. And she despised herself for it.

While St. James droned on endlessly, Justin folded his arms and tilted his head as his gaze flowed up and down her body. She was brought back to her wedding night, when he had given her the same appraising stare just before he stripped her of her clothing, her innocence, and a little piece of her soul. That was something she would never get back.

Setting her jaw with frustration, directed both at him and at herself, she began to draw her stare away when he smirked at her. *Smirked* like he was enjoying her discomfort, taking pleasure in the power he now held over her. Any panic, any fleeting desire she felt when she looked at him, was replaced by anger, indignation. The bastard. Well, she would be damned if she was going to let him win any quarter from her. Not ever again. Certainly she would not let him keep her from her duty.

"St. James, would you mind if I had a moment alone with . . ." Justin trailed off again and gave her an empty stare. "*Ria.*"

St. James looked between the two of them rapidly with a lewd grin, and then nodded quickly. "Of course, of course. Just don't forget who introduced you if you claim her for your own, Baybary."

Justin finally broke the stare that had been holding Victoria hostage and spared St. James a heated glance. "Oh, don't you worry. I will never forget."

Completely oblivious to the rage in Justin's tone, St. James gave a deferential bow and disappeared into the mass of people, leaving them alone. Or at least as alone as they could be in the midst of a milling, curious crowd.

"What can I do for you, my lord?" Victoria asked, quite proud that her own tone was as cool as his. At least her terror and confusion and other tangled emotions weren't reflected in her voice.

And to her surprise and pleasure, that cool tone seemed to incite *his* emotions. His dark gaze finally flickered with a hint of anger before he caught her arm.

"Not here," he grunted. With little of his reputed finesse, he began dragging her across the room and out the terrace door.

Victoria briefly considered fighting him, but thought better of it. If she battled him in the middle of a ballroom, everyone would see. It would provoke too many questions, too many whispers. It could ruin everything. It was better to face him alone.

Though the thought of that made her hands shake both with a desire to strangle him and with a need to touch his skin.

In the cool air of the night, he found a darkened corner of the terrace that wasn't occupied and hauled her behind a potted plant for the most privacy they were likely to find.

As soon as she was certain no one would see, Victoria yanked her arm from his. Now her anger was pulsing at the surface, and she allowed herself the pleasure of the most withering glare she could muster. The same one she gave wayward servants and tenants behind in their rent.

"What is the meaning of pulling me out of the ballroom? You have no right—" she began.

Justin's mouth fell open. "No right? Here you are at a ball, having men paw after you as they compete to be your new protector. And you tell me I have *no right*, Victoria?"

Oh, why had he said her name? In a flash of a moment, the sound of it leaving his lips brought her back to their wedding night and gave her the same erotic shiver it had then. No matter how much she despised and could not understand Justin Talbot, she couldn't forget the fact that she wanted him. Still. Despite everything she had endured thanks to him.

She shook away the emotions and smiled, though she felt no joy, or pleasure.

"What a surprise," she spat, hating the bitterness that tinged her tone and revealed too many emotions. "You recall my name."

Justin's hands gripped into fists at his sides at her reaction.

"Of course I know your name," he hissed, and she could tell that minding his voice took Herculean effort. "You are my wife."

She flinched before she shook her head. This was enough. "I haven't *ever* been your wife, Justin.

Not truly. And what I'm doing here and who I'm with is really none of your concern."

She moved to push past him and return to the house, hoping upon hope, but not truly believing, that he would let her go.

Of course, he didn't. In one quick, smooth motion, he caught her upper arms and backed her up until her rear end hit the side of the building. His hands were hot on her bare skin, marking her and forcing more of that hated, unwanted desire from her traitorous body.

He was so hard, so heavy as his muscular frame molded to hers. He leaned in, holding her in place with his weight. And she fought the urge to lift her chin up and offer her lips to him. Taste him and see if he still felt the same. Test if the perfection of their last joining was a false memory implanted by lack of experience and foolish hopes.

"I want to know what you are doing here, Victoria," he growled. "And I *will* have satisfaction."

Chapter 2

Lesson 2: Never take more than you can control.

Victoria swallowed hard. *Satisfaction* was such a loaded word, especially when Justin was touching her like this. She was certain he had chosen it with purpose. Did that mean he could read her reactions to him so clearly?

Did he know that she wanted to wrap her legs around his waist, tell him if he wanted satisfaction, he should take it? God, she hoped not. That knowledge would give him even more power in this untenable situation. She needed to steal back as much as she could, and quickly.

"Answer me, Victoria," he growled.

She flinched at the sound of her name rolling like silk from his lips a second time. That gravelly, low tone was still her undoing.

"You're no courtesan," he murmured.

She stared at him in surprise. He was smirking at her again, just as he had in the ballroom. And just as it had then, his conceit gave her the power to overcome her desire and find control.

"You think not?" She laughed, placing her hands against his chest.

God, he was so hot, and she could feel the coiled strength of every muscle beneath her palms. Fighting to forget those things, she shoved him back. Though her physical strength was nothing to his, he released her arms, and she was finally able to breathe again.

"Are you so arrogant that you think just because you didn't want me that no other man did? Or that because you forgot about me all these years that I haven't existed? You know nothing about me, Justin," she snapped, the truth of those words serving as a reminder to herself as much as to him.

His mouth thinned to a line of displeasure. "You are correct. I do not know you. I never did and I never desired that knowledge." He backed away even farther. "But I know that in three years a woman doesn't go from shy innocent to wild seductress."

Victoria arched a brow. "Doesn't she? How would you know? All you know are you own selfish desires and wants. That is all you've ever known. You have no idea of my life."

And he didn't care. She was almost grateful for that reminder, although it stung her in some deeply hidden part that she refused to acknowledge.

He shook his head. "I know enough. I know you have essentially taken over the running of my estate, and done a very good job of it. How would you have time to become some soldier's lover and learn all his sensual tricks?"

She thought she saw the corner of his lip twitch with anger, but couldn't be certain. Was he actually upset she might have taken a lover? How could he be? He didn't want her. He never had. He admitted that with no compunction.

But she didn't care about that. The farther away he moved, the easier it was to recall her true purpose in London. And it had *nothing* to do with Justin and their unresolved issues. In fact, she needed him to stay as far away from her as possible.

She had prepared for what she would say on the off chance she was recognized during this dangerous game. Now she found those practiced words and repeated them.

"Do you know how utterly boring running an estate is, Justin? And how exciting a man who has traveled and seen the world can be?" She smiled as his eyes narrowed. In some petty part of her, she liked frustrating him, flaunting her so-called affairs.

"Victoria—"

His tone was a warning, but she pressed on.

"I wanted to come to London, to have a share in the excitement and pleasures to be found here."

"But you are a wellborn lady. A woman of title. If anyone finds out about what you're doing, you could ruin yourself. Do you not even care about that?" he asked, astonished.

She shrugged. "It isn't as if I was ever that well-known in London circles. I never had a chance to visit the city as an adult, since our marriage was arranged before I even had a chance to debut. My former friends who now live here aren't coming to the kind of parties I attend. And even if I do see someone of my acquaintance, I made certain to alter my appearance enough that no one would recognize me."

She hesitated a moment. She *had* prepared, and yet Justin had known her instantly. She tilted her head as she murmured, "I'm actually surprised you identified me. You could hardly look at me when you did spend time with me."

He scowled. "No matter what you do to change your appearance, a man recognizes his wife."

She shook her head at his possessive tone. "Once again, I question how you can call me *wife*. We spent one night together in three years, and you could hardly wait until morning to leave. You've made a good show of forgetting me all this time, I suggest you simply do the same now. Put me and our unwanted union out of your mind. Soon enough I will return to the country and everything will be normal again."

His eyes were wide, angry, and wild. Actually, it was the most emotion she'd ever seen him show. She was almost proud that she had broken the shell he kept around him. At least she could make him feel *some* strong emotion, even if it was only irritation.

"So you have no intention of staying on in London permanently?" he asked, his voice now deceptively calm even though the firestorm of anger still raged in his gaze.

She shook her head. There was no harm in this little kernel of truth. "No. As you implied, running an estate takes a great deal of time, and I have duties to attend to back at home. In a few weeks, I shall likely bore of this game and depart."

He clenched his hands in and out of fists at his sides. "So you simply came here to find a lover for a few weeks and then leave?"

Victoria swallowed. That was her story, wasn't it? The one Marah had made her rehearse a hundred times on the way to London and since their arrival a fortnight ago.

"Yes."

He was moving toward her before she could react. She stumbled back and hit the wall again.

Instantly he bracketed his hands around her head, trapping her for a second time in less than half an hour. He leaned in close, his warm breath caressing her cheek, stroking her skin. All the emotional distance she'd managed to create while they'd argued faded in a flash. Desire rushed to the forefront once again with blinding speed.

"If you wanted a tumble, Victoria," he said, his lips almost touching her throat. "All you had to do was send word. I would have been most happy to oblige your . . . urges."

Victoria's eyes flew open. She could not let her baser urges win this war. She couldn't let *Justin* win. Even if she had to fight dirty.

"I've already had a tumble with you, Justin," she snapped. "I've had better."

He pulled his head away to stare at her. His anger had transformed to indignant rage. She had gone too far. Much too far. And now it was clear she was going to pay.

And pay she did. Justin cupped the back of her head and dropped his lips to hers in an angry, punishing kiss. Or at least, it began as angry and punishing. But the moment their mouths met, it transformed quite rapidly to something else. Something hot and wild and utterly out of control.

Victoria's protests faded the second his lips burned hers. She found herself opening for him, welcoming him in and reveling in how familiar his touch and taste still was. His tongue dueled with hers as she sank into his embrace. The entire length of his body pressed against her, pinning her to the wall fully and forcing her curves to mold into the hard planes of his body.

The erotic sensation was almost too much to bear.

And yet he gave her more. His hands began to move, cupping her breasts, massaging until her tingling nipples hardened beneath the sinfully thin fabric of her clinging red gown. No wonder courtesans wore such things, they magnified each touch. Better still, she had forgone undergarments, just like a real woman of the night, which meant with just a few tugs, Justin could touch her. Fill her.

And she couldn't deny that in this moment of utter weakness, she wanted that.

He seemed to read her mind, for he began to pull her gown lower until her breast peeked out over the scooped neckline. In the tiny rational part of her mind, Victoria knew she should have been horrified to be so exposed, but she wasn't. She found herself arching toward him as he broke the kiss to begin a slow descent down her throat. He cupped her backside and lifted her, granting his mouth access to her now revealed nipple.

The flame of heat set her skin on fire with

every moment he tugged at the sensitive tip. Sensation rushed through her, settling between her thighs. Soon she would be utterly consumed by his touch.

He sucked hard and her hips jolted, meeting his in an explosion of sensation. She felt the hard thrust of his cock, rocking against her core, demanding access she would not deny him.

He stroked his tongue over her nipple again and growled, "You see, if you want someone to satisfy you, all you need is me."

Victoria froze as his brash words pierced the haze of pleasure. They were like cold water on her soul. She *had* needed him once, and she never wanted that to happen again.

With a little cry, she twisted out of his embrace and pushed him away. To her surprise, he let her go with no argument, backing up to give her space. In the dim moonlight that pierced through the darkness of the terrace corner, he stared at her. She knew what she looked like. Her gown was twisted, one breast still shining from his mouth. Her hair was slightly mussed, her mouth swollen from his.

She looked like a wanton. She looked like the courtesan she pretended to be.

"I don't want you," she panted, tugging at her gown to cover herself.

Justin smiled at her denial, and Victoria cursed

her lack of control. It made her words so patently false. Justin knew that her reaction to his touch had been real. If nothing else, the physical connection they'd made on their wedding night still existed, even if time and other people had separated them.

"Don't you?" he murmured, reaching for a stray lock of dark hair that had come tumbling from her chignon when he touched her. She flinched away from his fingers, fearing the intimacy of that gentle touch even more than the alluring draw of his kiss.

"No. And you don't want me, not truly. You just don't like the idea that someone else could desire what you believe you own. Well, you do not own me, Justin. Not my body. Certainly not my soul. I just want you to leave me alone," she insisted, as she moved past him and began to walk toward the house. If only he would simply let her go. "It's what you are best at."

"Oh, *Ria,*" he called out to her before she had gotten three steps away.

She stopped, hands clenched at her sides, then slowly turned to face him. "What do you want?"

He gave her a thin smile. All the powerful emotion they had exchanged was gone. Perhaps it had never truly existed for him. Another good reminder that her husband was never what he seemed.

"I'm afraid I cannot simply leave you be. Not while you're attempting to cuckold me with the first buck who catches your fancy. A man has his pride, you know."

Victoria bit back a humorless laugh. Ah, yes. His pride. His bloody reputation. *That* was what he desired, not her. And as she stared at him through the semidarkness on the empty terrace, she realized *exactly* what she needed to do. For the first time since she turned to find Justin staring back at her inside, she felt calm. Controlled.

"You don't have any say in what I do, Justin," she said softly.

"Don't I?" He frowned. "If I wished, I could simply reveal your identity to the room. No one would touch you if they knew you were my wife. They wouldn't dare."

She folded her arms. "No. You won't do that."

He chuckled, challenge in his expression and posture. "And why wouldn't I?"

"Because doing that would hurt you far more than it would hurt me."

His brow wrinkled. "And how would it possibly hurt me for the world to know my wife is the most sought-after woman in the country?"

"Because I'm not just the most sought-after woman in the country. I'm Ria, the most sought-after *courtesan* in the country. And the reason so many men want Ria is that she was taught exotic sensual arts by a long string of talented lovers. None of which was you, husband."

Victoria almost crowed when his smug expression began to crumble and the truth of what she was saying sank in.

She continued, "So if you reveal that I'm your wife, you will also reveal that I turned to others to find fulfillment. And *that* would hurt your precious reputation more than anything else. After all, what kind of lover could you possibly be if your wife would prefer to become a courtesan than be with you?"

A long moment of silence hung between them, but Victoria made no effort to fill the emptiness. She wanted Justin to ponder what she had said. Be affected by the truth of it.

And in some cruel part of herself, she wanted him to be stung by it. That she, a woman he had thrown away, now held sway over the only thing he cared about.

Finally he murmured, "You would ruin me, ruin yourself, just to live out this charade of yours?"

She stepped closer, trying not to breathe in the heady, masculine scent of his skin.

"Oh yes, I most definitely would." She turned away. "I don't expect we'll have to have this tedious conversation again, Justin. Good evening."

And then she walked into the house without so much as a glance over her shoulder.

* * *

Justin stared at Victoria's retreating back, too shocked by her dismissal to say or do anything but sputter in her wake. What the hell had just happened?

He spun on the terrace, pacing to the wall and looking down over the gardens below. He'd been so happy to return to London, but then his wife had shown up and in one wretched evening ruined all his plans, his comfort, his life in general!

Worst of all, she had reminded him, without even trying, that he wanted her. Still. Despite everything.

"We saw Ria return to the ballroom," Shaw said as he and Caleb came out onto the terrace to join Justin.

He struggled to maintain a façade of control before he turned to face his friends. None of his family had attended his wedding or met Victoria, nor had Shaw, so neither man had any idea she was the infamous "Ria."

No matter how much Justin trusted the two men, he had no intention of revealing the truth to them. Not yet. Not until he was sure how he wanted to handle his wayward wife and her ruse.

"Did she?" Justin managed to croak as he relived every moment with Victoria in vivid detail.

Caleb nodded. "And she looked a bit mussed,

as well. It's a good thing we didn't formalize our wager, or I fear I'd owe you even more blunt than I already do!"

His brother's chuckle grated on Justin's nerves.

"Yes, trust you to win in one night what the rest of us couldn't touch in nearly two weeks," Shaw grumbled good-naturedly as he lit a cigar.

"I haven't won 'Ria' yet," Justin conceded, clenching the stone edge of the terrace wall in a steely grip.

He had shaken his wife, of that he was certain. And he'd realized that she wanted him with the same intensity that he craved her, which was utterly shocking and intensely erotic. But in the game he was now playing with Victoria, that was not winning.

"No?" Caleb said in surprise. "Well, then there is a chance for the rest of us. We can still make it interesting. What do you say, whichever one of us beds her first wins . . . what? Blunt, horses? Justin, I've had my eye on that new phaeton of yours; what say you put that up?"

"No bets," he growled.

Justin pushed from the terrace wall, gripping his hands into fists at his side as he tried to control the sudden burst of rage that hit him in the gut. He certainly wasn't going to bet on which one of them would bed *his* wife first.

No matter what, legally she was *his*. The idea

that she was tempting other men, that she had *been* with other men, perhaps even educated in Eastern sexual practices and God knew what else from some idiotic soldier . . . it turned his stomach.

"Baybary?" Shaw began, tilting his head with concern.

Justin turned away. He wasn't in any mood to discuss his wife with anyone at present. Because when he thought of her, it wasn't with any kind of rationality. It wasn't with his usually cool detachment.

No, his thoughts of Victoria were primal and possessive and entirely out of character.

They were simply: *Mine. Mine. Mine.*

By the time Victoria entered the small house she had let in the unassuming, rambling neighborhood of Soho Square, any bravado she'd managed to exhibit at the ball was long gone.

"Good evening, my lady," her butler intoned as he reached for her wrap.

Victoria held the garment for a moment too long as her mind spun away to dangerous, sensual territory. When the butler gently tugged, she released it with an apologetic smile.

"Thank you, Jenkins," she mumbled as she staggered up the hallway toward the front parlor.

"May I get you anything, madam?" he asked, concern plain in his deep voice.

She shook her head as she began to shut the door behind her. "No, I do not require anything."

Her hand was shaking as she grabbed for a bottle of sherry. Oh, she required something, but nothing the butler could provide. She required some sense.

As she splashed a healthy portion of the liquor into a glass, she tried to calm her nerves. An impossible task considering what had happened tonight.

She touched her lips and could still taste Justin on them. Her breasts remained heavy and hot with the brand of his hands and wicked tongue.

"You're home early."

Victoria jumped as her best friend, Marah Farnsworth, entered the parlor and closed the door behind her. She tried to appear calm as she smiled weakly at the other woman. It was clear she failed by the way Marah's dark blue eyes widened in concern. Immediately she crossed the room and put a comforting arm around Victoria's waist.

"Oh, it was a difficult night, wasn't it? Lord Richen didn't make some clumsy attempt to grope you again, did he?" her friend asked as she led her to the settee in front of the fire.

Victoria shook her head as she took a seat. An elderly gentleman's sad and easily dodged attempts to molest her certainly weren't enough to put her in such a state of upset. No, it took a very virile, very powerful man to do that.

"Justin is here," she choked out with no preamble before she downed the remaining liquor in her glass.

Marah jumped to her feet, one slender hand covering her mouth in shock. "No! Our sources said—"

Victoria set her glass on the table beside her with a clink. "Our sources were clearly mistaken. He was at the soiree tonight."

Marah sank back onto the couch beside her. "So he saw you then?"

Biting back a bark of humorless laughter, Victoria nodded. He'd seen so much. Even the things she'd fought so hard to conceal.

Her friend shook her head. "And even after all the trouble we put into your hair and making your dress so different and the way you move, he recognized you? After three years?"

Victoria nodded a second time, even as she willed herself not to remember every moment of their encounter again in powerful, hot detail. It was a losing battle. The things he had done. The things she'd *let* him do, despite all her intentions.

"Tell me everything," Marah said softly.

Victoria swallowed hard. How could she explain *everything* to her innocent friend? She wasn't certain she fully understood what had happened tonight herself, let alone had the ability to explain it to Marah. So, instead of everything, Victoria settled for revealing a selective *something*.

Carefully, she disclosed enough about her encounter on the terrace with Justin that Marah understood their tenuous situation, though she left out all the passion and pleasure that they had exchanged. There were some things better left unsaid, and unthought about.

As she finished with a shaky sigh, Marah collapsed against the back of the settee with a shake of her head.

"My," her friend murmured. But then she smiled wickedly. "But after all the hell you've been through because of him, it must have been gratifying to finally put the man in his place."

Victoria pondered that statement. Gratifying? No, nothing about tonight had been that. Confusing. Terrifying. Frustrating. But there had been no gratification, even when she left her husband sputtering out his rage on the terrace.

All tonight had served to do was remind her that Justin Talbot held a powerful sensual sway over her. Even after all this time.

"Victoria?" Marah asked, tilting her blond head to the side. "He shook you, didn't he?"

Victoria thought about refuting that statement for a moment, but decided against it. She was too shaken to cover her emotions on the subject. Marah would see right through any weak denials.

"I was surprised to see him," she admitted.

"And I'm sure he was shocked to see you." Her friend smirked briefly, but then she was all seriousness again. "But now that the unpleasantness is out of the way, we can return to matters at hand. Did you uncover any new information about Chloe?"

Victoria flinched. Chloe Hillsborough was one of her best friends. The young widow had come to London six months before to become a courtesan and had been very successful at it. She had even seemed to like it, going so far as to send her friends a list of "rules" a courtesan had to live by. Ones Victoria had begun to take very seriously since Chloe had suddenly disappeared without a trace. In her last few letters to Victoria and Marah, she had described a persistent suitor who was stubbornly against taking no for an answer.

Although Chloe had never mentioned the man's name and given only the briefest description, it had been clear their friend was afraid of what this stranger would do the longer she held out against his pressing advances. Both women were certain their friend's disappearance had something to do with him.

Victoria and Marah had quickly realized they could do no good unless they were in London, involved with the kind of people Chloe had mingled with daily. So the courtesan "Ria" and her erotic past had been born.

"I found nothing new," Victoria admitted with a frown. "I did see several of the men we have been tracking, but once Justin interfered, it was difficult for me to focus enough to approach them."

She scowled, hating herself both for her failure and for Justin's ability to shake her.

Marah patted her arm. "I'm sure all will be well. Lord Baybary will forget you again, as he did for so long before. A man like him will find other diversions, especially since you threatened his precious reputation. And we *will* find Chloe. I know we will."

"I hope so." Victoria sighed, covering her eyes. Suddenly her head was throbbing.

She wasn't as convinced that Justin would simply release his drive to pursue her. Their encounter on the terrace had been intense, desperate, driven. She'd lost control, but she wasn't convinced she was alone in that. She had felt Justin wavering as well. And she wasn't so certain he would let her go now that they'd had that brief taste of each other.

Worse, she wasn't so certain she *wanted* him to let her go. Not before she felt the full force of the pleasure he could bring her just one more time.

Chapter 3

Lesson 3: It is simple to make a man want you. Don't want him.

The more Justin thought about the situation with Victoria, the angrier he became. He paced across his parlor, fists clenching and unclenching at his sides, heat rising up his neck as he ran over the previous evening's events again and again in his head. It wasn't the first time, either. All night he'd tossed and turned, stewing over Victoria's sudden arrival in his world, her tempting appearance, her maddening behavior and words.

But the thing that had awoken him this morning, hard and ready, was the memory of her taste, her surrender to his touch. Despite his building anger, his lust hadn't abated even a fraction. It was entirely disturbing.

"If you keep circling the room in this fashion, eventually you'll bore a hole in the floor and we'll all end up in the cellar with the laundry wenches," Caleb said mildly as he took a sip of tea and ate another scone in one wolfish bite.

"You *are* in a mood this morning," Shaw concurred from his place beside the window, looking out over the grounds behind Justin's London estate. "Kept up too late last night by some mysterious woman?"

Caleb laughed. "Not Ria, that's for certain."

Justin glared from one to the other. "You two could try minding your own affairs for once."

Shaw pushed off the window and came toward him. "Ah, that *is* the source of your foul mood, is it? You were very secretive last night, but she must have given you quite a set-down. I don't think I've ever seen you so out of sorts over a bit of muslin before."

Clenching his teeth, Justin tried to remain calm. He was finding he didn't like his own wife being referred to in such bawdy terms. Damn Victoria for putting him in such an untenable situation.

"Great God, you have a scowl." Caleb laughed, setting his tea aside. "What is wrong with you? Certainly Ria is charming, but she's not worth all this trouble. She's just a courtesan, just a woman, nothing more."

Justin stared at the two men. There would be no putting them off a subject once they were interested. They would push and prod and bother until they knew all the details. That was their specialty, after all. And now that they weren't in the middle of a crowded party where anyone could overhear, Justin wasn't as hesitant to reveal the truth. Oh, he was certain he would get a good ribbing from both men, but they were trustworthy. They always had been.

"She isn't just a courtesan and she's far more than a mere woman," he admitted, pouring himself a scotch despite the early hour of the day. "'Ria' isn't even her real name."

Caleb was on his feet as though a fire had been lit under him. "Really? Oh, do tell. I would love to hear this since all that exists regarding Ria is rumor and conjecture. What *is* the mysterious lady's real moniker?"

Justin sighed. He wasn't looking forward to what would come next. "Her name is Victoria Talbot. The *lady* is my wife."

For an all-too-brief moment, the room was utterly silent. Justin could hear the faint pop of logs in the fire as they burned, the tick of the grandfather clock near the door. But then the blissful quiet was broken as both Caleb and Shaw began to talk at once.

"You jest!" Shaw said, shaking his head in disbelief. "That isn't possible."

"But Victoria is sequestered in the country!" Caleb spoke over Shaw. "Doing . . . whatever it is she does there."

"Taking care of your estate," Shaw added helpfully. "Which I never understood why you let her do that, by the by. But that isn't important now. Are you certain that she is your wife?"

Justin clutched the crystal tumbler in a death grip. "Absolutely certain. That was why we were alone on the terrace for so long last night. I was confronting her."

"Why didn't you tell us?" Shaw asked, his jaw still gaping.

Justin shrugged. "It wasn't something I was happy to admit. And I feared being overheard at the party."

Caleb leaned forward in growing interest. "What did Victoria say when you spoke to her?"

With a shake of his head, Justin muttered, "She said if I reveal the truth about her identity, it will reflect poorly on my reputation. That she would make it clear I was not . . . *talented* enough to keep her attention, and that is why she is looking for a lover so blatantly."

The two men stared at him, again stunned into silence. Then his brother shocked him by throwing back his head and letting out a loud, booming laugh.

"There is nothing funny about this," Justin cried as he set his drink down with a jarring smack.

"Oh yes, there is!" His brother continued to chuckle. "In short, she's got you by the balls. Honestly, if I'd known what a spitfire and a beauty she was, I would have insisted you bring her to London long ago. Why in the world didn't you tell me?"

Justin's nostrils flared, and the vibrant heat of emotion warmed his cheeks. "Damn it, Caleb! When I left Victoria, she wasn't the kind of woman who would come to London posing as a courtesan, looking for a lover under my very nose and practically blackmailing me into accepting it!"

"Perhaps you should have gone home more," his brother said with a wide grin. "It appears your virginal bride of convenience turned into something so much more interesting while you were away."

Justin scowled. *That* was certainly true. Memories of his wife collided with the new images from the night before. Three years ago Victoria had been hesitant, timid. There were times on their wedding night when he'd actually thought she was afraid of him. Of course, he'd never been certain if her behavior was all an act or not. With a father like hers, he'd never even fully trusted her innocence until he'd actually breached her maidenhead.

There was only one thing he'd been completely certain of that long-ago night. Passion. The passion had been real. A passion and a driving need more powerful, more *overpowering* than anything he'd experienced before or since, and that was saying something considering the skilled lovers he'd had in his bed. Touching Victoria, awakening her desires, had been an utter pleasure and a complete surprise, as well.

But he had no interest in living some fairy tale with a woman whose father held the key to his family's demise. A woman who might be just as cunning as the man who sired her. Justin had been blackmailed into the marriage, but had sworn it would be a union in name alone. So he'd left.

And spent three long years trying to forget Victoria. Trying to erase that one night from his mind. But now she was back, forcing herself into his life, into his dreams.

Shaw stepped up with a shake of his head. "I always felt you gave Victoria too much leeway, Baybary. I mean, you hardly knew the woman, yet you allowed her to run your estate."

Justin threw up his hands in annoyance. "I never questioned that decision. She has run it well. My holdings have almost doubled since she became my wife. Allowing her that freedom took the burden off me and it gave the woman something to do."

"Clearly not enough." Caleb laughed again.

Shaw ignored Caleb's irritating interjection. "There is something else I never understood. Explain to me again why you married this woman in the first place, and in such quick fashion. One moment you were free and vowing to wait until you were sixty to settle down with some young, fresh miss and produce your heirs, the next you were leg-shackled to a woman whose father had been at odds with yours for years over some monetary transaction."

Justin shot a look toward his brother, but Caleb was still too amused to notice the importance of that question. Justin forced his face to be still, to not reflect any of the tangled emotions that surrounded the circumstances of his marriage.

"As Caleb said, it was a union of convenience. A business agreement between Victoria's family and my own, to balance the scales of whatever it was her father felt he had been cheated out of," he explained, carefully leaving out the unsavory parts of the bargain.

Shaw tilted his head, unappeased. "But what did *you* gain from it?"

Justin fought the urge to tell the truth. *Silence.* That was what he had received from the union. And so far Victoria's father had kept up his end of that agreement, although Justin was always waiting for the day when Martin Reed went back on the terms of their bargain and began his threats again. So far the money and prestige he received had kept him quiet. Not to mention whatever perverse pleasure Reed took in besting the son of a man he despised.

"Justin?"

It was Caleb who spoke this time, and the humor was gone from his voice. There was a rare expression of concern on his brother's face. Justin shook off his thoughts and paid attention.

"I gained land, of course," he lied. "And peace. You remember how father and Martin Reed fought, Caleb. It was all-out war at times. That ended when I took Victoria as a bride and united the two families."

"But Father was furious when he heard of your marriage," Caleb pressed, looking at him with a strange expression. "It was one of the few times when his anger was turned on your bad choices, rather than mine."

Justin shifted uncomfortably. His younger brother was often distracted by frivolity and pleasure, but beneath all that Justin knew a serious man lurked. A man who was desperate to prove his worth. To Justin. To their father. To himself.

If he ever uncovered the truth . . .

"Father came around eventually," he hurriedly explained. "He ended up appreciating how all the frivolous court battles ended. Reed no longer showed up at the house drunk to make a scene in front of guests."

Their father had never looked further into Justin's reasons. And for that, he was happy.

"The motives of the past are not particularly important," Justin hurried to add, hoping to maneuver both Caleb and Shaw away from the nasty subject of the particulars of his marriage agreement. "The present and future trouble me more. Victoria is my wife, for better or worse, and she is now in London parading herself under my very nose. Furthermore, I cannot stop her for fear of hurting my own reputation."

Shaw nodded, a solemn frown on his face. "A quandary, indeed. If you don't stop her, someone might uncover her true identity, and that would bring even more trouble. The gossip, Justin. It would go far beyond mere whispers. You could be shunned socially. There are rules, boundaries, even when it comes to ladies and gentlemen taking lovers."

"Don't remind me," Justin groaned, thinking of the laughingstock he'd become if Victoria was unmasked. The idea alone was bone-chilling. And when her father found out, it might be the very thing he needed to loosen his tongue and destroy Justin's world.

"So what will you do?" Caleb asked. "How do you intend to get your pretty little minx of a wife under control?"

Justin pondered the question. It was the very

one that had been tormenting him since he'd met with Victoria the night before. That and her taste.

"Last night, when I confronted her, there was a cunning to her eyes." Justin winced. The same cunning that had always been in her father's stare, as well. "But there was something else. I couldn't quite place it, but there were times when I caught a flicker of . . . I don't know, other emotions. I wonder if taking a lover is not her only purpose in London."

Shaw folded his arms. "Interesting. If she does have an ulterior motive, it could explain why she suddenly arrived here *now*."

"And why she doesn't intend to stay for more than a few weeks," Justin mused.

The night before, he'd been so distracted by Victoria's appearance, not to mention her touch, he had not fully recognized the signs that something was amiss. Now that she wasn't in his arms, he recalled a brief flash of fear when he said she wasn't a courtesan and the expression of longing when she spoke of returning home in a few weeks' time.

"But what could bring her here?" Caleb asked.

"It could be anything," Justin admitted on a sigh. "I hardly know the woman, remember?"

His brother folded his arms. "I remember her father from our childhood. He was a blustering tyrant of a man with all kinds of theories and secrets and lies swirling around him. Perhaps there's something Victoria is hiding about him."

Justin straightened up. He hadn't considered that, but it could be true. Although his servants reported to him that Martin Reed never visited his daughter and she rarely made trips home to Stratfield to call upon him, the two did correspond through infrequent letters. Victoria *could* be here to settle something for her father. Justin wouldn't put it past the bastard to allow his daughter to parade herself around like a whore just to save his own hide.

If that was the case, the truth could set him free in more ways than one. If Justin had something to hold over Reed's head, he never again had to worry about his own family secrets coming out.

"I could do a bit of poking about," Shaw offered. "My brother's connections in the War Department could come in handy. And secrecy is practically his middle name."

Justin nodded. "Do that, thank you, Shaw. In the meantime, I must find some way to curb her search for a new lover until we uncover the truth. I don't want her unmasked."

Caleb pursed his lips. "Perhaps we could provide someone discreet for the job. Hell, Shaw, you're between women, aren't you?"

Justin realized he had lost all control over his expression the moment Shaw held up his hands and started retreating backward across the parlor toward the door.

"Oh, hell no!" Shaw cried, locking gazes with Justin. "It's one thing to have a bit of fun with the long-separated lover of an old friend after he's given you his blessing. It's another entirely to take that friend's *wife* to bed, even for a good cause."

"Come now," Caleb interrupted, either unaware of his brother's upset, or enjoying the show. "My brother has never been interested in Victoria, despite how fetching she is. You would be doing him a favor."

Justin blinked, trying to make the cloud of red go away from his line of vision. Why he was suddenly so possessive, he could not fathom. He had never before minded sharing a lover he had lost interest in.

Except, despite his brother's words, he hadn't lost interest in Victoria. Not yet. Not ever, despite every attempt.

"We are *not* finding Victoria a lover. Not Shaw, not anyone," he ground out through clenched teeth.

"But that would solve your problems," Caleb pointed out.

"No!" Justin roared, fighting not to grab his brother and give him a good shake. "I don't want her taking *any lovers*."

None but him. Only he hadn't meant to voice his opposition to her plans so strenuously. Now Caleb and Shaw both stared at him. Justin stifled a curse.

"Why don't you?" Caleb asked, this time quiet.

Justin turned away, staring into the fire. He pictured Victoria again. Arching, moaning, her breasts spilling from her gown, her head tilted back in pure pleasure. He pictured all that, but this time with another man, and his stomach turned.

"By law, she is mine. And I have a reputation to uphold," he growled, though that explanation didn't ring completely true in his head. "Leave it at that."

But he knew that wouldn't be possible. Not anymore. Now that Victoria had forced his hand, he was going to have to be in very close quarters with his wife. There would be no avoiding her or the desire that coursed between them. Eventually it would all come to a head.

And he couldn't wait.

Victoria smoothed her gown and gave her cheeks a pinch to bring color to their paleness before she stepped from her carriage onto the packed drive. She looked up at yet another opulent house. From the outside, it looked utterly respectable. Inside, she would encounter something entirely different. Another raucous party filled with randy men, outrageous women . . . and possibly danger, both in the form of whatever person was responsible for Chloe's disappearance and from Justin.

She shivered as she recalled her husband's hot

mouth on hers, branding and burning her. Taunting her with the way he could force her to want, making a lie all the years she had claimed she had forgotten him entirely.

She might see him tonight. But even if she didn't, she was under no illusion that she wouldn't *some* night. They were moving in the same circles now. Though she didn't truly know her husband, Victoria had been fully aware that taunting him, flaunting her intentions before him as she had the night before, was akin to waving a red flag in front of an agitated bull.

It had been a foolish mistake, one made out of her own pride and a desire to slash away some of his haughty exterior. But her investigation into Chloe's disappearance should have been her top priority, nothing else. If Justin interfered in the search for her friend, everything she had sacrificed to come to London would be for naught.

She moved into the ballroom with the crush of the crowd and shook her head. That was enough thoughts of Justin. She could do nothing about what had already transpired, so she would do better to focus on Chloe.

Tonight one of her friend's former protectors was rumored to be in attendance. Victoria's duty was to find the man and talk to him, subtly bringing the topic of conversation to Chloe in the hopes he might have information about her whereabouts. Or at least some information about the frightening gentleman who had been pursuing her friend just before her disappearance.

The moment Victoria entered the crowded ballroom, she was surrounded by admirers. Men who stared at her blatantly, complimented her openly, made suggestive statements that often made her skin crawl.

But sometimes, just sometimes, she felt a burst of pride when they made it clear how much they wanted her. After so many years spent feeling as if no man, and especially no man of experience, would ever want her, the fact that so many did was good for her confidence, if nothing else.

As her "suitors" flowed around her, she let her gaze move over the buzzing crowd. It was strange for her to see all the very proper gentlemen moving around the room, laughing and smiling and having fun with their mistresses and lovers.

It gave her a sting since she knew their wives were at home, not invited to these kinds of events. How many of those women were sitting abandoned with broken hearts? How many faced tragedy and torment alone, just as she had after Justin's departure?

She sighed. The empty marriages she saw evidence of around her were a mere reflection of her own. No amount of heated exchanges with Justin would ever change that.

"There you are, my dear!"

Victoria turned with the false smile she'd perfected since her arrival in London. She watched as her hostess, Alyssa Manning, crossed the room, arms outstretched. Victoria braced herself for the other woman's attention, anxiety coursing through her every vein.

It wasn't that she didn't like Alyssa. The courtesan had never been anything but kind and welcoming to her. In truth, Victoria was terrified of the other woman. Alyssa was everything she wasn't. Calm. Collected. Comfortable in her sensuality.

And each time the celebrated courtesan approached, Victoria was certain she was about to be publicly unmasked.

Alyssa pressed a kiss to each of her cheeks. "I'm so glad you could come, darling Ria. Welcome."

"Thank you. It is a l-lovely home," Victoria stammered, searching for something to say that would rouse no suspicion. And her statement was the truth. The large, airy town home was as fine as those that some of the most celebrated ladies of the *ton* resided in.

Alyssa laughed. "Thank you. It was a gift from a duke, you know."

Victoria's eyes widened. She hadn't known. Certainly the man must have cared for Alyssa to give her such an estate. It made her wonder . . . had Justin given such extravagant gifts to other women?

She forced the unwanted thought from her mind.

"I—I see," she finally choked out. "Well, I couldn't miss the gathering of the Season, now could I?"

"Not if you're looking for a new protector, you couldn't," Alyssa agreed. "My parties are the best places for a young lady of your position to meet a man. Come, who do you want to be introduced to? I have a very handsome, very rich general here tonight . . ." Alyssa looked at her carefully. "But no, you've already had your fun with a man in uniform, haven't you?"

Victoria blinked before she remembered her lie that a mysterious soldier had taught her ancient erotic secrets after time spent in India. That had been Marah's idea, after her friend had found a few very graphic books hidden amongst some of her late parents' items in her guardian's attic. Victoria shivered as she thought of the sexual positions detailed within the worn pages. The images had haunted her for many nights, leading to fantasies involving Justin more often than she cared to admit.

"Ria?"

Victoria shook away her wayward thoughts and nodded. "You're right. I am looking for someone quite different."

Alyssa pursed her lips in thought, then her blue

eyes lit up. "I know the perfect man for you. He hasn't taken a regular mistress in a few years, but his status as a lover is celebrated. He will certainly appreciate *your* rumored talents. And he just returned to London. Have you ever met the Earl of Baybary, Justin Talbot?"

Victoria squeezed her eyes shut briefly. Had Alyssa truly just offered to introduce her to her own husband? Dear God, if it weren't so awful, it would be funny. Almost.

"Yes, I'm afraid I have met Lord Baybary," Victoria said through clenched teeth. "And I don't care for him at all. I would rather avoid him, actually, if it is all the same to you."

Alyssa leaned back and looked Victoria up and down slowly, as if she were expecting her to sprout a second head. "My goodness, I've never met a woman who didn't lust after Baybary. That body, those eyes, his reputation for leaving no woman unsatisfied . . ."

A strangled groan made its way from Victoria's lips before she could stop it. Damn it, those words made thoughts enter her mind. Thoughts about Justin's infidelity, of course. But other ones, as well. Thoughts of the way he'd left *her* well satisfied on their wedding night. The promise of pleasure that had been left unspoken in every touch they'd exchanged the night before on the terrace.

Alyssa cut short her list of Justin's attributes. "I see, you truly do not like him. Well, to each her own. Is there a certain gentleman you *do* wish to meet?"

Victoria swallowed hard. Despite all her bumbling and distraction, somehow Alyssa had opened a door. This was the perfect and natural chance to speak to one of Chloe's former protectors.

Drawing a deep breath, she said, "I've heard a few things about Viscount Wittingham."

The other woman's eyes widened. "Alex? Yes, he is very handsome, of course. But . . . are you certain you wish to meet *him*?"

Victoria straightened up at Alyssa's hesitation. "Why? Are there things about him that make him unsavory?"

Here she had thought Wittingham would lead her to whoever had spirited Chloe away, but perhaps there was something much more sinister about the man her friend had broken ties with only weeks before her disappearance.

"Nothing specific," Alyssa reassured her, but there was doubt in her expression. "If you would like, I will make the introduction. He is in the billiard room."

Victoria smiled and shoved her shaking hands behind her back. This was the moment she had been waiting for. Now she simply had to make the best of it.

Chapter 4

Lesson 4: When one man wants you, a second will follow.

Justin couldn't keep himself from staring at Victoria as she stood chatting with Alyssa Manning, one of London's most notorious courtesans. Alyssa's beauty had been celebrated for years, with men going to ridiculous lengths to have her. Duels had been fought over her. Men had all but given up their status to stay in her bed.

Tonight Victoria outshone her by far. His wife wore a light green gown that matched her bright eyes to perfection. The lacy neckline swooped dangerously low, offering up her gorgeous breasts on display to every man who was currently leering at her. And her shiny black locks were bound up loosely so that free curls left tempting trails along her back and shoulders.

The two women seemed utterly at ease with each other, smiling and laughing as they talked. It made Justin's blood boil, because with every unpracticed gesture, every toss of her dark hair, Victoria's claim that she wanted to be the lover of some other man, that she had already *been* the lover of other men, rang more and more true.

He watched the two women move toward the billiard room with a sinking heart. Men played in the back, spent time with their mistresses, looked for new ones. His fists clenched at the thought that a huge number of men were looking at *his wife* for their next sexual conquest.

"That's right. Look like you want to kill everyone in the room. That's the way to keep attention from yourself and your wife," Caleb said with a sarcastic snort as he brought Justin a tumbler of scotch.

Justin glared at his brother, but quickly smoothed his emotions from his face. Caleb was infuriating, but correct. The last thing he wanted was for anyone to notice his possessive attention toward "Ria" and start to make connections between the sultry courtesan and Justin's quiet, shy little wife, abandoned on his estate far away. That someone would be so observant was only a slight possibility, but it wasn't a risk he wanted to take.

"Did you uncover anything of interest?" Justin asked.

Caleb shook his head. "No. My very discreet inquiries made it clear that while every man knows a man who bedded Vic—"

Caleb broke off when Justin glared at him. They had agreed to refer to Victoria as "Ria" while in public to reduce the chance of discovery.

"Every man knows a man who has bedded *Ria,*" Caleb corrected. "But not one of them has actually taken her to bed himself. Though not for lack of trying. For being labeled 'London's Greatest Courtesan,' she has had a shocking lack of verifiable sex."

Justin let out a long breath.

"Relieved?" Caleb asked with a wink.

With a shake of his head, Justin shot a look at his brother. "Of course I am happy that her infidelity cannot be proven. Any small fact could be of assistance if the worst happens and she is unmasked."

"So it is all about your reputation, eh?"

"Of course." Justin stared off in the direction Victoria had headed. "What else could it be?"

His brother chuckled. "I have no idea, but it is fascinating to watch."

Justin jerked his attention back to Caleb. He understood perfectly the implication his brother was making, and it was beyond irritating.

"So where is she now?" his brother asked.

"Billiard room." Justin downed his entire drink in one burning swig. "With Alyssa Manning."

Caleb turned to him, mouth gaping. "Really? Well, she certainly does move in the right circles. If anyone can find her a protector, it's Alyssa."

"I am aware," Justin answered in his most withering tone.

"Are you certain you don't want to set Vic—*Ria* up with a lover of your own choosing, at least until we uncover more information? That would certainly occupy her time and keep her separate from all these people who know you so well."

Justin shook his head. "No. Absolutely not. I don't want her bedding anyone."

"No one but you."

He hesitated. There was no use denying it.

"Yes, I do want her."

His brother seemed surprised by his easy admission of that fact. "Well, no one could blame you for your desire. She is very beautiful."

That she was. Normally Justin had trouble recalling what a woman looked like when she left a room, even one he was pursuing. But it was far too easy to conjure an image of Victoria, wrapped in his sheets, beckoning him with those dangerously bewitching eyes.

Just the thought made him rock-hard. But this neediness, this wanting, if Victoria recognized it, she could use it against him. So he had to control it. And her.

"Beautiful or not, I have no idea if I shall actually pursue my desire. Certainly I could have equally spectacular women in my bed who would cause me far less trouble." Of course, Justin couldn't think of a one to save his life. He shook his head. "No, for now, my priority is to discover if there is any alternate motive for her sudden arrival. One way or another, I must force her out of London before she rips both our worlds apart. If something else happens between us . . ."

He waved his hand in the air dismissively, but he felt anything but dismissive at the idea of having Victoria in his bed. He felt . . . off-kilter.

He never felt like this. Ever. And it infuriated him.

"There you are," Russell Shaw said as he strode up to the two men and blessedly ended their troubling conversation.

Justin nodded in acknowledgment to his friend. "Did you find any new information?"

Shaw cocked his head. "And a very good evening to you, as well." He exchanged a meaningful glance with Caleb before he continued. "I have uncovered a bit about Miss *Ria's* activities. She arrived in London about a fortnight ago. Before her arrival, rumors were already swirling about her . . . skills."

Justin flinched. "We already knew all that."

Shaw's eyes widened. "Yes, I'm getting to new information now. Good God, man, calm yourself."

Justin glared at his friend, but kept his remaining comments to himself.

Shaw drew a breath. "No one knows much about her past or her intentions. Hell, I haven't met anyone who knows her last name. Aside from her outings to these gatherings, the lady is a veritable ghost. She vanishes at dawn and reappears only to dance the night away."

Justin cursed under his breath. He had been hoping for some kind of indication that Victoria's plans went beyond the obvious. But her infuriating desire to take a lover was all that existed for now.

"Speaking of which, is that Ria now?" his brother asked, motioning toward the terrace doors that led to the gardens behind the ballroom.

Justin swung around in time to see Victoria's expensively slippered foot disappearing outside. And she was on the arm of Viscount Alexander Wittingham, a man known for his voracious sexual appetites and string of former mistresses. Justin took a step toward the door, but Caleb caught his arm.

"Wait, Justin. If you make a scene, you could very well cause even more trouble than you have already," Shaw insisted.

Justin pulled against Caleb's grip, but his brother held fast. In his rational mind, he knew Shaw was correct. Confronting Victoria in the state of mind he was currently in would only raise suspicions. But somehow that didn't matter as much as getting her away from the other man, keeping her from acting on her desires.

Justin yanked his arm free from his brother's grasp and started his way across the ballroom.

"I don't give a damn."

Victoria laughed at something her companion, Viscount Alexander Wittingham, said, but the sound was hollow and empty. Since they had begun their tour of the gardens, the gentleman had been nothing but charming and handsome and amusing, just as Chloe described him in her letters to Victoria and Marah over the weeks they were together. So far, Victoria felt no threat from him. But neither did she feel any connection to him.

Although he certainly seemed to feel one to her. The viscount had been staring at her quite blatantly since they began their walk around the pretty gardens behind Alyssa's home.

"I must say, Ria, you are even more beautiful than I'd heard. I'm quite flattered you agreed to walk with me tonight," the viscount said with a deferential nod of his head.

Victoria stifled a sigh and put on the flirtatious persona she and Marah had perfected with the help of Chloe's "lessons." With a gentle pat on his arm, she laughed. "It is I who is flattered, my lord. I have heard nothing but good things about you."

He tilted his head. "Good things, eh? What kind of things?"

"The kind ladies are not supposed to speak about loudly." She swallowed. This act still wasn't natural to her. When she returned home, she would never again complain about the modesty and decorum Society expected of her.

Wittingham drew back, and the gleam of interest had doubled in his stare. "Really? How intriguing. And from whom did you hear these very complimentary things?"

Victoria all but held her breath. This was her chance. "From another lady who was lucky enough to spend a bit of time with you. She spoke very highly of you."

He turned toward her. "I am at a loss. What lady must I thank for her high praise?"

"It was Chloe Hillsborough, my lord."

As she spoke the words, Victoria leaned forward ever so slightly and focused on gauging her companion's reaction.

Wittingham's smile faltered a fraction, and the good humor faded from his expression, replaced with a faraway brooding.

"You heard this from Chloe?" he repeated, her name rolling slowly off his tongue like he was savoring it.

Victoria nodded, watching his face closely. Chloe had never written with anything but the highest praise for her former lover, but perhaps that wasn't enough for Wittingham. Judging from the emotion in his eyes, there were strong feelings that lingered on his part. Perhaps he hadn't been able to accept it when Chloe ended their affair.

"That is high praise indeed," he said softly, his gaze moving away from Victoria as he looked over the moonlit gardens. "Was this a recent statement?"

Victoria examined his face. The emotion she'd seen had been wiped away, and she couldn't read his intent or feelings any longer. Was that because of pain or anger . . . or was he purposefully hiding something to determine what *she* knew about her missing friend?

"Not particularly. I actually haven't heard from Chloe in some time. I was hoping to see her during my trip to London, but so far I've been unsuccessful."

She hesitated. How far did she dare push the man? Too much and he would become suspicious. Then again, this could be her only chance to interrogate him.

"Do you happen to know of her whereabouts?"

Wittingham flinched slightly. "No. I'm afraid I do not. We were once close, but . . . but that ended some time ago." He shook off his distance and turned to look at her. "I'm surprised you would bring me out into the garden to talk to me about another woman, Ria. Is that really the topic you wish to discuss?"

Victoria dipped her head with a blush she didn't have to force. She wanted more information, but she didn't particularly want to end up in Wittingham's bed tonight. There had to be a way to accomplish her objectives.

"A very straightforward question, my lord," she said with a light laugh.

He leaned in closer. "I have a feeling you are a woman who appreciates that sort of thing."

Before Victoria could answer, a voice from behind them sent all the fine hairs on the back of her neck to stand up.

"Back. Up."

She spun around and watched in shock as Justin stepped from the shadows. The full moon cast half light on his face, revealing the thin set of his sensual lips and the intense focus of his eyes. The anger and possessiveness in his expression stole both her breath and her voice.

Wittingham arched a brow with what appeared to be genuine confusion. "I beg your pardon, Baybary. Are you speaking to me?"

Justin took a jerking step forward. "You heard me plainly. I said *back up.*"

If Victoria had been in Wittingham's position, she would have done as Justin ordered, if only because a barely controlled violent intent was so clear on every line of his face. But Wittingham merely looked at her mildly.

"Is Lord Baybary a friend of yours?"

She swallowed hard. She and Marah had prepared for all contingencies but this. She never would have guessed that Justin would interfere in her business after she so handily set him down and threatened him with the destruction of the only thing he cared about. His damned reputation.

"Yes. I am a friend of"—Justin glared at her—"*Ria's.* And I think she has been outside long enough. I shall escort her back into the ballroom."

Wittingham looked Justin up and down, then glanced to Victoria. "Do you wish to go with this man?"

Victoria stared at the viscount in surprise even as Justin made a growl of displeasure. It was impossible to read Wittingham's feelings, for his face was completely impassive. Still, his question spoke of a desire to . . . protect her. Was it an act or a genuine concern?

"Ria," Justin growled.

She shot him a look, then smiled at Wittingham. She would have to tread carefully, lest she risk offending him and cutting off all chance of obtaining more information about Chloe later.

"It seems Lord Baybary has something important he wishes to discuss with me. I have no objection. But I do hope we can talk more later, Wittingham." She pursed her lips in Justin's direction. "Without interruption."

The viscount released her arm and gave her a short bow before he turned on his heel and headed toward the house. Without looking at Justin as he passed, he murmured, "Baybary."

"Wittingham."

Justin kept his stare trained squarely on Victoria, dark eyes flickering in the dim lamps on the garden pathway. Despite her frustration that he had intruded upon her private conversation, and had perhaps ruined her chances to uncover more details about Chloe's life and disappearance, Victoria couldn't help but be moved by Justin's expression. There was something so very possessive and sensual in the way he stared. As if he didn't just *want* to own her . . . he already did, and it was only a matter of time before he staked that claim.

Victoria shivered at that thought. God help her, she did want his touch. But she was more than her mere physical urges. She had a mind, as well as a body. She knew full well that all Justin wanted was to *claim*. Not because he cared for her or even really wanted her, but because his pride pricked him.

And she wasn't about to allow him to keep her from her duty to Chloe. No matter how tempting he was.

After the viscount had gone far enough up the path that they would not be overheard, Victoria advanced on her husband.

"How dare you intrude upon my private conversations?" she hissed, her voice just above a bare whisper.

"I think a husband has every right to at least *see* the men his wife is planning on cavorting with," Justin retorted softly. He glanced over his shoulder. "You could do far better than Wittingham, trust me."

She shook her head in frustration. "You don't get a say, Justin. I don't want your comments or advice."

"We don't always get what we want," Justin said with a feral smile.

Victoria's heart thudded, and she stood frozen in place as her husband advanced on her, one slow step at a time. She recognized what he was about to do. She knew it was all a manipulation. But she couldn't turn away when he slowly slipped an arm around her waist and pulled her against his chest.

"But I could give you what you need, Victoria," he whispered, his voice rough. "Better than anyone else."

"You don't know what I need," she whispered, but her broken tone spoke louder than her weak words.

He examined her face, and Victoria shivered at the intensity of his stare. In a terrifying moment, she realized he was searching for something in her eyes. Something beyond desire.

Truth.

She pulled against him, but he held firm.

"What do you *really* need?" he insisted.

Her heart was pounding now, and she was certain he could feel it as they were molded chest to chest.

"Nothing from you. I don't trust you with anything."

"Not a thing?" he murmured as he cupped her chin and tilted her face up.

And then his full, tempting lips were descending rapidly, covering hers with hotly possessive pressure. All the fearful emotions that had plagued her since her arrival at the ball that night suddenly faded, leaving only Justin. Only the moment between them.

Just as it had the last time he touched her, the kiss spiraled rapidly out of control. She found herself rocking against him, leaning into him, clutching at him, and wanting more. Wanting everything.

He pulled away first, leaving her staggering and dizzy as he stepped back into the shadows toward the house. "Trust me or don't, Victoria, but never forget that you are mine. And if you will not freely give me the answers I demand, I will find a way to take them."

Justin made his way through the thinning crowd, his mind reeling with every step. All he could think about was Victoria.

Their encounter in the garden had been many things. Intensely passionate. Angry. And something else. When he questioned her about what she needed, her response had been far more than sexual.

It had been fearful. She had wanted to escape him, and for the first time, he didn't think it had anything to do with their past. She was hiding something. He just had to determine *what*.

But it wouldn't happen tonight. Victoria had fled the instant he broke contact with her lips. No one had seen her since, and Shaw had reported that her carriage was gone.

From the corner of his eye, he saw Caleb standing with Shaw. The men were entangled in deep conversation with two young women, laughing and grinning like a couple of fools with no cares in the world. He supposed they didn't have any. They certainly didn't have his troubles.

With a curse, Justin let his gaze move over the remaining guests. Perhaps if he stared at them long enough, he would forget Victoria. But it was not meant to be. Within moments, Justin realized that one of the few remaining partygoers was Alexander Wittingham. His stomach turned as he thought of Victoria alone with the man in the moonlit garden. Their conversation had seemed comfortable, and Wittingham had been leaning in far too close.

Clenching his fists, Justin moved toward his rival. Even if he couldn't yet end Victoria's quest, at least he could *discourage* her potential suitors.

He stalked across the room and stepped up to tap Wittingham's shoulder. The viscount turned and frowned when he saw it was Justin who had interrupted him.

Justin glared back. "I would like to talk to you."

Wittingham nodded a farewell to the two gentlemen he had been conversing with and motioned toward a hallway. "I believe Alyssa has a parlor just behind the ballroom. I assume you would like privacy?"

Justin nodded. He stared at Wittingham's back as they left the ballroom and walked down the hall. Never before had he had a problem with the viscount. In all honesty, he'd never spared the other man a thought beyond passing politeness. He knew Wittingham was good at cards, and had even more luck with the ladies. He was about Justin's age, and they had both done well in school in some of the same subjects.

But right now Justin was having a difficult time not putting a fist through the other man's nose. Especially when his errant mind kept creating vivid images of the bastard touching Victoria.

The viscount closed the parlor door behind them and turned to face Justin. "I can only assume this private audience has to do with Ria and that unpleasant scene you made earlier in the evening?"

Justin considered his answer carefully. He didn't want to reveal too much. "Just steer clear of the lady, Wittingham."

The other man tilted his head. "I beg your pardon, Lord Baybary, but I have no intention of doing that. From what I understand, *the lady* is not yet attached to anyone. She has not named you as a keeper or a lover, so I am not going to assume you speak for her until she tells me so herself."

Justin gripped his fists. Normally he wouldn't have batted an eyelash at Wittingham's pursuit of a woman he was interested in. Justin would have gone to her and simply wooed her away, depending on his own charms rather than threats.

That didn't seem possible with Victoria. *She* seemed to delight in denying him, even as she invited every other man closer.

"I'm warning you, Wittingham," he began.

The viscount folded his arms. "Your warning is quite clear, Baybary. And I will tell you this, if Ria chooses you, then so be it. But I've never been influenced by the posturing of other men. I won't start with you, no matter how powerful you are. Good evening."

With that, Wittingham turned and left the parlor. Once he was gone, Justin let out a stream of loud, lewd curses that echoed in the quiet room around him, but did nothing to better his mood.

He was accustomed to getting what he wanted. He was always in control, always the one beginning or ending affairs, always the one determining his own fate. That control had been an obsession. He never wanted to find himself forced into anything as he had been when Victoria's father managed to blackmail him into marriage.

But now he felt anything but in control of the situation. Hell, he didn't even know where his wife *was*, let alone what she was doing and with whom.

It was time he found out, though.

With renewed purpose, Justin made his way back to the ballroom. Shaw and Caleb still lingered in the corner, though Caleb had gone from mere discussion with his lady friend to pressing her against the wall and kissing her. There was no doubt where that little encounter would end. Justin flinched when he flashed briefly to a memory of Victoria's body rubbing against his, setting him on fire.

"Shaw," he snapped as he stepped up to his friend.

Shaw turned away from his purring paramour with a scowl. "I'm a bit busy, Baybary. Can this wait?"

"No." Justin motioned his friend away from his conquest. Shaw let out a harried sigh, but followed his direction.

"Your brother, the one in the War Department." Justin dropped his voice to a mere whisper. "Could he determine where someone was living, as well as their activities?"

"Easily," Shaw said with a shrug. "Do you want to know where Vic—where Ria is staying?"

Justin nodded. "Yes. She may be letting a place under her real name; it might be something else. I want to know."

Shaw sighed as he shot a longing look toward the pretty young woman who still waited for him. She gave him a little wave.

"And I assume you want me to start this tonight?" his friend groaned.

Justin nodded. "The sooner the better."

"Damn friendships anyway," Shaw grumbled. "I don't suppose you want to entertain Camilla while I do your bidding? You look like you could use a night of pleasure."

Justin stared at the woman. He hadn't really looked at her before, but now he recognized her as one of the dance hall girls from a bawdy revue he and Shaw had attended months before. With auburn hair, bright blue eyes, and pale, luminous skin, the young woman was absolutely striking. And if her flirtatious stares at both men were any indication, he could easily find solace in her bed. Normally his erection would have been raging with just that one glance.

Tonight, however, was another story. His cock didn't even stir.

"No. I'm afraid until I manage to talk to Victoria without her running away every time I get too close to the truth, I'm in no mood for any entertaining."

Shaw tilted his head, and surprise sparkled in his bright eyes. "That woman is entirely under your skin. I've never seen anything like it." Justin opened his mouth to speak, but Shaw waved him off. "Just skip the arguments. I'll do what you wish, though I expect you understand what a sacrifice I will be making."

His friend shot a meaningful glance toward Camilla. Justin rolled his eyes. "I do. And I swear that someday I will make a similar sacrifice to help you."

Shaw laughed as he walked back toward the lithe dancer to make his excuses to her. "Trust me, Justin, I will *never* find myself in a situation that requires such a sacrifice. Good evening."

Justin scowled. His friend could say what he liked, but Justin had never intended to be in this kind of situation, either. He'd left his wife behind on a country estate so that he could forget she existed. Who could have predicted that she would burst into his world and set him on his head?

He turned to say good night to his brother, but Caleb was already staggering toward the door, his conquest fitted against him, whispering in his ear. With a groan, Justin went to his own carriage.

Unlike his brother, he faced a long drive home and an empty bed to greet him when he arrived. And dreams of the woman who he had never wanted to see again and now couldn't manage to stop thinking about, no matter how hard he tried.

Chapter 5

Lesson 5: No man can make you lose control . . . unless you let him.

Justin stared up at the modest home that stood before him along a line of similar abodes. The house was small, but tidy and utterly unassuming. Certainly it didn't look like the kind of place that housed "London's Greatest Courtesan." And yet inside these four walls, Victoria lived. Justin didn't even want to know *how* Shaw had uncovered that fact in less than twelve hours.

He stepped up to the stoop and gave a sharp rap across the wooden surface. Within a few moments, the door opened to reveal a tall, broad-shouldered butler who looked Justin up and down with a disapproving sniff.

"Sir?"

Justin held out his gold-foiled card. "The Earl of Baybary to see—"

He stopped. How in the world was he to address Victoria? To his surprise, she had let this town home under her real name, but should he call her his wife? Ria? Lady Baybary?

He didn't have to make that decision. Suddenly a young woman appeared over the shoulder of the servant, but it wasn't Victoria. She had dark blond hair and even darker blue eyes that were wide with shock and recognition, though Justin was certain he had never met the lady before.

"You!" she cried, face draining of color as she stepped in front of the butler. "What are *you* doing here?"

Justin drew back at the venom that poisoned both her stare and tone.

"I apologize, dear lady, but I'm afraid I do not recognize you," Justin said, treading carefully since the butler was now looking at him askance over the stranger's head. He was a fairly large man for a servant of his rank, and Justin didn't particularly want to scuffle with him on the front stoop if he could avoid it. He had enough problems without adding *that* to the list.

"But I recognize you," the blond spitfire retorted as she folded her arms. "You are not welcome here. Please leave."

Justin leaned back, his patience wearing painfully close to the end. "I don't think so. If my *wife* is letting these apartments, that means she is doing so with my money. I have every right to be here."

"We don't want you here," the woman hissed, but Justin could see that his reference to Victoria being his wife had hit home with both the unknown woman and the butler, who was now staring at him with more surprise than menace.

"I suggest you let me inside," Justin said, settling into the cool and collected affectations he was most comfortable with. The ones he couldn't seem to muster when Victoria came within five feet of him. "Or else I can start declaring my intentions right here on the front step where all the neighbors can see and record them."

The woman glared at him long and hard, but he could see he had won even before she drew aside and motioned him in. "Come in, Lord Baybary."

He stepped into the foyer, and the butler closed the door behind him. The servant cast a side glance toward the woman. "Should I send for Her Ladyship, Miss Farnsworth?"

The woman, now identified by a name, shook her head. "Her Ladyship is abed. There is no reason to rouse her. Lord Baybary will not be staying long. You may go; I will take care of this matter."

As the butler bowed away, she motioned to a room off the foyer. Justin followed her gestured order and found himself in a small but comfortable parlor. The walls were plainly hung with just a few seascapes, and the furniture was upholstered in plain, serviceable fabrics. There was nothing particularly sensual about the room.

As he had been with the external appearance of the home, he was surprised by the decor. He had always been generous when providing for Victoria's comfort. With her monthly pin money alone she could have let a beautiful home in the middle of Bond Street that would have been the perfect place to bring her gentleman callers. One with velvet settees and sensual wall hangings, not to mention a fantastic view of all the comings and goings of Society.

The fact that Victoria had chosen this home, where she would likely never bring an upper-class lover, raised his suspicions. It was more hide-out than love nest. But what was Victoria hiding from?

He was torn from his thoughts when Miss Farnsworth folded her arms and cleared her throat noisily. He turned to his unpleasant companion with what he hoped was a dashing smile, not a pained grimace of frustration. This was the perfect time to exercise some of his famous charm.

"Now, Miss Farnsworth, is it? I assume you are a servant of my wife's and—"

She snorted in a very unladylike fashion and

placed her hands on her hips. "I am Victoria's friend, not her servant. And you can save your breath. All that charm doesn't work on me. I know far too much about your true character. Victoria did not invite you here, nor does she desire your company."

Justin clenched his fists at his sides. "I assure you, I mean Victoria no harm."

The young woman's cheeks flushed. "Oh yes, I am certain that is true. I'm certain you *mean* nothing you say or do. And you think nothing of the consequences of your actions, just like you—"

She broke off suddenly and turned away. Justin wrinkled his brow. What would she have said if she hadn't censored herself?

"Victoria has no desire to see you," Miss Farnsworth repeated, though the heat was gone from her voice.

Justin gritted his teeth at her stubbornness. "Why don't you summon her, and we shall see if that is true, madam?"

She turned back, and her jaw was set like steel, her arms folded over her chest. "I have no intentions of doing so, my lord. You would do better to depart."

For a moment, the two stared at each other. Justin was surprised by how much utter disdain rolled off a woman who had never met him before in her life. It made him wonder what kind of ogre

Victoria had made him out to be that her friend would despise him so thoroughly.

Clearly, he was going to get nowhere with Miss Farnsworth blocking his every move, but he had no intention of leaving until he had seen his wife. Even if that meant setting aside all pretense of propriety and manners.

"You leave me no choice," he said on a sigh, then strode from the room and headed up the stairway toward the home's private chambers.

Miss Farnsworth was at his heels before he'd made it to the first step. "Stop this instant, Lord Baybary."

He ignored her, making his way down the hall and throwing open the first chamber door he came to. Empty. The second was the same, and by that time he had actually succeeded in blocking out Miss Farnsworth's outraged demands and calls for servant assistance until they were nothing more than a buzz in the background. He reached for the third door, but before he could check inside, it opened before him.

Victoria stood in the entryway, staring at him with eyes so wide they could have been saucers. Instantly he forgot everything he had come to say as he stared at her.

Her dark hair was down around her shoulders, just as it had been on their wedding night, but that was where the girl of his memory ended and the woman of reality began. Unlike that long-ago night, she wasn't wearing a virginal cotton night-shift. Instead a silky black robe clung to every full curve of her lush body, outlining all the things he had been fantasizing about since her sudden reappearance in his life.

Immediately the spark that had flared between them on their wedding night returned. But even it was different. Hungrier. More desperate. And tinged with anger and betrayal from both sides, rather than the virginal fear Victoria had worn like a cloak on their wedding night.

The moment hung between them, silent as they stared at each other, but then it was disturbed by all hell breaking loose. The butler arrived at the top of the stairs, flanked by two equally large footmen. Miss Farnsworth began shrieking at him even as she tried to talk to Victoria, seemingly at once. And a maid entered into the hallway, saw the uproar, and promptly collapsed into a theatrical heap.

The two footmen caught Justin's arms and began to pull him away when Victoria's voice lifted above the fray.

"All of you be quiet!"

The entire circus came to a sudden halt as everyone in the hallway, including the maid, who had regained her senses during the excitement, stared at Victoria.

"Wilson, Petry, please release Lord Baybary," she said softly. When the servants did as they had been told, Justin smoothed his coat and glared at the two men.

Miss Farnsworth spun on her friend in horror. "Victoria!"

Victoria set a hand on the other woman's shoulder. "Throwing him out will not change anything, Marah." She shot a brief glance in his direction. "Justin will keep coming back until he has gotten his way. But once he has, he'll leave."

Justin flinched at her pointed reference to his departure the day after their wedding. He was annoyed and chagrined at once.

"Justin, you may come into my private parlor," she said, motioning behind her. "We will talk there. Jenkins"—she looked at the butler—"no tea, please. And someone help Rebecca up from the hallway floor. She's going to get a splinter."

With that, she turned on her heel and coolly entered her chamber, leaving everyone in the hallway to stare at her retreating back before the servants rushed to fulfill her orders. Justin couldn't help but stare along with them.

If he had wondered before where his shy, uncertain bride had gone, the question was even stronger in his mind now. The woman who had just given all those orders was someone entirely different. She was neither the tempting courtesan from the scandalous parties, nor the shy young woman of his memories. So Victoria had at least three personas. Three lives. But which ones were the lie? Which the truth?

Or was there any truth to her at all?

"You had best not hurt her again," Marah Farnsworth whispered with a glare before she stomped over to the maid and grasped her hand. "Great God, Rebecca, you do faint at the slightest things."

Justin stepped into Victoria's chamber and shut the door behind him. She was standing at the window, her back to him, and she flinched, just the slightest bit, when the door clicked into place, but she didn't speak.

He took advantage of her silence to look around. Just like the parlor below, the room didn't appear like that of a courtesan, which gave him a strange relief. The small dressing room they stood in had an armoire, dressing table, and settee, as well as a little writing desk in the corner. Next to the desk was an open door leading to Victoria's bedroom. Through that, he could see her bed. The coverlet and sheets were rumpled and tangled.

She had been sleeping when he arrived, just as Marah implied. He couldn't help but shut his eyes and picture his wife all alone in that big bed. Only his imagination took the image further. To the *two* of them in the bed, their bodies writhing against each other.

"Why did you come here, Justin?" Victoria said softly, interrupting his thoughts.

He shook away the fantasies, though he couldn't erase the erection they had so easily caused. His cock throbbed, despite the frustration his wife inspired.

"You and I have much to discuss," he answered, shifting in an attempt to relieve his discomfort. It didn't work.

She turned, and he thought he saw her gaze flit down to the obvious signs of his arousal, but she didn't react. Her stare almost immediately returned to his eyes.

"Every time you have seen me since we met at that ball, you have cornered me to 'talk.'" She shook her head. "There is nothing left to say."

He moved forward. "How can you say that? I have *tried* to speak to you, yes. But you have run away from me without giving me any real answers every time. Now there will be no running. Not anymore."

Her eyes narrowed. "You are the last one who should lecture about running, Justin. You are a master at abandoning your responsibilities. If I don't wish to discuss anything of import with you, then that is a consequence of your own making."

He flinched at the raw anger in her green eyes. Eyes that had darkened with her emotions. How pretty they were. He'd all but forgotten that.

"Stop staring," she said, her face coloring red with a blush as she looked away from him.

"I can't help it," he said softly. He was as surprised at his own admission as she seemed to be when she spun back on him with a gasp. "I—I cannot fathom how different you are, Victoria. And how much the same. So beautiful."

Her lips pursed. "Did you come here to whisper pretty lies in my ear in the hopes it will give you what you desire? I am not as naïve as I once was."

He shook his head. "No, you are not. But you aren't as jaded as you pretend to be, either. And I am not lying when I say that I cannot help but stare at you. I am also not lying when I tell you that my preoccupation with your beauty is not my reason for coming here."

Victoria swallowed hard. "Why then?"

"Last night there was a moment between us," he began.

"You mean the moment where you molested me in public . . . again?" she bit out with enough sharp sarcasm in her voice to cut a lesser man.

He shook his head. "Don't pretend that the heat between us doesn't originate from both sides. You trembled when I touched you, and I wager you imagined what would have happened if instead of walking away, I took you to my bed."

Her lips parted in shock and more than a little desire. But the wall she had built around herself remained intact. "You arrogant—"

"I imagined it, too, Victoria," he interrupted quietly.

That admission stopped her cold. So her pointed tongue could be silenced.

"But that isn't the moment I meant. Last night, when I asked you what you needed, for the first time I saw real emotions in your eyes. Not Ria's false simpering or the anger that accompanies our every exchange. I saw something deeper." He moved forward a fraction. "I think you are hiding something. Tell me why you really came to London."

She snorted out a laugh sharp enough to cut. "You are so damned certain that I am not truly here to find a lover. Your conceit is staggering. Why can't you simply accept that fact?"

He frowned. "You have run my estate with prudence and skill. My staff respects you entirely. These things make me think that you aren't that kind of woman."

Now it was Victoria who advanced. If he had searched for true emotions on her face before, now they were displayed openly. Her hands shook at her sides, and her cheeks were flushed with so much upset that it was palpable.

She had never looked more beautiful.

"As if you know anything about the kind of woman I am from some distant reports you receive from strangers," she all but hissed. "We've been married for three years, and I would wager you haven't thought of me once during that time, let alone bothered to find out anything about me. The only interaction you have that has anything to do with me is through the solicitor in regard to the estate." She turned away. "I'm assuming those exchanges don't include how many lovers I've taken recently."

Justin clenched his fists. Whether or not her statements were true, Victoria was saying these things to bother him. And perhaps she deserved her chance at vengeance. But she was dancing very close to the fine line of his self-control.

"And how many have you taken, Victoria?" He cocked his head.

She blinked, her cool façade broken for just a moment by a flash of regret, of fear.

"Perhaps I'm more like you than we both imagine," she whispered. "Perhaps I've lost count of my lovers."

Justin fisted his hands at his sides in frustration. Every conversation with Victoria was a game, one where she changed the rules whenever it suited her purpose. And there was only one way he knew to bring her under his control. To break down the barriers she put around herself and perhaps finally uncover the truth he had been seeking since the first moment he saw her in London.

Without a word, he closed the distance between them and wrapped his fingers around her silk-encased arm. She gasped at the touch, but had no time to resist before he pulled her against his chest.

"I remember one lover," he murmured before he kissed her.

Just as had happened every time before, her lips parted beneath his, her body went soft and pliant. It was complete surrender and the sweetest thing Justin could have imagined. Only this time, there were no interruptions to come. No chance of being caught and their secret uncovered.

There was nothing to stop him from taking her into her bedroom, splaying her out on that big, empty bed, and claiming her until she whimpered his name in pleasure. And, oh, how he wanted that. More than anything he could recall for a long time.

Victoria felt Justin backing her up, maneuvering her into her bedchamber. And though she knew she should stop this madness, deny him, she made no move to do so. It was as if she couldn't. The moment he touched her, all her plans invariably fled, leaving her a wanton mass of quivering flesh and empty, clenching sheath. Was it wrong to want him to fill her? Claim her?

Yes, of course it was. This man was a cad who had abandoned her with no thought for anyone but himself. A bastard who could very easily put her investigation into Chloe's disappearance at great risk. Yet those things didn't matter when he cupped the back of her neck with warm, rough fingers and delved his tongue into her mouth, melting her with claiming kisses that hinted at the promise of so much pleasure to come.

She arched into him, rubbing her hips against his, moaning when the hard shaft of his erection bumped the juncture of her thighs. Beneath her robe she already felt the heated wetness between her legs. That fact should have humiliated her, but it didn't. She just wanted him to end the ache. To give her the pleasure she'd been denied for all these years.

Perhaps once he did, she could finally forget about him. Put him to rest, put her curiosity and longing for him away. Free herself, at last, from his influence, which had loomed over her since the morning he walked out of her home and her life forever.

His fingers fumbled at her robe tie, and then the silk was gliding away. When Justin saw she was nude beneath, he sucked in a breath.

She couldn't help it. She shut her eyes, blood rushing to her cheeks as he examined her from head to toe. She could pretend to be a courtesan all she liked, but when the man was staring at her like that, she couldn't help but feel stripped bare emotionally as well as physically.

"So lovely," he breathed as he let his fingers travel down her throat, cupped her shoulders, skimmed downward until his thumbs just teased over her already pebbled nipples.

"Justin," she groaned, grasping for his forearm to steady herself as her knees threatened to buckle.

Although the pleasures of her wedding night had resonated with her and she had quickly learned that she could bring herself a shadow version of that explosive feeling, she wasn't prepared for how good his touch was. Like lightning, it shocked her, then traveled with molten heat through her entire body, settling as a pulse between her thighs.

He examined her face for a brief moment, his expression almost as bewildered as she felt. But then his mouth came to her throat and she forgot to watch him. Forgot to breathe as he let his lips move in a downward path. He sucked her skin, lightly bit at the sensitive flesh, and made her come alive with little tingling pleasures. His lips closed around her nipple, and he sucked.

Victoria couldn't control the ragged cry of pure pleasure that burst from her lips and rang in the silent room. Oh yes, *this* was what she had missed.

This desperate, needy thrill. And for once, she didn't care about the consequences or calculate the costs. She just *felt* Justin's skillful touch and reveled in it every moment.

Then his mouth moved lower, and she felt his lips crest over her stomach. Her eyes flew open, and she stared as he dropped to his knees before her. She was pinned between the edge of the high bed and his hot, hard body. There was no escape, even if she wanted to run. Which she didn't.

"What are you—?" she began.

One dark eyebrow arched in her direction, and she cut the question off. If she were really an experienced lover, she would have felt this before. She'd seen such things in the erotic books she and her friends had shared. A man giving a woman an intimate kiss.

"I have wanted to know your taste for so long," he growled as he parted her legs with his shoulders.

She shivered at that declaration. It had to be a lie, but she was too weak with desire to argue. Justin hadn't wanted her, it wasn't possible that he had fantasized about—

She sucked in a breath as all thoughts left her mind. He cupped her sex, parting her lips with his fingers and exposing her to his seeking eyes, his gentle touch. She grasped at his still fully clothed shoulders and clung to him for dear life.

He pressed a kiss against her. It was gentle at first, just grazing the tender flesh that tingled between her thighs. She couldn't help but arch toward him, offering herself shamelessly, reaching for more.

His second kiss was far more intimate. He stroked his tongue across her weeping slit, awakening nerves she hadn't even realized she had. She tilted forward, but Justin caught her, cupping her backside to keep her upright. His hot fingers burned into the sensitive skin of her bottom, setting off a firestorm of pleasure that was only intensified by his seeking tongue.

She shifted her weight helplessly, widening her stance to grant him greater access, though she knew that invitation only made her a wanton. But she needed the pleasure he could give more than anything. And he seemed more than willing to grant her that boon.

He stroked his mouth over her, seeking out every hidden crevice, every tingling inch. Finally he found the hooded bud of nerves that was pulsing and aching for his touch. Justin glanced up at her, a wicked expression darkening his already dark eyes. And he sucked her.

Victoria leaned back against the edge of the bed, hips thrusting out of control as he tormented and pleasured her in equal degrees, taking her up one crest of need, but keeping her from the top every time. Desire overcame her like madness, forcing her body to do things she no longer controlled, making her breath come in needy pants, her voice nothing more than a series of loud moans.

Finally, when she feared she could no longer bear the pleasure or the anticipation, he suckled her hard, swirling his tongue over the little bud. The pleasure exploded, washing over her, stealing her breath. Her hips crashed against him, but still he licked and sucked on, driving her further than she'd ever gone, making her weaker than she'd ever been.

She collapsed against him as the last tremors of pleasure faded. Her body was heavy and her bones liquid as a sense of fulfillment warmed her. She hardly noticed when Justin swept her into his arms and laid her gently on her bed. She stared at him through hooded lids as he backed away, watching her.

But her attention was regained the moment he shrugged his jacket from his shoulders and went to work on the fine shirtwaist beneath. She watched him divest himself of his clothing, one button, one hook at a time. And was surprised when her desire, which had so recently been slaked, returned as more and more of his taut skin was revealed.

Three years had been exceedingly kind to her husband. If anything, he had even more lean coils of muscle beneath his skin. If there was one thing for certain, it was that he hadn't neglected his own care while they were apart.

And now the sight of him as he kicked his trousers away and stood before her in all his naked glory wasn't as shocking as it had been the first time. Since their parting, she had read books, seen realistic drawings of man and all his forms. And she'd had her memories to keep her all too aware of what a fine specimen Justin Talbot was.

Her palms ached to touch him, to explore all the forbidden activities she'd read and heard about while they were apart. No longer was she the shy, naïve flower. She knew what she wanted.

Justin stalked toward the bed, his intent sketched on every tense line of his face. The mattress bowed beneath his weight, and then he covered her body. His mouth merged with hers again, and she tasted her own sweet, earthy essence mingled with the familiar flavor of his lips. It was infinitely erotic to know what that wicked mouth had just been doing and to taste the response he had coaxed from her.

She wrapped her arms around him, sliding her hands over his skin as if she could memorize the map of his body. His muscles bunched and twitched beneath her palms as she smoothed over his contoured back. Downward lower to the base of his spine, and then she cupped his backside as he had done to her when he pleasured her.

Justin groaned into her mouth and his hips thrust, grinding his hard body against the juncture of her thighs and forcing the tip of his cock to nudge inside her wet sheath. The friction of the touch brought a shiver through her body.

Victoria actually felt the thin wire of his self-control break when she brushed her bare breasts against his chest. Justin muttered a curse beneath his breath as his knees forced her legs open wide. He positioned himself at her entrance, stroking the head of his erection back and forth over that hidden nub before he slid into her just a fraction.

Then he stopped, locking gazes with her.

Everything around her seemed to come to a halt as the moment hung between them. Victoria was only aware of him. Of her. Of the nearness of their bodies and how much nearer she wanted them to be.

"Justin," she whispered, her fingers digging into his skin.

He drove forward, shutting his eyes with a harsh cry as he filled her to the hilt in one shattering thrust.

Victoria's long-neglected body relaxed around the invasion. There was no pain this time, only a pleasing fullness that spread though her like a hot bath. She squeezed around him, the ripples of pleasure already building again.

He cursed a second time and held her tighter before he withdrew and thrust forward again. Instantly he set a hard, driving rhythm, totally different from their wedding night when he had been gentle, despite the circumstances.

And unlike their wedding night, Victoria knew what to do in response. She had certainly dreamed about it enough. She rose up to meet him on every angry, passionate stroke. Their bodies ground together, warring and merging at the same time. It was a battle for pleasure, a battle for truth, a battle for everything being waged between them.

But Victoria felt she was destined to lose. Already pleasure wrapped around her, drowned her with its tempting caress, and she was lost. She tumbled over the edge of release, arching up, digging her nails into Justin's back, screaming out his name against his shoulder as he took her ever higher, ever harder, and finally stiffened against her and spilled his seed into her womb.

Chapter 6

Lesson 6: Pleasure is the ultimate weapon.

Victoria didn't know how long they lay entangled in each other's arms, their bodies joined. It could have been a moment; it could have been an hour. Time seemed to hold still as her body shivered and glowed with pleasure.

The sex had been at turns gentle and angry. A surrender and a battle. But there was one constant: it had been utterly fulfilling. Better than all her most vivid memories.

Yet Justin was not someone she could ever form a bond with. And as if to prove that fact, he let out a low groan and rolled away from her. Without so much as a backward glance, he grabbed for his trousers.

The movements were so familiar that they took her off-guard for a moment. So it was to be like last time, then. Searing passion followed by abandonment. Almost as if she really *were* a courtesan that he could use and discard at his pleasure.

Except this time, she refused to let those facts break her. She had grown in the years they were apart, come into herself. She now ran an estate, so well that even her husband had to admit it. She had friends and interests that had nothing to do with the man whose scent now clung to her skin.

No, she was not the same person she had been that night long ago. Even if Justin was. In every way.

She swallowed back a sigh of resignation and forced a wicked smile. Back to the game. "You see, I told you. Running is what you are best at."

He didn't glance in her direction. Hardly acknowledged her at all beyond grunting, "Something like that."

Victoria's smile fell just a fraction. He was so unaffected by her that she couldn't help but be a little embarrassed, especially since she was lying splayed out on her bed, stark naked. The urge to pull the blankets over herself was almost overpowering, but she resisted. She still needed Justin to believe she had become the kind of woman who took lovers with no thought to the consequences.

Now that they had made love, she was certain his desire for her, or at least his desire to mark her so that she wouldn't forget she belonged to him, would fade. Thankfully her own desire would be equally purged.

Except that she couldn't help but watch in fascination when the muscles in his back bunched as he grabbed for his discarded clothing on the floor.

She shook her head to clear her mind.

"Very good, I'm glad we still understand each other," she said. "May I assume I can conclude my business in peace now that you have gotten what you wanted?"

Justin pulled his linen shirt over his head before he turned back to look at her. His gaze smoothed over her nude body, taking in her form with utter familiarity. To her surprise, renewed heat flared in his dark gaze.

She blinked. He wanted her? She had always assumed that once he slaked his need, he lost all interest in her, but he looked as though he could spend the next few hours in her arms quite easily. Except for the smugness in his smile, he looked just as ready to take her as he had when he entered her room.

"Oh yes, my dear. I got what I wanted." He took a step closer, and she gripped her hands at her sides to keep from covering herself. "I got *exactly* what I wanted."

"My body?" she asked, motioning to herself. "It never interested you until you realized someone else had had it."

She was goading him, she knew it. And she also knew how foolish it was. But this time, her set-down didn't seem to frustrate and anger him as it had before. In fact he chuckled.

"Your body tells secrets your pretty little mouth won't."

He took a long step in and leaned toward her. There was no escaping him when he flattened one palm on either side of her head on the headboard. She tensed, though she wasn't sure whether to expect a kiss or something worse. With Justin, she never knew *what* to expect.

"I know you haven't had a lover, Victoria," he whispered close to her ear.

His hot breath stirred both her hair and the pit of longing low in her belly, though she hated herself for the desire.

"At least not for a long time. Perhaps not even since that night three years ago when I claimed your maidenhead." His voice was low and seductive, despite the cold harshness of his words. "I felt it. And even if I hadn't, I guessed it from your reactions."

Victoria fought for breath. "My reactions?"

"You still have that endearing innocence from all those years ago, despite how you might dress or how shockingly you speak to me. Under it all, that appealing artlessness remains." He brushed the side of her cheek with the tip of his nose. "London's Greatest Courtesan wouldn't blink at sharing the most intimate of kisses, Victoria. But a woman who has never enjoyed those pleasures might."

Her eyes went wide as his statement sank in. Her body had betrayed her. Her true, passionate reactions had shown her for a fraud in a way her words and affectations never had at any party.

And *that* was why Justin had made love to her. To force from her what she wouldn't share. But it could hardly be called making love when it was used as a weapon, could it?

A little niggling sting worked its way through her, but she ignored it. This was no time for such indulgences like hurt over a man from whom she had come to expect far worse. Right now she had to find a way to convince Justin that he was wrong.

"Perhaps my lovers simply never indulged in such intimacies," she said with a shrug.

He cocked his head. "Then you have been fucking the wrong men."

She flinched at the indelicate reference, and he had the gall to laugh. "Yes, so innocent that the word *fuck* makes you cringe. So untried that your sheath was like a virgin's tonight."

He reached out to brush a lock of hair from her cheek. She jerked her face away even though every touch lit a fire in her traitorous body. How could she feel such a powerful draw to him, even when she knew his true character?

She shivered as he stared at her. Her control was too shaky and weak to face off with him now.

"Get out," she whispered.

He pulled his hand back, and for a flash of a moment, she thought she saw regret on his face. Before she could be certain, he stepped away with a low bow.

"Of course, my lady. I have what I came for, after all. But do not for a moment mistake my departure for retreat. Now that I have uncovered one of your lies, I intend to ferret them *all* out. Until I have"—his gaze moved over her a second heated time—"utter satisfaction in this matter. Good evening, Victoria."

She kept her gaze focused anywhere but on him and didn't respond to his mocking goodbye. But when the door shut behind him, she was out of bed in an instant. She grabbed for her robe and shoved it on. Not that covering her body did anything to erase what she had done. The ground she had surrendered. The desire that had been rekindled.

"Damnedable man!" she cried, bringing her fists down on the wooden footrest at the end of her bed with a jarring smack that only served to send pain shooting to her elbows.

"He is gone now," Marah said as she slipped into Victoria's bedchamber quietly. "What happened?"

Victoria stifled a humorless laugh. What had happened was the inevitable. She could admit that to herself, though she doubted Marah would understand. Virginal, unmarried Marah, who considered men no more than an unwanted distraction best studied from afar. Victoria could never explain how passion could overwhelm good sense in an instant.

"Victoria," her friend breathed as she looked her up and down. "Did he . . . *rape* you?"

Instantly Victoria spun on her friend with a gasp of horror. "No, of course not! Justin would never do such a thing."

And it was true. Despite his other failings, if she had said no . . . really *meant* no, he wouldn't have touched her. Even to prove his point. Even to prove her lies.

"Then I take it by your disheveled appearance and flushed chest that you took him to bed by choice." Marah's tone was suddenly flat, and there was accusation in her blue eyes. As if Victoria had betrayed her by taking Justin to her bed.

Victoria straightened her shoulders. There was no reason to be ashamed of what she had done.

Justin was her husband, after all. Even if it was in name alone.

"Yes. I took him to bed," she admitted. "That was why he came."

Marah cocked her head. "And why would he come for you now, after all this time?"

Victoria's shoulders slumped. That was getting to the heart of it, wasn't it? Justin might have wanted her, but that wasn't why he'd taken her. As always, he had ulterior motives.

"In order to determine whether or not I'd had a man recently. And that was the one thing we didn't plan for, Marah. My body and my reactions to him betrayed me. He knows I've had no lovers since him."

Marah's eyes fluttered shut, and she let out a gasp of breath. "That bastard. He used you. Again."

Victoria flinched. Yes, she had been used. Yet, behind the embarrassment and anger that fact caused in her, she was still tingling and satisfied from the encounter. And she wanted more. Why in the world did she have to want so much more?

"You must stay away from him, Victoria," her friend said, interrupting her tangled thoughts. "Lord Baybary can determine too much with a touch. His interference could very well undermine our purpose. You cannot trust him."

Victoria nodded. Marah was right, of course. Justin was the last person she could ever trust. Too bad he was the very person driven to expose all her darkest secrets.

By the time Caleb and Shaw arrived at Justin's fashionable town home in Mayfair, he had already drunk half a bottle of his finest bourbon and was sprawled out across his settee at an angle that did nothing to ease the tension in the aching muscles of his neck.

"Great God," Caleb said with a shake of his head as Justin's butler showed the men inside and wisely shut the door behind them without offering refreshments.

"Is the Lord of Control stone drunk?" Shaw chuckled as he stepped up to Justin. "Come on, on your feet, mate."

Justin shoved away the hand Shaw offered and muttered, "More comfortable here."

That was a lie. Even in his inebriated state, with the room spinning merrily around him, his neck was cricked and the corner of a pillow was jabbing his arm. But he didn't want to get up. He *deserved* to be uncomfortable after what he had done to Victoria.

Caleb sighed before he crossed the room and snapped his fingers in front of Justin's face. "Hey, hey!"

Justin struggled to sit up and shot his brother a glare. "I'm not that drunk, you ass."

Caleb's eyebrows came up, and he turned to Shaw. "Ah. I'm not the one sprawled out half drunk with my hair sticking up in four different directions . . . but *I'm* the ass."

"Apparently." Shaw shrugged.

"So what brought on this bout of self-loathing, Justin?" Caleb asked as he folded his arms. "And why call on us to witness it? I haven't seen you like this since . . ." His brother trailed off. "Since you came to visit me in London the week before you married Victoria. And you never told me what caused that stint, either."

Justin flinched at the memory of that night. He'd come to London, aching from the terrible secret he knew. Wanting to talk to his brother, who was his very best friend. But by the time Justin was face to face with him, he'd known he couldn't tell Caleb the truth. If he did, it would only bring one more person into the pain. Caleb, especially, didn't deserve that.

"Don't recall," Justin slurred. God, he felt like hell.

"I assume this little turn with the bottle was inspired by your visit to Victoria's town home," Shaw said as he poured sherry into a tumbler.

As he held out the glass, Justin made a grab for it, but Caleb got to it first.

"That's enough for you," Caleb said as he took a sip. "Is Shaw correct in his assessment?"

Justin flopped back on the settee, and his head bounced off the arm. With a wince, he groaned, "Yes. I saw my wife today."

"And did you determine anything?"

Images of Victoria arching beneath him, moaning as he stroked his tongue across her, crying out as she came, flashed through his mind.

"She hasn't had a lover in a long, long time."

Shaw snorted out a laugh. "With that body? I think you are indulging in wishful thinking along with spirits, old friend."

"Her reputation—" Caleb began.

Justin shook his head. "Poppycock, the lot of it. I know Victoria hasn't been with a man in a good, long while. Her body told me."

The moment he said it, he wished he could take back the words. His brother and Shaw froze in their places, staring at him.

"Am I to infer that you took Victoria to bed?" Shaw choked out.

The question inspired even more images of their heated coupling, and also of the look on her face when he told her in no uncertain terms that he had only made love to her in order to force the truth from her. It was a damned, dirty lie, but he'd still said it. He made her believe that he reveled in humiliating her, when in reality it made him feel something he rarely did.

Regret.

But he couldn't tell her the truth. He couldn't let Victoria know that being in her bed had brought him a pleasure he'd never experienced before.

If he'd told her that, it would have given her far too much ground. And ammunition to use against him. Given the lies she'd already told and threats she'd been making since their first encounter, he didn't trust her.

"So, do tell all," Caleb said as he sank into a nearby chair and rubbed his palms together.

Justin sat up quickly enough that his head throbbed. "What?"

His brother shrugged. "You always give us the details of your paramours, Justin. I want to know what brought you from going to Victoria's home for a confrontation to peeling off her clothing and having her. Don't leave out a bit of the story."

"I'm not telling you about Victoria," Justin said as he staggered to his feet and to the bell at the door. When his footman appeared, he ordered strong coffee. He obviously needed a clear head to deal with Caleb and Shaw.

"Why not?" Shaw asked, interest lighting in his focused stare. "Caleb is correct. You have never been shy about sharing the intimate details of your other lovers. What makes Victoria different?"

Justin slammed a hand down on the sidebar next to the door with enough force that the picture hanging above it shivered. "Because she's my wife, damn it!"

The strength of his statement surprised him as much as it surprised the other two men. His relationship to Victoria shouldn't have made a whit of difference, and yet he couldn't bring himself to share even a moment of the passionate encounter with her. It was too private, too intimate, too personal.

He was kept from having to explain himself by the arrival of his coffee. He took the set from a surprised maid at the door and immediately poured himself a cup. Wincing at the bitter flavor, he attempted to pull himself back together.

"What happened with Victoria is not important," he said, ignoring both Shaw's and Caleb's incredulous expressions. "The significant fact is that I've proven Victoria false. She is most definitely lying about her past, and I believe she's lying about her purpose here as well. That proves to me that there is something far deeper going on."

"Why?" Shaw pressed. "Perhaps she made up the story of her experience in order to garner more interest in potential lovers. After all, it worked. The men of our acquaintance are ready to battle to claim her."

Justin shook his head. "I don't think so. Victoria is a beautiful, desirable woman, and from the way she has run my estate, she is also a reasonable and careful one. If she really wanted a lover, she could have easily obtained one quietly and discreetly. Instead she came to London under this outrageous guise and false identity. To me, that says she desires attention and quick exposure to as many men as possible."

Caleb nodded. "That does speak of desperation, not prudence."

"Exactly." He downed the rest of his coffee. Now that his mind was working on something less troublesome than his passionate reactions to Victoria, it seemed to be clearing. "But why would she be desperate? There must be something else driving her to come here and be exposed to such a shocking lifestyle."

Why did he care? Justin shut his eyes. After all, his goal was to get her the hell out of London, not delve into her past or her future or her heart. And yet he was driven to know what made his wife so reckless. If only just to have the answer for himself so he could forget her again.

"Debts, perhaps?" Shaw offered, interrupting Justin's troubling musings.

"No. I have always been more than generous with Victoria when it came to money. She has more than she could spend in years."

Justin ignored the voice inside him that said he had always been so generous to Victoria to make up for his utter failure as a husband. A payout of sorts.

"What if she has secret expenses?" Caleb asked.

Justin turned to his brother with a shake of his head. "No, Victoria keeps meticulous records that my solicitor reviews monthly. Any discrepancy would be instantly caught."

Shaw's brow wrinkled. "Which again points to her steady nature."

He nodded. "Yes."

"Did she give you no clue as to her true motives?" Caleb asked. "Even after your encounter?"

Justin pursed his lips. After how coldly he had treated her, he'd certainly made no headway in obtaining Victoria's trust. No, she seemed to *expect* him to behave in such a way. She wouldn't confide in him under the current circumstances. She would have to be convinced or forced into doing so.

"No."

Shaw leaned forward to rest his elbows on his knees. "So she is the first woman I can think of who hasn't given you exactly what you wanted, when you wanted it."

Caleb laughed at their friend's assessment.

Justin glared at Shaw. "She most certainly gave me what I wanted."

Shaw arched a brow, and Justin turned away. He wasn't so obtuse that he didn't know exactly what Shaw meant. It wasn't Victoria's body that she withheld. He had a sneaking suspicion if he returned to her home at this instant and pressed her, she would surrender to him again. But she would always keep a part of herself separate.

And though he had never wanted anything more from his lovers than brief passion, he found himself curious about all that Victoria kept locked away from him. And not just the parts that had to do with her true objective in London.

Chapter 7

Lesson 7: A kiss means nothing, but it can change everything.

As a child, Victoria had dreamed of attending fashionable soirees and glittering balls. Some of her most vivid memories were of lying on her mother's bed, watching her maids prepare her for a night out. Her mama had told her stories about what would happen and who would be in attendance. And then her father would come into the room and teach her to dance.

Those nights had been some of the happiest of her life. Before death claimed her mother and alcohol and creeping madness altered her father.

But now she was older. In the past few weeks, she had attended enough balls and parties to make her wish she had never laid eyes on a dance floor or felt the heat of a man's leering stare on her chest or heard the opening strains of the scandalous waltz.

If she had the option of running away, she would have. But because of Chloe, she could not. So here she was, at one more Cyprian gathering. She'd already walked the gauntlet of men when she'd arrived and now enjoyed an all-too-brief moment alone as she moved deeper into the crowded room.

She didn't expect the blessed peace to last long. Soon enough, someone would find her and she would be forced into the role of "Ria" again.

Or, more disconcerting still, Justin would be the one who invaded her privacy. After their angry, passionate exchange and his uncovering of her lies about her lovers, she knew it was likely he was in attendance here tonight, looking for her. In fact, she wouldn't put it past him to be watching her from a distance, waiting for the perfect moment to pounce and threaten and demand.

Justin was out for truth, for secrets . . . He wouldn't stop until he had stripped each and every one of them from her grasp as easily as he had stripped her of her clothing in her bedchamber. She shivered at the memory. It was clear she could never repeat that lapse in judgment. Surrendering her body meant surrendering far more when it came to her husband.

And her true purpose in London left no room for such mistakes. The longer she remained without uncovering any evidence of Chloe's whereabouts, the more frightened and uneasy she became. Someone was hiding the truth about her friend, and if that someone uncovered Victoria's real identity and purpose, it could put her in terrible danger, not to mention Chloe.

A woman's voice pierced through Victoria's troubling fog. "Ria!"

She turned to find one of the nameless mistresses of the hordes of gentlemen in attendance coming toward her. This one was wearing a dress cut so low that Victoria could see more than a hint of the dark circles of her areolas below the neckline. She did her best not to look scandalized, and smiled.

"Good evening," she said, hoping she wouldn't be expected to recall the young woman's name.

"I have been asked to make an introduction to you, if you are amenable to meeting a gentleman," the other girl said with a sly smile.

Victoria nodded slowly. This was her least favorite part of her charade. Her objective for being here never allowed her to turn down an opportunity to meet a gentleman who was interested in becoming her protector, for fear he would be the one who could unlock the truth about Chloe's disappearance. She had no name for the last man who had pursued her best friend, all she had were hints of a description. Flashes of menace and chilling obsession. All the men were suspects until she could determine otherwise.

"Of course, I am most agreeable," she said, tilting her head with what she hoped was as vapid an expression as the young woman before her possessed.

"Very good!" The girl all but clapped her hands. "You are lucky that he wishes to meet you. Although he is not titled, he has made ample funds in shipping and is building himself quite a reputation."

Victoria fought to keep a smile on her face. Money and power had never had much meaning to her, but she knew many of the courtesans cared little for their partners' characters and more for their purses.

"Who is this man?"

Instead of answering, the young woman motioned to someone to join them. Through the crowd, a very tall, broad-shouldered gentleman came toward them. Victoria sucked in a breath at the very sight of him, he was so impressive.

He was older than Justin by at least fifteen years, with the beginnings of gray entering his temples. But he looked anything but frail, like some of the men so anxious to have her join them in their beds. His age only distinguished him, made him all the more imposing.

Victoria wouldn't have called him handsome, exactly. His features were too strong individually to mesh with a sense of beauty. But he was striking, and she found it difficult to look away from the piercing focus of his steely gray stare.

"Mr. Darius Evenwise, may I present Ria?" the young woman said with a deferential nod to the gentleman.

"Thank you, Tabitha," Evenwise said, even as he bowed over Victoria's hand without breaking his intense gaze into her eyes. "I so appreciate your assistance in this matter."

Even the empty-headed chit knew when she was being dismissed. With another little curtsy, she scurried away to find whoever was her own protector, leaving Victoria alone with the new gentleman. And she *felt* alone with him, despite being in the middle of a crowded ballroom. There was something about him that demanded attention, focus, no matter what else was going on around him.

"It is a pleasure to m-make your acquaintance, sir," Victoria managed to stammer, withdrawing her hand from his.

She tried to smile, but the expression felt less than convincing. There was something about this gentleman's presence that rattled her and broke the character she had so carefully built around herself.

"I have heard so very much about you, my dear," he said with a thin smile. "I could no longer keep myself from making your acquaintance."

A group of laughing courtesans stumbled past them, jostling Victoria and causing her to stagger to regain her footing. In an instant, Evenwise caught her arm, keeping her steady even as he glared at the women with a flash of anger.

"Heathens," he muttered beneath his breath. He held steady to Victoria's arm. "Perhaps you will join me for a stroll through the gallery? We will encounter less frivolous behavior there."

She choked on her answer. Something about this man made every fine hair on the back of her neck stand up, but she ought not refuse him. It was her duty.

"I would enjoy that very much," she said, her throat suddenly parched.

With a smile, he slipped her hand into the crook of his arm and maneuvered her with grace through the rowdy ballroom, where some of the crowd had begun to deteriorate into rather public displays of affection. Victoria blushed at their outrageous conduct.

But as uncomfortable as the groping hands and open kisses made her, they also brought her thoughts to Justin once again.

"Are you still with me, my dear?" Evenwise asked, impatience in his tone.

Victoria started. Damn her wandering mind. It seemed Justin could endanger her investigation without even being in the same room. She banished all thoughts of him as she gave an apologetic smile.

"Of course."

"You looked as though you were far away in your mind," he said, none too gently. "If you are not interested—"

Victoria hurried to repair the damage her flighty thoughts had caused. "Of course not, sir. Please forgive my distraction. It shall not happen again."

He frowned as they continued to move forward. "I hope not."

As they moved farther from the safety of the bright, full room, Victoria's unease increased. Away from the peering eyes of Society, this man could truly do anything to her, no one would come to her aid.

Ridiculous. Though he was imposing, aside from an apparently short temper, Evenwise had given her no reason to think he was truly dangerous. Even if he were, he would be a fool to do something to her just a short distance from a crowded ballroom. It was only her overactive imagination playing tricks that made her so wary.

She smiled as they stepped into the gallery that linked one wing of the large estate to the other. Pictures hung at every level from the high walls.

Ancient ancestors glaring down in disapproval, no doubt. Not that she blamed them. The owner of this estate had turned it from a reputable house to one of sin and excess.

"I am flattered you would seek out my attentions, Mr. Evenwise," Victoria said, hoping the tremble in her voice would ease before he commented upon it.

He looked down at her, his focus entirely on her and nothing else. "It is I who is flattered, my dear. You certainly know that you are the most sought-out beauty at present. Any man allowed a moment of your time is the lucky one."

She blushed, and it wasn't forced. The compliments that flowed from the lips of the men pursuing her always made blood rush to her cheeks. It was so strange to be an object of desire after so long spent thinking no man could want her after Justin's desertion. But then . . . he *had* wanted her two nights ago. With a burning drive even she couldn't ignore.

She had to stop thinking about that.

"I would give a fortune to know what crossed your mind just now," Evenwise said. Victoria jumped as he leaned in closer.

"I—I apologize again, Mr. Evenwise—"

"Darius," he interrupted with a smile. "I hope we will soon be comfortably acquainted enough that you will call me by my first name."

Victoria swallowed hard. "Will we?"

He nodded. "You *are* looking for a protector, are you not?"

She leaned back just a fraction to gain some distance. "Y-yes."

"A good idea. A woman as beautiful as you are needs protection. Not just financially, but physically. A man could lose his senses with you."

Victoria sucked in a breath before she could control the action. The way this man was looking at her, with such focused intent and sexual interest, it seemed he was commenting not in a general sense, but on something specific.

Other men had commented on her need for "protection" before, but none had made it sound so much like a threat. Suddenly, being alone with Darius Evenwise seemed like a very bad idea.

"I-I'm sure I'm being looked for in the ballroom," she said, motioning back toward the hall. "Perhaps we should return."

"I only desire a moment to make my case, Ria," he said, holding fast to the hand he had tucked into the crook of his arm.

Her instinct was to tug hard and run, but that would be folly. It would either incite him further, or make her look an utter fool, perhaps even unmask her as a fraud. So she merely stood by, heart pounding wildly against her ribs, staring up at the man.

"Ria, there you are," a masculine voice drawled from the hallway entrance.

Both she and Evenwise turned. Justin was leaning against the entryway in a casual posture that Victoria didn't believe for a moment. She saw his clenched fists and the tension in his neck, even from so far away. But despite the fact that she knew he was angry, she almost sagged with relief. Justin's anger was dangerous, yes, because it always incited her own emotions, ones she would rather have controlled. And it also invariably led to a passion she could not afford.

But the danger she felt with Evenwise was very, very different. She pulled her hand from his grip and staggered a few steps toward her husband.

"I have been looking all over for you, my dear," Justin said, giving her a false smile as he shoved off the doorjamb and moved toward her.

"And here I am," she managed to say with a tight little laugh.

He reached for her, taking her arm much more gently than she had expected or perhaps even deserved. But then he utterly shocked her by drawing her against his body and pressing a soft kiss directly on her mouth. Victoria flinched in surprise, but then she couldn't help but respond. She clutched at his arms, lingering over the taste of his lips a moment too long to be taken as a charade.

When he drew back, she stared up at him. Why had he done that? And why had she allowed it?

Justin glanced down the hallway toward Evenwise. With a shiver, she followed his stare. The other man hadn't moved since Justin's entry. He remained in the middle of the hallway, staring at the two of them with a clear expression of anger.

"Ah, Evenwise. I see you've met my new mistress."

Victoria spun on Justin as all the gratitude she'd been feeling toward him bled away. The bastard! He knew perfectly well what claiming her, especially so publicly, meant.

"Just—" she began.

He glared down at her briefly, his face a stone mask that clearly told her to play along if she knew what was good for her. Even if she wanted to deny him, she couldn't. Not after the way she had kissed him with such utter abandon.

She struggled to find some way to repair the damage, but before she could say anything, Alyssa Manning stepped into the gallery.

"Ah, Ria, there you are. I was looking for you." The courtesan looked at the two men. The tension that coursed between them could not be denied, but she made no acknowledgment of the awkwardness. "And Mr. Evenwise, Lord Baybary, how lovely it is to see you both."

Justin turned to the courtesan with a smile that was suddenly genuine. Victoria pursed her lips in annoyance. For not the first time, she wondered if the two of them had been to bed. Justin was obviously fond of the woman by the warm expression in his eyes. He certainly never looked at *her* that way.

"Good evening, Miss Manning," Justin said with a tilt of his head. "Ria and I are planning to depart as soon as I gather our wraps."

He shot Victoria another glance that told her not to argue, and Victoria gritted her teeth. "Very well, Justin."

"Perhaps Victoria will come with me while you do that, my lord," Alyssa said, though her smile was more than a little confused.

Victoria's heart sank. Had the other courtesan seen their shocking kiss and heard Justin's claim that "Ria" was now his mistress? If she had, there would be no hiding it.

Justin stared at the two women for a moment. By the way his hand tightened on her arm, Victoria could tell he didn't like the idea of letting her away from his side, but finally he released her with a quick bow.

"Of course. I would like a moment with Mr. Evenwise, at any rate."

Victoria's heart lodged in her throat. Dear God, what in the world would Justin say?

"Come, Ria." Alyssa caught her hand and drew her from the room.

Victoria managed a quick glance over her shoulder, but all she saw was Justin stalking toward Evenwise. Then Alyssa was chattering in her ear, and she couldn't see what was happening anymore.

"When I heard you had gone out of the ballroom with Darius Evenwise, I had to look for you," Alyssa whispered.

Victoria peeked over her shoulder again, straining to hear whatever encounter was going on behind them, but it was for naught.

"Someone introduced me to him. A woman . . . Tabitha perhaps?" she said in distraction.

Alyssa's mouth turned down in a frown. "Wretched little chit. That makes perfect sense. Many of the mistresses are threatened by you."

Victoria drew back, her attention now entirely on Alyssa. "They are?"

Alyssa laughed. "Sometimes you seem so innocent." Her smile melted away. "At any rate, I wanted to warn you to be careful of Evenwise."

Victoria straightened. "Careful, why?"

"Well, it hardly matters now." Alyssa shrugged. "For it appears you don't need that advice. I overheard when I came into the room. It seems you have found your protector after all and without my help! Now you are with Justin."

Victoria stifled a moan. Damn, her fears were true! Of all the women to see Justin's claiming, Alyssa was the worst. The matchmaker would quickly spread the word that she was off the mistress market, and no men would dare pursue her until Justin made it clear he was finished with her.

Tears pricked her eyes at the thought that all her work and sacrifice had been for nothing, all because Justin had done the one thing she hadn't expected.

Claimed she was his. The biggest lie of all.

"But I thought you told me you didn't care for Lord Baybary?" Alyssa said with a frown. "When I offered to introduce you, I recall you declined quite strenuously."

Victoria cursed her husband one more time before she shrugged. "My first impression of the gentleman turned out to be wrong."

Wasn't that the truth?

Alyssa laughed. "I know all about that. So he swept you off your feet, eh? Well, enjoy him, Baybary is rumored to be a fantastic lover. Perhaps you'll have better luck keeping him at your side than most. I've certainly never seen Justin look at another woman with as much passion as I saw him look at you."

Shocked, Victoria came to a standstill as they entered the foyer. "No. That cannot be true."

"Oh yes. I know passion when I see it." Alyssa patted her arm. "You should not underestimate your charms, my dear."

Victoria almost laughed. How much time had she spent doing just that before she'd finally stopped allowing Justin's abandonment to dictate her life? And yet here she was, back in the same situation. Justin held the keys to her future. At least for now.

"You said you heard Justin was a good lover. You haven't experienced that yourself?"

Oh, why had she asked that? She knew full well that Justin slept with every woman he so much as tripped over. She had long ago stopped caring about his infidelity. But she certainly didn't need to hear the details from Alyssa's lips.

The other woman wrinkled her brow in surprise at the question, but shook her head. "No. I'm afraid I've not had the pleasure."

Relief flooded Victoria unexpectedly. Well, so much for not caring if Justin tupped every woman in London. Apparently she *hadn't* killed all those jealous feelings after all. She would have to work on doing so once this nightmare was over.

Alyssa tilted her head. "Are you certain you are quite all right, Ria? You are very pale."

"Just tired, I suppose," Victoria murmured.

Alyssa looked over her shoulder with a smile.

"Well, there is the man who will take you home and no doubt get you right to bed."

Victoria turned, her stomach flipping as Justin stepped forward, her wrap held out for her and a wide smile on his face that did not reach his eyes.

"Ah, yes," he drawled. "Ria will be tucked away soon enough. Come, my dear."

She scowled. There was no refusing him. Not with Alyssa standing by, watching them. She had no choice but to turn and allow him to press her wrap over her shoulders. His body heat clung where he had held it, almost as if he were touching her, even when he stepped away.

"Good evening, Miss Manning," he said with a smile.

Alyssa said good-bye, but Victoria hardly heard it. All she could think about was Justin and how she would now have to live with the consequences of the claim he had made.

Chapter 8

Lesson 8: Leave him wanting more.

"What the hell were you thinking, Victoria? Do you have any idea what could have happened to you tonight?"

Justin was becoming aware that he was yelling even though he and Victoria were just a few feet apart in his carriage as it rumbled over the cobblestone streets toward Soho Square.

He didn't mean to shout. He simply couldn't help himself when he thought of everything that could have happened to his wife. Picturing a thousand different and equally horrifying scenarios made him frustrated and angry and—

And afraid.

He stopped short at that thought. Justin hadn't been afraid of anything since—God, he must have been a youth. But right at this moment, the utter terror that gripped his heart was so strong that he could almost taste it.

Victoria had been alone with Darius Evenwise, whose reputation was whispered about in all kinds of circles. There was talk of his violent sexual deviancies . . . and the fact that at least one of his previous mistresses had vanished without a trace nearly two years ago. Evenwise claimed she had returned home to her mother, and perhaps that was true.

But the idea that it wasn't made Justin cold down to his very soul.

A terrible image of Victoria's crumpled body flashed through his mind, raped or even worse.

"Damn it," he snapped, gripping his hands in fists at his sides. "What the hell is wrong with you?"

Victoria stared at him, unflinching, apparently unmoved by his outburst. "You have no right to interfere with me, Justin, or to judge my decisions. You gave that up when you marched out of my life."

He tried to control his emotions with a few long, deep breaths, but it didn't help. He was spiraling out of control, and his feelings were only stoked by Victoria's complete disregard for her own safety or for his thoughts on the matter.

"Perhaps I don't have any right to interfere

with you," he conceded, frustrated that his voice was still unnecessarily loud. "But judging your decisions is absolutely my right, especially when you make ones that could have gotten you killed. Do you know what kind of man Darius Evenwise is rumored to be? Did you even ask before you strolled into a darkened hallway alone with him?"

Victoria straightened up at that comment, her green eyes brightening with interest. "Alyssa also made mention that there was something unsavory about the gentleman but would say no more on the subject. What is it that made you both so uneasy about my safety?"

Justin stared unblinking at her as he tried to fathom her reaction. Here he had just told her she was in danger, and Victoria looked like he'd offered her a purse full of gold.

That fact added another troubling layer to her already leaning tower of lies. From her business decisions over the years, he'd judged her to be prudent, but asking for danger was anything but.

Once again he wondered which was the real Victoria. The woman who seemed aroused by the fact that she had been, albeit briefly, in peril? Or the one who had common sense?

It seemed he would never uncover the truth. And yet he was compelled to continue trying, if only to rid himself of her presence in London.

"Why are you here?" he asked for what seemed like the hundredth time.

"To find a lover," she retorted without flinching. "We've established that fact over and over."

"You are a liar," he growled. "Just like your father. Everything about the story you've created to lure men to you is a lie. And that makes me think that your supposed motives are also false. You are here to find something, yes, but a lover? No."

"Please." She laughed, but the sound was hollow. "Don't try to convince me that you've spent any time dissecting my motives. You don't give a whit about me. You only want me to disappear again so you can pretend I don't exist."

"Is that what you want?" he asked, a horrible thought dawning on him. "For me to care what happens to you? Is that why you came here, why you insist on putting yourself in jeopardy? To garner my attention?"

She stared at him in utter shock, and that, at least, did not seem false. "Great God, no!"

A strange relief filled him. In all the years they had been apart, Justin hadn't considered what kind of pain or loss Victoria had suffered when he'd left. He'd thought of her, yes, dreamed of her touch occasionally, but not really pondered the consequences of his abandonment or that she might wish for him to return home and be a real husband to her.

Hearing she hadn't been pining away, plotting to throw herself into his path at any cost was a good thing. Mostly. He ignored the tiny twinge of disappointment that accompanied her expression of horror at the thought.

But all that still left his initial question unanswered.

"So you didn't come here for me. Then why? Just tell me the truth, and I shall stop badgering you. This is as tedious for me as it is for you."

She arched a brow in silent disbelief.

He clenched his teeth. "You are the most stubborn woman I have ever encountered!" he burst out, his emotions overflowing. "Did you come here for a debt? Are you being threatened? Is your father involved?"

He held his breath after saying the last, but her face remained as impassive as it had after every suggestion.

"Just a lover, Justin." She gave him an infuriating smile. "Nothing more."

Justin was across the carriage and had her pinned against the wall in less time than it took for her to gasp in surprise. He pulled her hands away from their shielding of her chest and lifted them above her head to keep her from pushing him away. He leaned his weight into her, loving how her soft curves molded perfectly against him.

"Let us say for a moment that I believe you," he whispered, nuzzling her ear. God, she smelled good, that intoxicating combination of lavender and vanilla. He had never been able to touch a woman who wore either since he spent the night with her. "You are choosing awfully dangerous potential suitors. If you want danger, I am happy to oblige you, my dear."

Then he pressed his mouth to hers, connecting with her in the only way he knew how. The only way that allowed him to bypass her lies, his own emotions, their shared past that seemed to stand before them like an insurmountable wall. And just as she always did, Victoria allowed him in, her normal hesitation gone the moment they touched. Her body arched of its own accord, her lips parted, and she surrendered with that sweet desperation that made him wild and out of control.

He released her wrists to glide his fingers down her bare arms, reveling in every satin inch of skin. As he devoured her mouth, he tangled his fingers in her hair, tilting her face for better access, taking what she gave and demanding even more.

Victoria moaned as her freed arms came around his neck to pull him even closer. Her hips gyrated, her breasts rasping against his coat, her breath in pants between searing, burning kisses.

"Tell me the truth, Victoria," he murmured as

he started to work on the dainty buttons on the back of her dress.

She shook her head even as she shoved her hands beneath his coat. Her fingers shook when they glided over his chest to fumble with the fastenings of his waistcoat.

He tugged at her gown, drawing it over her shoulders and around her waist. The chemise she wore beneath was sinfully sheer. It revealed the hard, pink tips of her breasts, the smooth curve of her belly. He dipped his head and captured one nipple through the cloth.

Victoria's head tilted back and her hands clenched into fists against his stomach as she hissed out a sigh of pleasure. He sucked hard on her nipple, swirling his tongue around the bud until the thin chemise became transparent.

"Tell me," he ordered again before he bent his head to the opposite nipple and repeated the treatment.

"Damn you," she groaned, but she didn't push him away. Instead one hand slipped into his hair, holding him in place as she arched into his mouth.

Justin glided one hand down the curve of her spine, cupping her backside and fitting her against him. He rocked into her, letting her feel the erection that tormented him.

As always, the intensity of their physical connection shocked him. No other woman had ever made him feel like he did with Victoria. Wild. Out of control. Randy as a green boy. He wanted to have her in every way. Any way. He wanted to keep her in his bed until he was satiated, though he didn't know when or how that would ever be possible. Touching her never seemed to ease the ache, only intensified it.

He fought for focus as he pushed her skirts aside and glided his fingers up the inside of her calf, her knee, skimmed her thigh. She tensed beneath the touch, her lids fluttering shut. She was trembling by the time he stroked his fingers over her swollen, wet body.

"Tell me the truth," he urged as he parted her folds and petted his thumb across her entrance. "Trust me."

Victoria stiffened, but it wasn't in pleasure or release. Her eyes came open, angry and wild, and she stared at him for a flash of a moment.

Then she placed her hands on his chest and shoved. As she did so, she staggered away, nearly depositing herself on the floor of the moving carriage before she managed to make it to the other side of the vehicle.

"Trust you?" she all but hissed as she frantically tugged at her twisted gown. "How can I? We know each other no more than we did on our wedding night."

He barked out a laugh as he watched her try to fasten her gown in the back. "You know me better, Victoria. And I know you. Your taste lingers on my lips; I can feel the way your nails rake across my back—"

He thought he saw her eyes flutter shut for a brief moment, but then she glared at him.

"If you took a common lightskirt off the street and to your bed, you would know those same things about her. Would you know *her*? Would you trust *her*?"

Justin flinched at the harsh, pointed tone of her words. He stared at her across the carriage as she tried in vain to fix herself. She was so lovely, her dark hair tangled around her face, her soft skin bare and touchable even while she made an attempt to button her gown. She looked utterly kissable, and he wanted so desperately to lose himself in her. Brand her with his touch.

Only he wanted one thing more. And it surprised him how much. He *wanted* her trust.

He was an idiot of the highest order for desiring such a thing from a woman he had every intention of shipping back to the country as soon as was humanly possible. But he did. He wanted Victoria to look at him with faith as much as lust. For her to open up to him and tell him what made her gaze flash with fear, what made her willing to take chances with her very life.

He wanted to . . . *protect* her somehow.

He shook his head in frustration, this time self-directed. It was a foolish, stupid wish. Trust was never prudent, whether given or taken. He should not want it. Especially not from Victoria, who was the spawn of one of the country's greatest liars and cheats. Who had already proven herself to be just as deceptive.

But what choice did he have?

He shrugged. "So what is it you want to know?"

She tilted her head in surprise. "What?"

"You say you cannot trust me until you know me. Give me a subject, and I will enlighten you to your heart's content."

She stopped fumbling with her gown and stared at him. Her green eyes had gone impossibly dark and filled with so much emotion that he almost wished he could take his offer of information back. It was a ploy that could easily backfire if she delved too deeply.

"Anything, Justin," she finally whispered. "Tell me *anything*."

"Turn around," he said softly.

She stared at him, wary, and he cocked his head.

"I'll button your gown," he explained, but as she slowly put her back to him, he knew his request had a deeper purpose. He didn't want to look at her while he whispered confidences.

Justin moved to the edge of the carriage seat and began to fasten her buttons with much the same efficiency as he had opened them. It was a shame to see such luscious skin disappear beneath layers of satin, but he ignored his body's desire to lick every inch and did his work.

"I have a home in Mayfair," he began, his voice low. "I fence in my club twice a week. It is my favorite diversion. On every Wednesday, I attend a card game with Shaw and my brother."

He closed the last remaining button of her wrinkled gown and let his fingers drag across the satiny skin on the back of her neck before he pulled away.

"I enjoy riding," he continued. "My favorite stallion's name is Firefox. And my favorite color"—he smiled—"is green. Or it has been since we wed."

As she moved to face him, she blushed, but it didn't seem to be in pleasure.

"Is that all?" she asked.

He shook his head. "Of course not, but I think it is a start. Now reward me. Tell me what is going on."

She laughed, but the sound was harsh. "Do you truly expect me to share my darkest secrets in exchange for these empty, meaningless facts?"

He frowned. Empty? Meaningless? This was his life she maligned. The one he enjoyed thoroughly. Or, at least, he *had* enjoyed it before she'd reappeared. Now her pointed stare made him almost ashamed of the frivolity that made up his days and nights.

"I don't trust you, Justin," she whispered, and her expression was sad. "I will never trust you. And I won't let you seduce or deceive me into revealing what is my business alone."

Justin clenched his fists. Here he had thought he could murmur a few facts and she would surrender. But he was learning, with every moment he spent with Victoria, that surrender wasn't something she understood. Unless it was in his bed.

Some part of him couldn't help but grudgingly respect that. Most people in his acquaintance were all too willing to sacrifice their "honor" when it came down to it.

"Victoria," he said on a long sigh. "I realize you have reservations about revealing whatever your secret is to me. And perhaps . . ." He hesitated. "Perhaps I deserve that."

The anger that had lined her face faded, replaced by genuine surprise.

"But—" He hurried to continue. "I'm afraid I am not *asking* you for the truth anymore. I'm *telling* you that I will have it."

She jerked back, and her glare returned. He found he missed the more open expression.

"I've told you time and again that you have no

right to do so," she said, but her voice and eyes were tired.

He frowned, making a slow count to ten in his mind.

"Whether you like it or not, you know perfectly well that I have many avenues to force you to do what I desire. I could reveal your secret . . ."

She opened her mouth to remind him of his precarious position, but he didn't allow her interruption.

"Yes, I realize that would reveal mine as well, but it would also ruin whatever it is you're trying to achieve." That statement sobered her, and he pressed on. "I could call upon the courts to declare you unfit. Hell, I could haul you back to the country and lock you in your chamber until all your fire is put out."

Victoria's eyes went wider and wider with each threat. "And yet you demand I give you my trust."

Justin shook his head. "I don't *want* to do any of those things. Perhaps I am not capable of giving you whatever you want to hear in order to gift me with your trust. And I truly regret that." He was surprised that the words were true. "However, denying me is no longer an option. You and your friend *will* tell me the truth about your purpose in London, or you will force my hand. So, please tell me."

The carriage pulled to a smooth stop outside the unassuming town home that Victoria had taken for the Season. Justin reached over and pushed the door open. He met her gaze and hoped she would see reason. But her jaw was set as stubbornly as ever before.

She glared at him. "No."

Chapter 9

Lesson 9: A whore trades in money. A courtesan trades in far more.

Victoria watched Marah pace back and forth in front of the fire, hands fluttering around her with every step. From time to time, her friend would cast a glance in her direction, but her attention was directed mostly at Justin.

Damn the man. He had been filling her friend's mind with all the very worst outcomes to their ruse since he had forced himself into her parlor half an hour before.

The worst part was that Victoria could not deny anything he said. For once, Justin was telling the absolute truth. There were no embellishments. He was simply laying out the story of that night's events and explaining, in chilling detail, all the horrors that could come of it.

She shivered. If his pointed words were frightening to Marah, they were absolutely terrifying to Victoria. Out of necessity, she had successfully blocked out many of the worst consequences of her masquerade as a courtesan. Now she had to face them.

"Don't you see, Marah?" Justin pleaded, his dark gaze focused on her trembling friend. "Victoria could be *killed* if you continue whatever foolhardy quest you two are on. Do you want that?"

Marah's gaze flitted to Victoria, and Victoria could see her friend was warring with herself.

"No," Marah finally whispered. "Of course not."

"I realize you two have painted me as a villain," Justin pressed, with just enough gentleness to his tone. "Yet you can surely see that I am the least of your concerns. I could even help you."

Victoria shook her head. He could have been a very successful barrister in another life. He was certainly smooth enough.

"Are you quite finished trying to frighten my friend into your confidence?" Victoria snapped, rising from the settee and placing a hand on Marah's shaking shoulder. "We will not be manipulated by your—"

Before she could finish, Marah looked at her. "But Victoria, what if he is right? What if something happens to you, just like it did to Chloe?"

Victoria shut her eyes and groaned.

"Chloe?" Justin repeated, rushing forward a long step. "Who is Chloe and what happened to her?"

"No one and nothing," Victoria said, even though she was fully aware that her house of cards was on its way to utter collapse. "You are simply confusing Marah with your endless haranguing, that is all. Now leave."

Justin glared at her, then refocused his attention on Marah. "Please."

A tear trickled down her friend's cheek as she glanced at Victoria again. "I couldn't bear it if I lost you both."

Victoria swallowed. Desperation clawed at her. "Not him," she pleaded on a whisper. "Trust *anyone* but him."

She thought she saw Justin flinch from the corner of her eye. Marah covered her face. Her voice was muffled by her fingers when she said, "Chloe Hillsborough is our friend, and she disappeared. *She* is why we came to London."

Victoria let out a string of curses that made even Justin's eyebrows rise. But when Marah sank onto the settee and began to cry, she sighed and took a place beside her. Wrapping an arm around her friend, Victoria comforted her while Marah sobbed loudly. Victoria couldn't blame her friend for this. It had been coming since the first moment she'd seen Justin in the ballroom.

"Tell me," Justin said quietly, and for the first time it didn't seem like an order.

She scrubbed a hand over her face. Now Justin had Chloe's full name and the fact that she was missing. If Victoria refused to reveal anything more, it wouldn't matter. He would use his resources to quickly determine the rest of the tale and be back on her doorstep, likely by morning.

At least if she revealed the truth herself, she would have the opportunity to choose her words. And maybe she could find a way to convince him to stay out of her way.

Although she doubted that.

"After you abandoned me in Baybary, I . . ." She hesitated and found herself looking at Marah. Her friend smiled back with gentle support in her eyes. With the same friendship Victoria had depended upon for three years. It gave her strength. "I turned to some of the women in the shire for friendship."

Justin frowned at the word *abandoned*, but for once he did not interrupt.

"I grew close to Marah, who was unmarried, after I had dealings with her grandmother. And eventually to a widow, Chloe Hillsborough." She looked at Marah with a teary smile. "We became like sisters, although our situations in life were far different. Chloe's husband had very little to leave her after his untimely death, and her finances were difficult at best. She longed for freedom and independence, as well as excitement. About a year ago, she began talking about entering into the life of a mistress."

Marah wiped away her tears and added, "I tried to tell her that bartering her body wasn't the answer."

Victoria drew a long breath. Her two best friends had exchanged many harsh words over the subject. Marah had never understood the draw of such an arrangement, and made her disapproval clear. And though Victoria had joined in discouraging Chloe, in some dark and secret place in her heart, she had known exactly why her friend desired such a life. Victoria had felt the pleasures of the flesh, the intimate joining of two people. She understood her friend's desire for both a financial and a physical union.

"And did she follow through on this plan?" Justin asked, his gaze locked on Victoria's face. She flushed at his close scrutiny.

She nodded. "Yes. Chloe knew a courtesan who was retiring and agreed to help her. About six months ago, Chloe departed to London to make her fortune. And she was quite successful, being as beautiful as she was—"

"Is," Marah interrupted sharply, and Justin's stare shifted to her.

Victoria nodded. *"Is.* Within weeks, she was

sending us letters telling us about Society life in London, all the parties she was attending, she spoke of the handsome gentlemen who courted her, and eventually the lovers she took."

Justin sat up straight, and his eyes were suddenly wide. "She actually told you about her lovers?"

"Do you think men are the only ones who talk?" Victoria asked. "Chloe told us *many* things about London and its inhabitants."

She swallowed back the fact that Chloe had often told her of Justin's antics before he left for the Continent. Although she had never been under any illusions about his behavior, some of those reports still stung.

"How did that bring you two here?" Justin pressed.

"In time, her letters changed," Victoria continued, staring at the fire with unseeing eyes. "She started talking about a man who was pursuing her. One who frightened her. He followed her, calling at strange hours and sending her gifts that were far too extravagant and personal for someone who had no relationship to her. Each time she refused his advances, he became angrier and angrier. She never said his name, but her descriptions troubled us both. And then . . . then . . ."

Her voice cracked. She couldn't bring herself to say it.

"Chloe vanished," Marah finished in a flat, pained tone. "She used to write twice a week. When several weeks passed with no letter from her, we grew frightened and decided to come here to look for her. Victoria became 'Ria' in order to determine who the man in Chloe's letters could be and if he was somehow involved in her disappearance."

Justin rose to his feet slowly. The smooth, unhurried action drew Victoria's attention to the long, lean lines of his strong body. But when he turned on her, for the first time seduction wasn't on his face. It wasn't even anger in his expression.

It was horror.

"So you came here to find a friend you think might have been the victim of some nefarious man who wanted her in his bed? You are pretending to be a courtesan in order to lure him out?" he asked, his voice deceptively quiet.

Victoria nodded. Said in that harsh tone, the scheme seemed ridiculously foolish.

Justin shook his head. "How could you put yourself in such danger?"

Victoria drew back at his tone and expression. He seemed genuinely concerned for her welfare, which was completely unexpected. It had become her habit to believe Justin totally selfish, especially when it came to her. Now he challenged that with the hint of fear in his eyes.

"I had no choice," she said, lifting her hands in a mute request for understanding. "When I thought of all the horrible things that could have befallen Chloe, I couldn't pretend it hadn't happened."

"And *this* was your solution?" he asked in a shocked tone.

"I needed a way into the world she lived in, the people she associated with. Chloe's benefactress had long ago departed London. Since there was no one else to turn to for help, masquerading as a courtesan myself seemed the best answer. It was certainly the quickest way to obtain entry into the secret underground society of mistresses and courtesans."

He shut his eyes and whispered a dark curse that only she heard. His breath came harsh and heavy before his stare snagged her own.

"I forbid you to continue this," he said with a jerking gesture of his arm.

Victoria clambered to her feet.

"Forbid me?" she repeated. "I didn't ask for your permission, Justin, and I have no intention of doing so. You asked my true motives, and there they are. I *won't* stop searching for Chloe until I know what has happened to her."

Justin moved toward her in one long step. "You cannot possibly fathom what you are risking each and every day you pursue the truth about her. It's too much to sacrifice, even for a friend."

"We know exactly the kind of danger," Marah interrupted, shoving her way between the two of them. She glared up at Justin. "Chloe might very well be dead."

Victoria couldn't control a little pained cry from escaping her lips. She spun away from Justin and Marah and staggered to the window to stare out into the darkness. That was the one possibility she and Marah had never voiced aloud, although it weighed on her mind every single day and night. Now that it had been spoken, it sat like a pit in her stomach, eating at her.

"Yes, that could very well be true," Justin said, but his tone was gentler than it had been before. "And *you* could be next if you continue this foolishness."

Victoria spun on him, swiping at the tears that were now flowing down her face against her will. "I am not a fool, Justin. Of course I've thought of that. But what would you have me do? Abandon her? What if she isn't dead, but being held somewhere against her will? Or what if she is simply injured and no one knows who she is?"

Justin let out a noisy sigh. "Does the woman have no family to conduct this investigation? Why not turn the facts over to the authorities rather than put yourself in jeopardy?"

Victoria moved toward him. "The only family she has left is from her late husband's side. If she vanished forever, those vultures wouldn't think twice about her. As for the authorities in London, what would you propose I say? That a woman they consider half a step above a common street whore has vanished? What do you think the Watch's reaction to that would be, Justin?"

He pursed his lips, but she could see he had no argument for her reply.

"I don't like the idea of you being in danger, Victoria," he ground out through clenched teeth.

She tilted her head to look at him closely. Every single fiber of his being spoke of his frustration, of the upset he was only just keeping in check.

"Ha!" Marah said from behind them, the disdain she had always felt toward Justin back in her eyes. "Do you expect us to believe that after all these years? Victoria could have been hanging about in dangerous taverns and inviting highwaymen to the house for all you know, Lord Baybary. So don't pretend as if you give a whit about her except that you want her to go away and pretend she never came back into your sorry existence."

Justin turned on Marah with a fire so intense in his stare that Victoria jumped at it.

"You know nothing about me," he said. His tone was soft, but it lacked nothing in power. "Or what I feel and do not feel for Victoria. And you are even worse than she is, Miss Farnsworth. An unmarried miss living with a supposed courtesan? If you are discovered, you'll be ruined completely."

Marah shrugged one shoulder. "If I am to look forward to a marriage like the one you 'share' with Victoria, I'm not certain ruination isn't the better option."

Justin's fists flexed at his side, but he didn't respond to Marah's pointed barb. Instead, he returned his attention to Victoria. "Do you have any inclination about how foolish this plan of yours is?"

She folded her arms. "It was working perfectly well before *you* interfered."

"You call being threatened 'working perfectly well'?" Justin asked.

She shook her head. "I had the opportunity to openly talk with several men Chloe kept company with. I was even able to slip her name into casual conversation and judge their reactions."

His lips pursed. "Great God, woman, let me stress again the danger that kind of behavior courts."

"Noted," Victoria said with a cold glare for him.

He stared at her a long moment before he let out an exasperated sigh. "You are determined to flout my direction and stay in London?"

She nodded once. "I must. This isn't about you, Justin. It isn't about me. It's about a friend I care deeply for and her well-being."

He hesitated at that statement. "*If* that is true, I cannot argue with the honor of your cause."

She wrinkled her brow. *If* that was true? What reason did he have to doubt the veracity of her statement? She had certainly omitted the truth in the past when it came to Justin, but on no subject that he was aware of.

He scrubbed a hand over his handsome face and let loose with another curse, this time loud enough that Marah blushed.

"Very well, Victoria. You are the winner."

Victoria's mouth dropped open. She could not believe his words. "You will not argue with me any longer? You will leave me alone and let me finish my search?"

Justin shook his head.

"Oh no. But I shall help you determine the cause of Chloe's disappearance. And if it is possible, I will help you find her."

Victoria blinked. Help her? She had never even considered that possibility.

He leaned toward her. "But there are conditions."

Victoria shivered at the sudden look in his eyes. The same hint of sensual wickedness and manipulation that had been present in the carriage was in his stare. If he was to help her, that meant they would be working closely together. And they both knew what that meant. Justin was no fool. He recognized her weakness for him, even if she denied it until the moon fell from the sky. And he would use that desire to control her if he could.

"With you, there always are," she whispered.

"Marah," Justin snapped without looking at her friend. "I would like a moment alone with my wife. You are excused."

Gasping out her outrage, Marah stomped toward Justin, hands on her hips. "Of all the nerve, to order me—"

Victoria sighed, holding up a hand to stop her friend's tirade. She locked gazes with her and whispered, "Lord Baybary has agreed to help us, when he could have made things very difficult. So I don't mind hearing his 'conditions' in private. Please."

Marah opened and shut her mouth, but finally let out a noisy sigh. "Very well. But I think you both know how I feel about the subject. Good night."

After her friend had departed the parlor and slammed the door behind her, Victoria turned to Justin. He stared at her, a feral smile on his face. And she realized she was alone with a man in some ways even more dangerous than the one she had found herself alone with in the hallway earlier that night.

Because Darius Evenwise might have hurt her body. But if she ever let him too close again, Justin had the ability to break her heart.

Chapter 10

Lesson 10: A mistress is not a wife, no matter how much she may wish to be.

Justin had never met a woman he couldn't control. Hell, there were few *men* he couldn't manipulate with a smile or a well-placed order. But Victoria wasn't like anyone he'd ever met. She turned him on his head. She spun him off his axis. She was at once everything he thought her to be and nothing he expected. But there was one area where he still had mastery.

Victoria wanted him.

Just the slightest touch made her shiver. The pressure of his lips on hers had her at his mercy. Since that was the only arena where he had the upper hand, it was the only way he knew to regain control of the situation.

And as long as he ignored the fact that touching her tested his own restraint as much as it shattered hers, he was certain he would be fine.

"What are your conditions, Justin?" Victoria asked quietly.

She folded her arms across her chest and looked at him with a stubborn, businesslike expression that would have seemed cold from any other woman, except Justin could see the shimmering gleam of desire in the depths of her green eyes. She knew what was going to happen between them as well as he did. They were both fully aware that before the night was over, they would be naked in each other's arms.

"Tonight I claimed 'Ria' as my mistress," he said softly as he began to circle her. She stood stock-still, refusing to watch him as he stalked around her, taking a slow perusal of her beautiful body. "And by the next gathering we attend, everyone will know that you are mine."

Her shoulders stiffened. "So tell them all that you don't want me after all."

He shook his head. "If I discard you, the interest in you will vanish like a mirage in the desert, and you don't want that. So I expect you to go along with my statement." He stopped just inches behind her and leaned in so that his hot breath stirred the little curls around her ear. "In every way."

An almost imperceptible shiver worked its way through Victoria's body. It was such a tiny movement, but it hit Justin in the gut like a sucker punch. Damn, but he wanted this woman. More than that, he wanted to make her crave him day and night. He wanted to be certain she left London with memories of him burned on her for life.

A cruel desire, when he had no intention of living as her husband in anything more than name only. That hadn't changed. The obstacles that stood between them in the past still existed. He was even more uncertain of her motives than ever. Yet he still wanted her to surrender to him in every way.

He really was an unbearable bastard.

Victoria turned slightly and gazed up at him. Her lower lip was trembling, her eyes slightly glazed. "I didn't think you kept mistresses, Justin. What will people say?"

He shrugged.

"That you are the most desirable woman in the Empire," he said softly. "And I only take the best."

Her gaze darted away. "You don't think I'm the most desirable woman in Britain," she said, her voice barely carrying even with the minuscule distance between them.

"Don't I?"

She shook her head. "You never have."

He tilted his head in surprise and examined her face carefully. She lifted her chin, daring him to refute her words, but behind her bravado and contempt, he sensed a long-buried hurt. Though he doubted she would ever admit that to him.

He should have let it be. Let her think that he never wanted her for more than a few moments, but there was some part of him that couldn't let that belief exist.

"You're wrong," he murmured as he slipped his fingers into her hair and cupped the back of her head. With a gentle tug, he forced her to look into his eyes. "You are so very, very wrong."

He dipped his mouth and kissed her. He had intended to take and claim and seduce, but things didn't work out that way. Instead he found himself wanting to be gentle. Reassuring. To let her know just how much she was desired.

He wrapped his arm around her waist and molded her body to his. She shuddered against his lips, and he knew he'd won her body, at least.

And oh, how he wanted that body. He was going to have her. If he could convince her to participate in this new ruse, to play his mistress both in public and in private, he could have her as often as he liked.

He massaged her scalp gently, and pins scattered out of her hair. "Doing this, it's a way to protect you during our search," he said softly. He leaned down to feather a few light kisses along the curve of her cheek. "And can you deny that you want me?"

She hesitated, stiffening as he trailed his lips down to her jawline, up to her ear. He felt her fighting, warring against their past. But it was a losing battle. He knew because he'd already fought it.

"I can't," she finally admitted on a shuddering sigh. "Denying I want you is like denying myself breath."

He didn't answer for a moment, simply enjoyed the warmth of her slender frame against his, the soft scent of vanilla that wafted up from her hair, the taste of her on his lips.

"Neither can I, Victoria," he whispered.

Her eyes widened, the green darkening to a glorious emerald that pierced to his very soul. "Don't toy with me."

"I may toy with you in a hundred other ways, but not about this." He brushed a lock of hair away from her eyes. "The want for you washed over me, and I can't fight the tide. So let me drown in it, Victoria. For a little while. And maybe by the time we've solved your mystery, we'll both be done with this wanting and we can go back to the way things were before."

A little groan broke free from her lips, and she tried to twist away, but he held her fast, keeping her from escape, from distance.

"Be my lover," he said softly. "Just for a while."

She looked at him, their faces mere inches apart. Her expression was cloaked, he could tell nothing about her heart.

"And if I say yes, you will help me in my search for Chloe?"

Justin frowned. Was she only bartering her body to get what she wanted? He shifted against her, and her eyes fluttered shut. No. When she said she wanted him, that was true. She was simply smart enough to negotiate despite her own needs.

Which he respected her for.

"Yes," he murmured.

"But I will be your mistress, not your wife," she said, still denying him what he craved.

He wrinkled his brow. "No one will know you are my wife, if that is what you mean."

A shake of her head was her reply. "I mean *you* will treat me as your mistress. Passion, but no expectation of emotion."

He stepped back, shocked by both her statement and the fact that he could not read her purpose. "Do you *want* emotion?"

Victoria flinched, just a little. "No. Not anymore."

He frowned. So once she had desired that. He should be glad her goals had changed. Shouldn't he?

"Then we will have passion and no emotion," he promised.

Her stipulation should have been an easy one to make, but something made it stick in his throat. Shouldn't *he* have been the one to maintain distance, telling her he wanted nothing more than her body?

"Then I will be your lover," she whispered.

Hesitantly, she stepped up to him. Her arms wound around his neck, and she rose up on her tiptoes to press her mouth to his.

She had never initiated a kiss before. He had always been the one to direct the merging of their mouths, as well as their bodies. But the gentle, almost innocent press of her soft lips to his was nearly his undoing. His lips parted in surprise, and she traced the crease with her tongue.

Justin gathered her closer, delving into the embrace with all the desire that had burned at him since he made love to her a few nights before. Perhaps it had even been dormant for longer . . . since their wedding night when her innocence had shocked and satisfied him in ways he never imagined possible.

It didn't really matter. Those desires were free now. And he intended to give in to them. To have Victoria in every way. To purge the need for her at any cost.

Her hands fluttered down from his shoulders to his chest, and then she was tearing away his jacket, pulling at the buttons and yanking it down his shoulders. Justin smiled against her lips, glad that she was as eager to be with him as he was to be with her. At least they shared in this madness.

He backed her toward the settee as she tugged his waistcoat away, her fingernails raking across his stomach through the linen shirt beneath. He sucked in a breath at the rough touch. She would unman him in a moment if he wasn't careful.

To regain some semblance of control, Justin stripped the buttons along the back of her gown with one slick movement. The sinfully silky fabric tipped forward, just as it had in the carriage, and revealed the satin skin beneath. He tugged at her chemise, and both gown and undergarments fell around her ankles, leaving her only in her stockings and slippers.

He stared at her, not even trying to mask his lust as he made a leisurely appraisal of her from head to toe. Where Victoria had once blushed or tried to cover herself, now she thrust her breasts out to their best advantage and tilted her hips in an invitation he had no strength to refuse.

Somewhere along the way, she had become aware of her sensual power.

And yet he had not been the one who made that happen. He was surprised to find he was disappointed about that fact, and not just because of a possessive jealousy that there *might* have been another man in her bed some time in the years they had been apart.

Instead he found he wished *he* had been the one to coax her into boldness. To make her aware of how much she could command with the mere twitch of her hips or the heat of her touch.

But he hadn't. Instead he was only the beneficiary of her daring. And when she reached for him, locked eyes with him, and began to unbutton his shirt without breaking their stare, he was ready to fall to his knees and worship at her altar.

She slipped her hand into the opening in his shirt and rested her fingers against his heart. He was certain she felt it slamming in response, rocking against his rib cage as he was overwhelmed with longing for her.

"Do you feel that?" he murmured as he slipped his arms around her and lowered her onto the settee.

"Your heart?" she whispered as she looked up into his face, now just inches away.

He nodded. "*You* do that to me, Victoria."

She gave a little smile before she leaned up and pressed her lips to his throat.

Victoria all but groaned as she tasted Justin's skin. She wanted to burn every second of this encounter into her mind and heart. She wanted to be able to conjure it up in its entirety later. But the moments were passing by so quickly. Justin was already shrugging out of his wrinkled shirt, tossing it on the floor beside them before he cupped her face and devoured her mouth.

Her mind spun as his weight came down on her, pressing her into the settee cushions and surrounding her with such heat that she felt as if she were on fire. She clenched her fingers against his skin, grasping for purchase as his mouth traveled down her throat. Her head thrashed against the settee pillow as he suckled her nipple, washing her away on a sea of desire.

She fought the tide, groaning as she threaded her fingers into his hair.

"No, wait, wait Justin."

His dark eyes came up, snaring hers with questioning.

"Don't tell me you plan to deny me now," he whispered as he caught her hand and glided it down his body to cup the erection that was making itself known through his trousers. "Not when I'm on the edge."

She stroked him with a groan that he echoed. "I want this, I do. But I'm always swept away by it. Overtaken. I want to *feel* it tonight. Please, I want . . ."

He locked gazes with her, exploring her face with that focused intensity that was so rare, but always made her shiver. Justin might have a reputation for debauchery, for sin, for frivolity. But the more time she spent with him, the more she realized there was something more behind all that. Something deeper.

"Being swept away is part of this," he said softly as he stroked just the tip of his index finger along her lips. "But I think I understand."

He shoved to his feet, leaving her sprawled wantonly across the settee. She stared up at him as he slowly removed his breeches and stood totally naked before her.

"You want to be allowed to explore this in your own time?" he said, a hint of question in his voice.

She nodded as she stared at the hard thrust of his cock. It was impossible not to want to touch it. "Y-yes."

"Then do it." Now his tone was husky.

She sat up and reached for him, taking him in hand and stroking him from base to head in one fluid motion. He let out a curse under his breath and braced his legs, but he didn't overpower her.

"Yes," he moaned. "Just like that. Slower now. Just a little slower."

She stared at his face, taut with tension, as she followed his directives. Beneath her palm, his erection grew harder and a dewy drop of moisture leaked from the tip. She stared at it, thinking of how good it felt when he exploded within her.

"You're a damned quick study, my dear, I will give you that," he groaned.

There was something utterly powerful about knowing she was giving him the same kind of intense pleasure he gave to her. Of having him at her mercy when she knew he could easily turn the tables on her any time he pleased.

When he allowed her that, it was a gift. One she took warily, but hungrily.

"I want to give you pleasure," she admitted softly. Yes, later, she might regret that moment of honesty, but for now it seemed like small reciprocation for the power he allowed her.

He stilled, staring at her with a strange and utterly unreadable expression. Then he dropped down to his knees in front of her and cupped her face to kiss her. The action was so surprising that Victoria didn't think to protest. She simply wrapped her arms around him and rode out the passionate storm.

He cupped her to him, wrapping her legs around his waist. She rocked her wet sheath against his flat stomach as she reached for more. More. For everything.

Then, in a blink of an eye, he lifted her away and reversed their positions so that he was sitting on the couch and she was straddling his lap, her splayed legs positioned perfectly over him.

She pulled back and looked into his eyes. His

lids were heavy, his gaze so dark and hungry that she could drown in it. His fingers caressed her arms, down her sides, and finally cupped her hips. He pushed, and she followed his unspoken order, sinking down over him. His cock slipped inside her inch by inch, a slow taking that she herself controlled.

And it was heaven. The only connection with Justin she had ever trusted.

Already her sheath fluttered and flexed at the fullness. Being positioned over him was a foreign feeling, but it wasn't uncomfortable or unpleasant. On the contrary, it was infinitely powerful, pleasurable.

"Roll your hips," he murmured before he caught one of her perfectly positioned breasts and licked her nipple with a lazy stroke. "Ride me."

She saw the tension in every line of his face. The way he was holding back, keeping himself from surging up and simply taking her. He was surrendering all his control to her. Even when he wanted more than she gave.

Something deep inside her shifted as she stared down at him in wonder. Passion overwhelmed her, desire for him that was more powerful than ever before. With a shuddering sigh, she curled her fingers around his shoulders and rocked forward. They expelled a sigh in unison as he slipped inside that final inch.

Doing as he'd ordered, she rolled her hips back, then forward. After a few strokes, she found a rhythm, one that drove her toward madness with every motion. He pressed kisses against her chest as he cupped her backside, helping her roll over him, holding her open to accept him fully.

She felt the release coming, building low in her belly at a steady pace. When she wanted to flex erratically, though, he wouldn't allow it, keeping her thrusts steady with the unending pressure of his strong hands.

"Reach for it, angel," he groaned. "I see it in your eyes. Take it. Let it come to you."

"Justin," she cried out as the first tremors of pleasure quaked through her.

"Ride through it, Victoria," he panted, his fingers digging harder. "God, I just want to—"

"Do it," she cried, tilting her head back as her hips thrust out of control.

He roared out her name and arched up, lifting her off the settee entirely with the power of his pleasure. He pounded into her from below, driving her already wild orgasm into a newer, higher realm. And then he stiffened beneath her and gave a choked cry as he poured himself into her with a final driving thrust.

With a shudder, Victoria collapsed against his chest. She rested her cheek against his shoulder, burying her face into the musky heat of his neck as her breaths tore in and out of her throat with a ragged sound. He hesitated a moment, but then his arms came around her in a gentle embrace.

She opened her eyes, staring at nothing while she allowed her feelings to wash over her. Warmth. Satisfaction. But something more. When Justin surrendered to her, it had forged a new bond between them. Tenuous, yes. But for the first time Victoria didn't feel like he was bound to run her over if it would grant him what he wanted.

But was that real, or just a manipulation? The last time, he had proudly admitted that he'd used sex to wage war on her resolve. Only time would tell if he was doing that again.

She pulled back to look at him. His head rested against the settee cushions, eyes shut, his breathing slowly returning to a more regular rate after their stunning union. He certainly didn't look like he was in any mood to dictate to her. In fact, he looked strangely peaceful, calm.

"Planning to paint my portrait, Victoria?" he asked without opening his eyes.

She laughed, a nervous sound that grated on her own senses. "What?"

"You're staring." He chuckled, and one eye came open.

She smiled despite herself. "You don't even know if I paint."

His laughter faded. "No, I suppose I don't. But I

soon will, won't I? We'll be spending a great deal of time together now that everyone believes you are my mistress. There is much to be arranged."

Those words were a reminder of the *real* reason she was here. And why they had made love. Their new bargain was one she could live with. More than live with. But she could never forget that Justin's help, his *gifts*, came with a price. Even if she was willing to pay it, she couldn't mistake it for real benevolence.

With a sigh, Victoria separated their bodies and got to her feet to find her discarded gown.

"What arrangements?" she asked, hoping the question sounded cool and unaffected.

"You will need to be moved into one of my homes in the city, for one," Justin said with a barely perceptible sigh. He shoved to his feet and scooped up his wrinkled breeches in one hand.

As he shook out the fabric, Victoria cast him a side glance. He was so utterly . . . beautiful, with long, lean muscles and that crooked, handsome grin.

And her traitorous body ached to merge with his again already. She could only hope that this new agreement would end that heated need. Certainly they would tire of each other at *some* point.

"I will install you in a more suitable place tomorrow," he continued.

His words sank through her disgraceful fog of lust, and Victoria jerked back. "Install me in a new home? Why?"

He arched a brow as he stepped into his trousers. "Because, my dear, my mistress wouldn't live in Soho Square, as attached to this house as I have become."

Victoria couldn't help but smile at his jest.

He continued, "I would put her up in the finest accommodations and parade her about for all my friends to admire and envy."

Victoria could make no argument. He was correct. When she was on her own, the private, quiet neighborhood where she had let her home was part of how she protected herself. But now they were playing a whole new game. With all new risks.

"Very well. I shall inform my staff to begin preparing the household this evening."

She stifled a sigh as Justin finished buttoning his shirt and shrugged into his waistcoat. Aside from being wrinkled, he didn't appear as though their encounter had left him any worse for wear. Versus herself . . . She cast a quick glance downward. She was only half dressed in her flimsy chemise, her hair was knotted around her shoulders, and she felt as if she'd been stripped in so many more ways than one.

"I also need to make certain that you and your

unpleasant little friend Marah are well guarded," he mused, almost more to himself than to her.

She shivered. When he said the word *guarded,* it conjured up so many unpleasant images. She didn't want to be in anyone's prison.

"Do you really think it is necessary?"

He nodded. "If something nefarious did happen to Chloe, your prying could have brought attention to you from very dangerous parties. I would rather be overly cautious than to see you . . ."

He trailed off before he finished his thought, and for a moment they simply stared at each other. Then he stepped forward and cupped her chin, stroking his fingers along her cheekbone absently.

"I should go now to start making my arrangements. But I'll leave instructions with your butler. I promise you, you'll be safe tonight."

His brow furrowed, as if he were trying to solve some difficult riddle. Then he leaned forward and pressed a kiss to her lips.

Lust was in his kiss, as it always was and always had been. But now, as he increased the pressure of his mouth on hers, she felt something more than mere need. Something warm and meaningful.

And as he released her and slowly bowed from the room, Victoria couldn't help but think that perhaps she had made a very bad bargain after all.

Chapter 11

Lesson 11: Scintillating conversation is a talent every woman should master.

"That valise will go into the master chamber," Victoria directed the footman who was carrying her things into one of Justin's London abodes the next afternoon.

The young man nodded, then headed up the stairs toward the bedchambers. With a sigh, Victoria looked around her. After the simple abode in Soho Square, she couldn't help but be impressed by this new home's sensual opulence. It looked every inch the kind of place where a man would keep his mistress.

Her cursory inspection upon her arrival an hour ago had revealed soft, velvet upholstery on all the chairs, most of which were built for two or more. She supposed that was to make afternoon trysts in every room all the easier.

The master bedroom was even more impressive. Her coverlet was made from expensive black silk and felt like pure sin when she stroked her hand along it. Even now, she wondered what it would feel like elsewhere. Or if Justin was the one gliding it along her skin.

A servant bustled past, and Victoria shook off her thoughts with a blush.

"Victoria, you really must listen to me," Marah said with a frown as she stepped from one of the nearby parlors.

Victoria drew a long breath before she faced her friend with a tight smile. That morning, before they departed their former home, Justin had sent a note telling Marah to pretend to be Victoria's maid once they arrived at his estate, since the servants he had hired would know nothing of their ruse. But so far, Marah had had difficulty following his direction.

"I *have* been listening to you, Marah," Victoria said on a sigh. "You gave me no choice all last night and all this morning while you railed on me about every action I have made since reuniting with Justin."

Marah's face twisted at her choice of words. "Is that what you think this is?"

Her friend glanced at a few servants who were

carrying more items in from the other house. With a frown, she caught Victoria's arm and dragged her into the nearest parlor, shutting the door behind them.

"Do you call this a *reunion* with your husband?"

Victoria shook her head at her friend's horrified look. "You know what I was trying to say. We have met again, that is all I meant by a reunion."

She certainly wasn't so foolish as to think she and Justin had any kind of future together. For some inexplicable reason, he wanted her, and she certainly burned for him . . . at least for the moment. If that desire allowed her to continue her search for Chloe, she would take advantage.

But they had already agreed that after this was over, they would return to their "normal" lives. And "normal" meant that they would live apart.

It was better that way.

"It is more than that." Her friend paced away in disgust. "You are back in his bed, and judging from the happy little flush to your cheeks last night after he left and the tangled appearance of your clothing, you are happy to be there."

Hot blood rushed to Victoria's face, but she fought her embarrassment. "Whether you like the fact or not, Justin and I *are* married, Marah. Coming to his bed isn't wrong." She shrugged. "If making love to him makes him more amenable to helping us find Chloe, isn't that what matters?"

Marah made an unladylike snort. "Are you trying to claim you are having sex with him just to get his assistance?"

Victoria hesitated. Marah was one of her best friends. Lying to her was a fruitless effort. "You don't understand. You've never experienced the pleasures a man's touch can bring."

Marah folded her arms with a harrumph. "I have read books, Victoria."

She couldn't help a small smile. "Reading books is not the same thing, I'm afraid. Whatever else has happened, when Justin and I are in the same room, there is a powerful spark between us. A draw I cannot deny."

Marah stepped forward and grasped Victoria's hands. "But the things he has done to you. Can you so easily forget them for a mere spark?"

Victoria yanked her hands away. "Of course I have not forgotten! *I* was the one forced into this marriage. Abandoned to a strange home in a place where I knew no one and expected to take over the running of a brand-new household and grounds."

Marah nodded. "And don't forget that he didn't give one thought to the fact that you might be—"

"Marah!" Victoria sent a sharp look to the parlor door. Pain, powerful and harsh, ripped through her. "Do not speak of that here."

Her friend dipped her chin with a blush. "I'm sorry. I know it is a difficult subject. I simply don't want you to forget that Justin flagrantly took lover after lover in London, with no thought to you whatsoever. And when you arrived here, he used your own desires against you in order to garner information you did not want to share."

"I know." Victoria paced the room. "Do not think so low of me, Marah. Just because I desire the man does not mean I have forgiven him for the past."

"What about trusting him? Can we truly do that?"

"What do you mean?" Victoria asked.

Marah shrugged. "About helping us find Chloe. He could easily promise to assist us while he moved you into a more controlled environment and busied you by pleasuring you day and night when he knows that is your weakness."

Victoria pursed her lips. "That thought has crossed my mind, of course. But Justin and I came to terms of a sort last night. For now, I am willing to have faith in his word."

When Marah snorted with disbelief, Victoria hastened to add, "In this and this alone. And I am on the lookout for signs that he could be untrue."

Marah sighed before she crossed the room and slipped an arm around Victoria's waist. "You are so good. And you may not see it, but sometimes I wonder if in your deepest heart, you want to believe that Justin is good, as well."

"Don't be absurd," Victoria said, but somehow her voice lacked the conviction she had meant it to have. Marah was correct in some ways. Once upon a time, she *had* longed for Justin to prove his worth. Come home. Be a true partner to her.

Those days were long gone. What she felt a twinge of now was only memory, not reality.

"I am glad you are going to be careful until he proves himself," Marah continued. "I wouldn't want to see you hurt like you were before."

Shaking her head, Victoria protested, "I was hurt before because I was foolish enough to open my heart to the man. I wished for more than he could give. This time I will not make that mistake. My body is all I will share with Justin."

Marah gave her an incredulous stare, but before they could continue, there were voices in the hallway outside that rose above the noise of the servants and their moving.

"And where is Ria?" one said above the fray.

Victoria jolted. Justin. And despite all her strenuous denials to Marah, her heart doubled its time just knowing he was near.

The door opened and Justin entered, flanked by the same two men Victoria had seen him with a few times. Now that she was closer, she recognized his younger brother, Caleb Talbot, from the portraits that hung in her family gallery at home. The other man, she couldn't place.

"There you are, Ria," Justin said with a broad smile. The smile faltered a fraction when his gaze fell to Marah. "And Miss Farnsworth. Welcome to my home. I hope you have found it comfortable."

"Oh yes," Marah replied, sarcasm dripping from every syllable. "Your hospitality lives up to your legend, if nothing else."

Justin's brother snorted out a laugh at her saucy retort, while his other companion simply stared at Marah. Justin merely ignored her rude reply before he reached back and pulled the door shut behind him.

"Careful now, miss," he said low as he moved toward them. "*You* are supposed to be 'Ria's' lady's maid, nothing more. Certainly you are in no position to speak to her protector so rudely."

Marah stepped away from him with a sneer. "What can I say? You bring out the worst in me."

Justin rolled his eyes, but ignored the comment. "Victoria, may I present my brother, Caleb Talbot. And this is my best friend, Russell Shaw."

She stepped forward to place a hand on Justin's sleeve. "You called me Victoria," she hissed beneath her breath.

He nodded down at her. "Yes. Caleb and Shaw know of our situation."

With a gasp, Victoria stepped back in shock. "You—you told them the truth?"

He wrinkled his brow. "Of course."

"I thought protecting my identity was key to this plan of yours," she said, casting a quick side glance at the men. And here she had just been declaring Justin's trustworthiness, yet he had shared her secret with strangers. "And what of Chloe's safety?"

Justin stared at her for a long moment, then turned to the other men. "Caleb, Shaw, perhaps you two could escort Miss Farnsworth into the dining room to ready for luncheon. I would like a moment with my wife."

Marah opened her mouth to argue, but Caleb stepped forward before she could say a word and caught her raised hand. He lifted it to his lips with a wink. "Come, my dear. You can war with my brother all through our meal, if it pleases you. I will even provide you with ammunition for your armory."

Marah blinked at him, stunned into silence. To Victoria's surprise, her friend followed him out of the room without any further fight. Shaw shared a long stare with Justin before he closed the doors behind them.

"It is entirely inappropriate for Marah to be alone with those two men," she snapped as she moved toward the door. "She is unmarried."

Justin snaked a hand out and caught her arm to keep her from walking away.

"You ought not lecture about inappropriateness when it comes to Marah. Everything you two have done thus far has put her reputation, and perhaps even her very life, at risk." His harsh tone softened, and he gave her a wink. "I swear to you that my brother and Shaw will not ravish her in the foyer."

He smiled as he said the words, but Victoria refused to return the expression.

"Your promises mean so little, Justin," she retorted.

Justin released her arm at that statement. He stepped back and stared at her in disbelief, almost as if her words had cut him.

"And where is that attack coming from? I thought we had come to some kind of understanding."

She gripped her fists at her sides. How could she feel *guilty*? Justin was the one who had lied over and over again.

"That was before you shared my story with two men I have never even laid eyes on before." She turned away and stared with unseeing eyes at the beautiful gardens behind the house. "You told me you would protect me, and yet less than twelve hours later, you have broken that vow."

He was silent long enough that she couldn't help but peek over her shoulder to look at him. He remained in the same spot, staring at her. Tension coursed through him, making him ramrod straight.

"You are correct in that," he finally said softly. "And I do understand why trust would be a difficult thing for you when it comes to me and my motives. I have not always treated you kindly."

She stepped toward him on instinct. This was the first time they had really talked about their past, not danced around it or alluded to it, but delved deeper. "You were not unkind. You just weren't . . . anything."

"Yes, well, I probably should have been more understanding. After all, it wasn't your fault that—"

He stopped, his cheeks paling, and Victoria took another step toward him. "What wasn't my fault?" she pressed.

He shook his head. "It doesn't matter now."

But it very much did matter. She wasn't immune to the emotions that suddenly weighted the air between them. They weren't lust, either. Something had happened, something she didn't know about, and Justin didn't want to tell her what it was, despite the fact that she had trusted him with one of her secrets.

Once again, it was a stark reminder that she couldn't trust him with anything else. Because he would never truly share anything in return, only hold what he knew against her.

"I see," she said softly.

"The best I can do now is to prove to you that my

word has meaning," he said. "I told you I would help you find your friend. I intend to do so."

He turned and picked up a file from the table. Victoria blinked. She had been so focused on *him* when he entered the room, she hadn't even noticed he carried anything with him.

"I realize you are angry that I involved Shaw and Caleb, but both of them have . . ." He hesitated, searching for a word. "*Associations* that I do not. I only told them the truth in order to utilize those things."

He pulled a sheet of heavy, expensive paper from the file and held it out to her. "With their help, I have managed to compile a rather incomplete list of everyone your friend was connected with. By tomorrow, the missing pieces should be filled in."

Victoria's lips parted in surprise at his offering. With trembling fingers, she took the paper he held out for her.

"Will you and Marah review this for me, please?" Justin asked. "Let me know if any names stand out or if there are men who Chloe never spoke of. I can provide you with descriptions, as well, in case she protected her paramours with false identities."

She stared at the long list of names. And he said this wasn't complete? "You did this already?"

"As I said, it is useful to have friends in connected places." He nodded, but then tilted his head to look at her more closely. "Why the frown? I thought you would be pleased."

"I—I am very pleased," she said with a forced smile. Inside, she was tormented. "But the quickness with which you have moved on this makes me very aware of how woefully inadequate my own investigation has been. How foolish I was to think I could actually help Chloe."

He stepped forward and held out a hand, like he was going to touch her. But he stopped, his fingers hovering between them for an all-too-brief moment before he pulled them back.

"You have done a great deal, Victoria. And only you and Marah can help us eliminate some of these people, or move them to a higher position as suspects. Plus I need you to do the one thing I cannot. It could be the most important aspect of the search."

"What is it?" she asked, shaking off a strange disappointment that he hadn't comforted her.

It was best. Every time he touched her, it only dissolved into a powerful sexual encounter. She didn't need that confusion now, not when Justin's actions and words were already confusing enough.

"No matter how much I hate it, you were right to insert yourself into the world Chloe inhabited," he admitted with a frown. "But I think you may have approached the wrong members of that world when you did your search."

She cocked her head. "What do you mean?"

"You need to speak to the women, the other mistresses, the courtesans, the actresses. Often when men look at a woman in Chloe's position, they only see lust, sin, forbidden pleasures. But the women are likely to see much more."

Victoria nodded in disbelief. So much for Justin being concerned only with pleasure. His charge made perfect sense, and his words caused her great comfort. For the first time in a very long time, she felt she had a partner in her woes. Oh, she had always been able to turn to her friends, but this was something different.

He continued, unaware of her thoughts, "We will attend a party tomorrow evening, and Alyssa will be in attendance. I suggest you speak to her first and foremost, as she has her fingers in every pie in London. Then branch out."

She nodded. "Y-yes, I will do that."

He smiled. "Now, on to more important things. How do you like the house?"

Despite her tangled emotions, Victoria stifled a laugh. *There* was the vain man she had come to expect, more concerned with how his home was perceived than with anything else. "It is very lovely."

When she hesitated before saying anything else, he cocked his head. "But?"

She squirmed. How had he so easily read her

questions? Was she so transparent, or was he simply becoming more attuned to her moods? She wasn't sure which option was worse.

"I—I simply noticed that it looks very much like the perfect house for a mistress. Very . . . sensual." She turned away. "I assume it is used often. You were not forced to evict another lady in order to give it to me, were you?"

Justin stepped forward, and slipped his warm hands around her upper arms. Slowly he forced her to look at him.

"You heard all the stories about me, Victoria," he said softly. "I have not kept a mistress since our marriage."

Victoria caught her breath. Yes, that was what she'd heard from several sources. Justin had lovers, but never anything more permanent than a few nights of pleasure.

She had always wondered why, but wasn't brave enough to ask him. She feared she might not like the answer. Plus it was too personal. They had already promised distance, she would be smart not to look for more, lest he do the same.

"As for why this house looks like that of a mistress, it is because my brother has kept women here in the past." Justin shook his head. "Never me."

Unexpected relief flowed over Victoria. Even though she never would have admitted it out loud, even under threat of bodily harm, she hadn't wanted to sleep in a bed where Justin had entertained another lover. There were limits, even to the stoniness of her heart.

He tilted his head closer. "I am not as much of a brute as you think me to be. I wouldn't be that cruel."

She nodded. "Sometimes I know that."

To her surprise, one corner of Justin's mouth quirked up and laughter lit in his eyes. "Sometimes, eh? Well, every man must be a brute from time to time, so I will accept that."

He motioned around them. "My home is not far from here. And with the busy park across the street and the adjacent home that I provide for my brother, it makes this place all the easier for me to arrange guard for. From now on, you will not be alone. You will always have my brother, Shaw . . . or me watching over you wherever you are."

Victoria nodded. The idea of Justin scrutinizing her every move was a very disconcerting one.

"And of course I will be spending a great deal of nights here to keep up the illusion that you are my mistress," he added with a wicked grin.

She shook her head with another smile. She didn't know what to make of the sudden ease of their discourse. It could very well be a trap, but she couldn't help but like it. The unexpectedly playful side of her husband was quite appealing.

"Of course. And may I expect you tonight?"

His expression grew serious and hungry in a moment, and the ease she'd been enjoying was gone, replaced, once again, with heat.

"Absolutely. I am already counting the hours until we will be alone."

She blushed and began to turn away, but he caught her arm and turned her back. His stare was no longer playful or even erotic. There was something more there. Something earnest.

"You can depend on me, Victoria," he whispered.

She shook her head slowly. "No, I cannot."

"In this you can," he insisted, squeezing her arm gently. "In this, I swear to you, you can have faith."

They stood frozen for a long moment, gazes locked, his fingers warm against her skin. Then he released her and motioned for the door. "Shall we join the others, then?"

Victoria opened her mouth, but no words would form. At least none that wouldn't reveal too much. Finally she nodded and led the way from the room.

Chapter 12

Lesson 12: A lady must dress accordingly, whether in the ballroom or the bedroom.

Justin leaned back in his chair and watched in utter wonder as his wife tilted her head and laughed at something Russell Shaw said. He didn't think he'd ever heard her laughter before. It was throaty and sensual and completely captivating.

It seemed Shaw wasn't immune to it, either, as he actually puffed his chest up with a grin before he continued speaking.

Justin frowned. Why hadn't *he* been the one to make her laugh first?

With a shake of his head, he turned to speak to his brother, but found Caleb leaning in close to Marah Farnsworth, murmuring something to her that had her blushing furiously. His lips pursed.

It seemed no one had a problem with the two women except for him.

Utterly frustrating.

With his brother so engrossed, Justin had no choice but to refocus on Shaw and Victoria. Now Shaw was leaning over, saying something conspiratorially to her. For a moment she simply stared at his friend, eyes wide, then both of them looked down the table and squarely at him.

Justin fisted his hand against the fine linen tablecloth and made an attempt to temper his tone. "And just what do you two find so amusing?" he asked through clenched teeth.

Victoria shot his friend another little smile that hit Justin in the gut.

"Mr. Shaw just told me how the two of you met, Justin. It sounds like a very interesting tale, indeed." Victoria's sparkling eyes and broad smile returned to him.

Justin groaned. Of all the stories Shaw could tell, he *would* pick an utterly humiliating one.

"Shaw is a liar," he growled, giving his friend a scowl that only made Shaw laugh harder.

"You don't even know what he told me," Victoria said with a laughing shake of her head. "So how do you know what is a lie and what isn't?"

Justin's gaze moved to her sharply. He searched her face, but saw no ulterior motive in what she had said. She wasn't referring to their own situation.

"He never tells the story correctly," Justin snarled.

Shaw's laughter boomed louder, and now even Caleb and Marah had managed to have their attention drawn. "My friend simply hates this story because he ends up arse first in one of the famous pools of Bath in front of two very lovely ladies."

Victoria dabbed at her lips with a napkin to cover her laughter.

"Women he wished to bed, I would wager." Shaw cast her a side glance. "This was, of course, before he married you, my lady."

Although Victoria's smile remained, Justin thought he saw a hint of color enter her cheeks. He didn't know why Shaw had said that. Clearly his wife knew he had taken lovers during their marriage. Hell, she wanted everyone to believe she had, as well. And yet the reminder seemed to bring her pain.

If Shaw sensed her raw emotions, he didn't show it, plowing on in his story. "Caleb, you were there, tell me I don't have the right of it."

His brother was in the thick, laughing along with their friend, completely oblivious to the way Victoria's amusement had faded or to Justin's own frustration.

Shaw winked at Caleb. "You and your brother were with your parents, enjoying the pleasures of Bath."

Caleb chuckled. "So far you are correct."

"Justin was attempting to enjoy a few *extra* pleasures with two widows who didn't care that the man was hardly out of short pants."

"Also right," Caleb encouraged, shooting his brother a wicked grin.

Justin saw a little flutter in the muscle of Victoria's jaw, as if her teeth were set.

"I was walking through the bathing room just as he . . . what was it exactly you were doing, Baybary? Making some kind of pose? I 'accidentally' nudged him, and he ended up in the pool. We've been fast friends ever since."

Shaw turned his attention on Victoria with a grin. For a moment, she stared at nothingness, her expression blank, but then she managed a weak version of her earlier bright smile.

"It sounds as if Justin has never had any trouble with the ladies," she said, her tone falsely light.

"He did that day," Caleb offered with a laugh that Shaw and even Marah joined in. "When he came out of the pool, he drenched both the women and sent them shrieking away."

Justin pushed back from the table with a screech of wood against wood. The sound brought the laughter in the room to a halt as all heads swiveled on him. All but Victoria's.

"Gentleman, we have a few things to do this afternoon." Justin gave the two men a look that brooked no refusal. "And Victoria and Miss Farnsworth must have time to look over our list."

Shaw pulled out his pocket watch, gave it a glance, and stared at Justin with an arched brow. "Very well."

Everyone got to their feet, including Victoria, though she still refused to look at Justin. His heart sank inexplicably.

In his entire life, he had never regretted his appetites. As long as he left his partners satisfied, he hadn't felt badly about loving and leaving them. Even with Victoria, who had ended up haunting him, he'd never felt guilt over bedding other women. Theirs was not a true marriage, if such a thing really existed.

And yet now a pang of remorse troubled him. A desire to explain himself to her, to make her see that those other women hadn't been a betrayal.

Even though they were. For the first time, they felt like a betrayal, and he was ashamed.

Caleb offered an arm to Miss Farnsworth, and she took it as they exited into the foyer. Shaw sent a questioning gaze toward Justin before he turned on Victoria.

"My lady, it has been a true pleasure to make your acquaintance. I do hope I will see you again, and soon."

Victoria's genuine smile returned, but it was

fleeting. "Thank you, Mr. Shaw. Talking to you has been . . . quite enlightening."

He bent a brief kiss against her knuckles, then shot Justin one final look over his shoulder before he left the two of them alone.

Victoria didn't so much as glance his way. Instead she picked at the pattern on the tablecloth.

"Your brother and Mr. Shaw are very nice," she finally said when silence had filled the room for a few moments. "Very entertaining."

Justin stepped forward, uncertain of how to proceed. Was he to apologize? And how exactly did one manage that?

"Victoria—" he began softly.

Her gaze came up, sharp. She didn't want to talk to him. Not about this subject.

"I shall be certain to look over your list this afternoon and make my notes," she interrupted. "I am sure you wish this to be resolved just as quickly as I do. The sooner things return to the way they were, the better they will be for us both."

Justin drew in a breath to speak, but Victoria was already moving for the door, acting the good hostess and saying her farewells to his brother and Shaw as they exited and moved toward the carriage awaiting the three of them at the foot of the drive.

Justin let out a sigh as he gathered up his hat and gloves from one of the servants and made his own way toward the doorway where Victoria stood waving to the other two men. She turned to move back into the house, but he caught her arm gently and held her in place.

"Victoria," he whispered, searching her eyes. Empty eyes. Ones that gave him nothing at all in return. Suddenly he missed her fire and anger. "I will see you tonight."

She nodded once, brisk and businesslike. "Yes. Until then."

A thousand thoughts rushed through Justin's head in that painful moment. He wanted to shake Victoria and tell her to be angry. He wanted to confess that for three years he had longed for her and dreamed of her. That she had spoiled every other woman for him, and that was why he never kept one. That he'd felt unsettled and unsatisfied until the moment she returned and he touched her.

Instead, he let her go and backed away.

"Good afternoon, Victoria."

"What kind of an idiot are you?" Justin snapped as he settled into the carriage and glared across the way at Shaw.

His friend wrinkled his brow and exchanged a confused glance with Caleb. "I beg your pardon?"

"You were talking about my conquests *with my wife*," Justin said, eyes widening in frustration. "Did you not notice her mood shift?"

"I noticed *your* mood shift, but not hers," Shaw said, folding his arms. "We were getting along fine until you started blustering at the end of the table. Besides, I was talking about conquests long before you even met her."

Justin shook his head. "Do you think that matters? All you served to do was remind her that I took lovers while we were married. It's a wonder that you ever get a woman in your bed if you are so obtuse."

Now it was Caleb's turn to look at him in surprise. "Good God, man, does that signify? You two are married in name alone. If you're taking her to bed now, it is a meaningless affair, no different from any other you've indulged in over the years. Soon enough it will be over and you will forget all about Victoria again."

Justin clenched his teeth. His brother's words were so dismissive, yet with any other woman, he would have agreed with Caleb's assessment. With Victoria, that kind of behavior seemed too cold. So wrong.

Caleb shook his head. "I like the woman a great deal, she's far different from what I pictured. However, you have made it abundantly clear that this is not a marriage you ever intend to make a reality. Why pretend as though her feelings in the matter make any difference to you?"

Justin pursed his lips. "They do make a damned difference to me."

Shaw drew back and looked him up and down. "Do they?" his friend said softly.

Justin glared at him. "And another thing. I don't like you flirting with my wife."

His friend's mouth dropped open. "Excuse me?"

"You were far too familiar with her this afternoon," Justin continued. "I don't like it. It will not happen again."

Caleb's eyes widened with every pointed word. He shifted his gaze between the two men as they faced off, then finally let out his breath in a whistle.

"What?" Justin snapped, snatching his gaze away from Shaw and piercing his brother with it instead.

"Nothing." Caleb held up his hands in mock surrender. "I've said my piece on this subject more than once. I am forever amazed by how much this woman has you under her spell."

Justin shook his head. "You delight in reading more into the situation than exists. Implying that there is more between my wife and me than desire and a long series of lies."

But the moment the words left his mouth, he realized how false they sounded. Since Victoria's arrival in London, he *had* been entangled in her web. Lost in lust and guilt, but, worse, he was plagued by a true interest in her. In finding out which façade she showed him was real.

And considering that her father held the keys to his demise, that he had threatened to use the information he had more than once, perhaps Justin's desire for Victoria made him a candidate for Bedlam.

Shaw shrugged. "I don't know. Perhaps there *should* be more between you. Of all the women you have shown any more than a passing interest in, she is the most suitable match for you yet. After all, Victoria is lovely and amusing, she's clearly intelligent, not to mention—"

"I think you had best stop waxing poetic, friend," Caleb interrupted, and his good humor was tempered. "My brother is turning purple."

Shaw searched Justin's face for a long moment before he shrugged. "My apologies. I meant no disrespect."

Justin grunted a response because he didn't trust himself enough to formulate words. Not when Shaw was treading on so many fire points he'd never known he possessed. He'd been best friends with the man for years, and yet he felt an inexplicable urge to throttle him.

Caleb leaned back in the carriage seat and put his hands behind his head. "Do you ever wonder what would have happened if you had met Victoria in London? Or if you didn't know her father? Do you think you would have pursued her? Or would you have avoided her like you did every other debutante?"

Justin flinched. Did he ever wonder? He wondered that every day. Even more since Victoria had returned to his life. What would have been different if he hadn't been *forced* into a union with her? What would have changed if there were no blackmail, no lies, no doubts about whether she was involved in her father's plot against him?

Would he have been able to see the passionate lover who lurked within her if he had met her on the dance floor at Almack's? Would he have been astute enough to catch a glimpse of the quiet strength that so impressed him about her now? Would he have seen past her beauty to the fiery spirit that so tempted and frustrated him?

More to the point, would he have pursued those things?

He shook the thoughts away. What would or could have been didn't really matter now. All that mattered was what was. He *had* been forced into this marriage. Victoria's father *was* Martin Reed. And Justin still wasn't certain that he could trust his wife, no matter how much he wanted her.

Victoria smoothed the starchy fabric of her gown and adjusted the high fluttering collar in the mirror above the fireplace. It had been weeks since she had dressed in anything but sinful satin and plunging necklines, so the formality of her current garb seemed strange.

Not that she normally wore such stuffy clothing. But after this afternoon, she didn't want to reveal anything more to Justin than she had to.

At first, it had been enlightening to listen to Caleb and Shaw jest with her husband. She'd seen and heard about a playful side, a jovial side to him that she'd never experienced. And she'd learned, by seeing how close he was to the two men, that Justin was capable of loyalty and friendship.

Just not with her.

However, Shaw's pointed story about Justin's wicked way with women had drawn her away from any fragile closeness she might have convinced herself she could share with her husband. Despite the humiliation of that reminder, she almost felt she owed Shaw a thank-you.

Still, his words had sat as heavy as a stone with her the rest of the day. Even as she and Marah reviewed Justin's list. Even as her friend went on about Caleb Talbot as if he were the first man she'd ever truly seen.

It sat heavy now as Victoria awaited Justin's arrival in the front parlor of the home he had put her in. As his mistress. But why couldn't their arrangement be as their marriage? One in name alone? If she didn't share his bed, it would be far easier not to forget . . . well, a great many things.

"Lord Baybary, miss," the butler intoned with a droning voice that seemed to echo in the quiet room.

Victoria turned as Justin stepped into the parlor. He was smiling, but when he saw her, his expression fell. Slowly his dark gaze moved up and down her frame. She knew what he saw, a woman far different from the one he had been seducing.

"Good Lord, wherever did you find that—that—"

"Gown?" she finished when he seemed to have trouble finding the words.

Justin pulled the parlor door shut behind him and shook his head. "I was going to say *thing*, but if you insist that it is a gown, who am I to argue? Why are you wearing it?"

She swallowed hard. It was so difficult to remain distant when Justin was shrugging out of his jacket, tossing it across the back of a chair with a casual elegance that spoke of a far more intimate and emotional relationship than they shared.

"Tonight I am not expected at any parties, I didn't see any purpose to dressing like a harlot," she said, proud that she managed to keep her tone cool and detached when she felt anything but.

One dark brow arched as Justin loosened his waistcoat and allowed it to join his other clothing on the back of the chair. That left him in only an expensive linen shirt and a cravat, which he was quickly loosening and discarding.

She sucked in a breath. Was the man stripping for her?

"So this is what you wear around the estate for comfort?" he asked, his tone revealing nothing about his thoughts.

She hesitated. At home she had a closet full of pretty gowns. Not as revealing as her costumes for Ria, perhaps, but certainly not as ugly and matronly as the scratchy dress she currently wore. She wasn't even certain where Marah had come up with it. Stolen from her maiden aunt before they left the shire, perhaps.

"Ah, so this isn't your normal garb," he said with a faint smile at her silence. "That must mean you are wearing this especially for *me*."

Heat flooded Victoria's cheeks. Even after so much time apart, he could so easily see through her. If she let him come too close, it would be even worse. She remembered full well how much worse.

"Why should we play games, Justin?" She sighed as she turned away from him to face the fire. "This arrangement we have made is purely business. I need your help finding Chloe. You want me to go away and leave your reputation intact. Must we make it something more?"

"No." She never heard his footsteps, but she felt the whisper of his breath against her neck nonetheless. Hot like the rest of him, tempting. "But I think we both want something more. And if anyone is playing games, it is you."

She drew in a breath and started to turn to protest, but he caught her arms before she could and tugged her against his body. Her back flattened against the muscled width of his chest, and her arms were useless as he pinned them in a firm yet gentle embrace.

"You have wrapped yourself in an ugly package, Victoria," he murmured against her ear. "But you cannot truly think that it will make me forget what is beneath. In fact, seeing you so hidden only makes me crave you more."

A shudder worked its way through Victoria's body from head to toe. Her eyes fluttered shut, her body arched against his. It betrayed her by growing hot, becoming wet. So much for strength against seduction.

"We made a bargain, my lady," he breathed, his voice so quiet against her ear, yet so powerful. "We agreed to be lovers. You cannot change the parameters of the deal simply because you wish to punish me."

He released her suddenly, only touching her enough to steady her. Then he stepped back.

"Now turn around."

Her hands shook as she did as he ordered. Facing him, she lifted her chin with what remained of her defiance. He smiled at the gesture.

"I'm going to unwrap you, Victoria," he said softly. "And then I'm going to burn that dress."

She started. "What?"

"You heard me. I have installed you in this house, with these servants, and everyone believes you are my mistress. No one except my brother and Shaw realizes your true identity. If you wish to keep it that way, you will behave accordingly. You will *be* my mistress. Dress like her." He smiled again, this time wicked. "And act like her."

Her nostrils flared as desire shifted and merged with anger. "And how would your mistress act, Justin? I have heard stories, but I still wonder. Would she run around in her chemise for the world to see? Would she bring you to completion beneath the table at a supper party? I can only imagine how your mistresses have acted."

Justin's face darkened, and the vein in his neck throbbed ever so subtly. "A very nice imagination you have. I certainly wouldn't be opposed to either one, if *you* were the one half naked and . . . *completing* me. But I think, right now, my mistress would merely kiss me. And then she would take me upstairs."

Victoria's lips parted in surprise. There was something in Justin's face. Something distant.

Something . . . longing. It was there in a flash, but then gone.

But it was enough to crush any resistance that remained in her aching body. Stepping forward, she placed one palm on his cheek. It was roughened with a day's stubble. She stroked her fingers to his jawline and traced the hard ridge until she found his lips. Then she tilted her face up, drew his head down, and kissed him.

His lips parted with a throaty groan, and he drank her in. She felt herself slipping, lost in sensation and desire. But before the kiss could change even further and remove the final remnants of her control, she pulled back.

"Then take me upstairs, Justin, if you want me in your bed."

Chapter 13

Lesson 13: Always be the one to walk away.

Victoria stood naked at the foot of the big bed in the master chamber, watching as Justin tore the ugly dress she'd been wearing in two in one motion.

"Tomorrow the servants will burn that thing," he said as he tossed it aside to move toward her. His eyes were lit with a hungry light in the flickering fire. One that increased as he drew ever closer. "I much prefer you this way."

"Naked and at your mercy?" she whispered past dry lips.

The hunger intensified as he came to a stop just a few inches before her. "Exactly."

She shivered. On a purely physical level, she

had always been at his mercy. Even when she had convinced herself that was over in the years they'd been apart, it wasn't true. Her desire for him had been dormant, not dead, and had come roaring back the moment she saw him.

And that desire had changed, as well. The more time she spent with Justin, the more she appreciated some of the better qualities he possessed. Like his quick intelligence. His wit, which could cut, but which made her smile despite herself. And his passion. Always his passion, smoldering under the surface.

Each moment they shared made her realize that he was utterly capable of weaving more than a mere sensual spell around her.

But she couldn't allow for more. After they found Chloe, *she* would return to Baybary and he would forget her. If she cared for him, the knowledge that he was having his fun with every willing actress and courtesan in London would not be bearable.

So she had to do something, and she had to do it fast. Something to keep her distance, to prevent him from entering her heart, even if she wasn't able or willing to keep him from her body.

"You told me that you wished for me to act like your mistress," she said, her voice cracking.

He nodded, even as he reached for her. His fingers threaded into her hair until black strands fell down around her bare breasts. He caught one lock and began to brush it back and forth across her distended nipple.

She caught her breath at the needy heat that blasted through her. "I will do so. But only if you treat me accordingly."

He stopped, and his gaze came up. "What?"

"Don't make love to me like I'm your wife," she explained, her back arching of its own accord. "Take me like you would a mistress. I don't want your tenderness, I don't want you to pretend you care about me."

His brown eyes focused with an intensity that almost made Victoria turn away.

"You don't know what you're asking for," he said.

She shrugged. "I'm asking that we don't play those games you accused me of playing earlier. If we are to go to bed together as part of the charade, then let us do it as mistress and protector, not man and wife." She held out a hand. "Is it a bargain?"

He caught her fingers and drew them to his lips. As she watched, he darted his tongue out and stroked it lazily along the length of her index finger, tracing it until his tongue probed the valley between her fingers. Instantly she was put to mind of the first time they made love in London. When he gave her the most intimate kiss.

Her body throbbed to life as the touch and the memory combined.

"Do we have a bargain?" she repeated, voice shaking.

"Turn around," Justin whispered, dropping her hand back to her side.

She looked at him with questioning, but ultimately did what he asked. It seemed resisting him came to naught. She put her back to him, tense as she waited for what he would do next.

"Put your hands around the bedpost, please," he murmured.

She heard the rustle of his clothing as he removed it and desperately wanted to look, but held back. She curled her fingers around the polished cherrywood of one of the bed's high posts and clung for dear life.

A moment later, she stiffened with a hiss of breath when he brushed his fingertip along the column of her spine. The touch was featherlight, but it sent a rush of heat and longing through her that made her nipples tingle and her pulse throb between her legs.

"I think I could look at you like this all day," he murmured as his finger continued to stroke over her skin. "Back arched, naked, my wanton little . . ." He hesitated. "*Mistress.*"

She shut her eyes. That was what she needed. That reminder that she was nothing more to him than a body to bury his own inside. A temporary passion. A kept woman who could and would be easily discarded.

"Only look?" she murmured, finally peeking at him over her shoulder.

He made a highly erotic picture. Naked and magnificent, he stood behind her, his body curling around hers though he did not yet touch her. He was dark and dangerous and hot as fire. And she wanted his embrace. She *wanted* his darkness.

"No, I've never been a man who believed in look but do not touch," he said with a smile.

Then he curled a muscled forearm around her belly and dragged her against him. Her backside fitted into the curve of his hips, and she felt the swollen, heavy length of his cock probing her from behind. Her earlier shiver was transformed into a shudder of pleasure as she realized his intentions. Her fingers tightened around the bedpost in preparation for the invasion to come.

But he didn't take her. At least not immediately. Instead he pressed a hot kiss in the center of her back. Nerves she didn't know she had fired as he trailed his lips along the sensitive skin, tracing her spine as he'd done earlier with his fingertip.

Meanwhile, his hands slipped lower. He cupped her hips, pulling her even closer to him, fitting her against his hard, muscled body until it seemed like there was no beginning or end to either of them. Just *them*. Together.

"Justin," she groaned, her fingers slipping against the shiny wooden surface of the post as she scrambled for purchase.

"I should make you beg," he murmured. She felt him rub the length of his erection back and forth against her weeping entrance and bit back a cry. "But this is as much torment for me as it is for you."

Then he was sliding home, fitting into her body and making her trembling knees buckle. But he caught her, holding her steady as he took the last few inches and filled her completely.

"You truly should have been born a mistress," he growled as he drew back and slammed forward again.

His rhythm was hard and rough, but it only served to ratchet Victoria's arousal higher and higher. To be *taken*, truly taken, was an experience she would never forget.

"Your body was meant for pleasure," he continued as he rocked her forward and back. "You were made to lie in a bed all day, sprawled out like a wanton, waiting for this. Waiting for *me*."

She tried to keep a cry from bursting from her lips, but his words, coupled with the rough slide of his hard cock inside her, stroking that hidden bundle of sensitive nerves just within her sheath . . . it was all too much. Her senses were overloaded and she lost control. Her back arched helplessly as tremor upon tremor of pleasure shook her.

Justin's hands came around her body, cupping her breasts, strumming her through the desire as he drove harder and faster into her. She felt his release building, heard it in the catch of his breath, the heat of his body, and then he exploded, clutching her close as he poured himself into her.

They stood like that for a long moment, half bent over the bed, their sweaty bodies molded as one, their breath heaving in time. Victoria reveled in the weight of him around her, the feel of him still buried inside her. For those moments, if none else, he was hers.

And no matter how hard she tried, she couldn't forget that she *was* his wife.

Justin breathed in the sweet scent of Victoria's hair. Since their wild, animal coupling, they had moved to a more conventional place on the bed. She was now gathered against him, her head tucked into the spot where his neck and shoulder met.

And he was comfortable and at ease for the first time in a long time.

Victoria shuffled at his side, and he felt her lift his hand from its position resting on her stomach.

He looked down to watch her stare at his hand in the dying firelight. Her expression was intense, focused, as if she could see his soul in the lines of his palm.

"There are Gypsies in Vauxhall who claim they can read the future in your palm," he said softly.

Her gaze turned up to his. "Yes?"

He smiled. "They say the lines tell the path of your life, if you know how to read them."

"I don't like to think that destiny or the lines of my hand determine my future," Victoria said with a low chuckle that warmed Justin unexpectedly.

There was something so comfortable about this conversation. About lying in bed with his wife and talking nonsense. It had been a long time since he had stayed with a woman for more than a few moments past orgasm.

Victoria continued, "I want to think that I have some choice in what will or will not happen to me."

Justin sighed. He certainly understood her desire to author her own life. He had been reaching for control over everything he did and experienced since her father's blackmail. He never wanted to feel that another man controlled his future ever again. And yet he had taken Victoria's choices away more than once. No wonder she had been so angry with him. Yet sometimes, like now, that anger seemed to fade away, leaving a more tender feeling.

She lifted his hand closer. "I certainly cannot see a future in your palm. I think I would settle for the past."

Justin stiffened. The comfort of the shared moment vanished in an instant. She was demanding secrets again. And they were not things he could reveal.

"What about your past?" he finally asked, spreading his fingers against hers and engulfing her hand. "It is as much a mystery to me as mine is to you."

"Yes, I suppose it is. You only ever knew my father as the raving drunk." Her tone was faraway and her lips drew down. "He wasn't always like that."

Justin cocked his head. Martin Reed was so big a villain in his mind, he had never considered him to be anything else. He'd never pictured him as a father or a man. Perhaps if Victoria explained more, he would understand his enemy better. Or even come away with some ammunition for their battle.

"What happened?" he asked.

She shrugged as she rolled over to lean her chin against his stomach. She looked up at him, and his breath caught. With her hair down around her bare shoulders, she looked so beautiful. So warm and fresh, with no hint of her usual guardedness or anger.

He wished he could paint a portrait of that moment, so he would never forget it.

"My father was once gentle, kind, even funny." Her smile softened. "Goodness how he made my mother and me laugh."

Justin remained silent as he tried to picture his wife as a playful girl. It was not difficult, and that made it feel all the more intimate.

"My mother died when I was eight years old. She was my father's world, and her death killed his laughter." Her face grew even more somber. "The bottle he chose to drown himself in afterward killed everything else."

Despite his attempts to remain immune, Justin couldn't help but feel empathy for Victoria. How she must have suffered as a child, both from her mother's death and from the loss of her father.

"Watching him change must have been difficult," he said as an encouragement for her to continue.

She nodded and blinked a few times as if she was fighting tears. For a fleeting moment, Justin wished she would allow them to fall, to trust him with that deeper emotion. But she didn't. She composed herself before she spoke again.

"He became a man I didn't know. Cold, distant. Hardly a father at all. We have no relationship to speak of anymore."

Her frown deepened, and Justin reached for

her. He touched her cheek, and she jolted at the contact. He expected her to pull away, but instead she leaned into his palm with a soft smile that warmed him in ways he didn't want to analyze.

"What about you?" she asked. "I know you are close to your brother, and I have seen portraits of your family in Baybary, but I know little of them, aside from my father's drunken ramblings, which are rarely accurate."

Justin drew in a long breath. After her honesty about her painful relationship with her father, he felt he owed her something. Perhaps there was a way to share his past with her without revealing everything.

"I was also once close to my family," he admitted. "But no longer."

He stopped. Had he ever spoken those words to anyone else? No. He didn't think he had. Even his closest friends knew very little about the breach between him and his family. But as he looked down into Victoria's eyes in the dim firelight, confession didn't feel out of place.

"What happened?" she asked.

He shook his head. "We—we grew apart."

She leaned closer. "Why?"

Again he searched her face. If only he knew what was in her heart. Perhaps if he did, he could have told her everything. Finally shared the burden of his secrets. But as much as he wanted to in that moment of weakness, he could not. There had always been that lingering question, that niggling doubt. Had she known of her father's blackmail?

And until he knew that for certain, until he was sure she wouldn't feed information back to her father or use it against him, candor was out of the question.

After he was silent a long moment, Victoria shook her head. "If it is too difficult for you to share, I won't pry. It was never my intention to force a confidence."

Justin drew back a fraction. If Victoria was playing a game, she was remarkably skilled and patient.

"I do have another question," she said. "Not about your family."

He nodded. On any other subject, he felt more comfortable being honest with her.

"I have always wanted to know—" She stopped suddenly, and a dark blush colored her cheeks. With a little shake of her head she began to turn away, but Justin caught her chin and kept her where she was.

"Ask me, Victoria."

She swallowed hard. "Why did you marry me?"

Justin released her, and Victoria turned her face from his, but he sensed her tension. Her complete attention to his every reaction.

Vowing to mask those reactions, he cleared his throat. "We have spoken of this before. Just as it was for your father, it was a business arrangement for me."

She continued to keep her gaze averted. "Is that all? Merely a business arrangement?"

He nodded slowly, and finally her dark green stare caught his from the corner of her eye.

"And what if I don't believe that?" she whispered.

He stiffened. "What more do you think it could be?"

"If it was a business arrangement, I think you would have stayed. At least until you had heirs. Or you would have made a 'business arrangement' with someone whose daughter you actually liked. I'm sure there were many lovely ladies whose company you enjoyed that would have made equally good, if not better matches. I brought very little to our union, after all."

Justin sat up, and the motion forced Victoria to do the same. For a moment, they stared at each other, raw emotion churning in the room. Then she blushed and slowly pulled the sheets around her breasts.

Flinching, Justin sucked in a breath. She looked exactly as she had on their wedding night. Dark hair down around her body, staring up at him in question.

"I heard you and my father arguing over something that night. I think I have a right to know if he did something to force you into our union," she continued, tilting her head to search his stare.

Those lingering doubts about her involvement in the circumstances of their marriage returned.

"And what makes you so curious now, Victoria?" he asked, doing his damnedest to temper his tone. "Why broach the subject tonight?"

"We had a moment of honesty," she began, then her lips pursed. "And after this afternoon, after hearing of some of your adventures, I simply wondered what could have tempted you into marrying a woman who you didn't want."

When his eyebrows went up, she shook her head.

"Very well, a woman you wanted in your bed, but not in your life." She leaned forward, bright eyes so wide that he could drown in their foamy depths. "Was it some kind of offer of money or land? Did my father blackmail you?"

Justin flew from the bed and turned on her. "Blackmail?" he repeated. "What makes you say that?"

His suspicions were now stronger than ever. Perhaps her "painful" confessions had been a ruse to make him admit something. Suddenly he questioned everything that had transpired, and he hated how their powerful joining had been tainted.

"Justin—" she began, moving toward him.

He shook his head. "Whatever you are fishing for, you shall not find it. My reasons for marrying you are my own. If you want more details for why you father behaved as he did, I suggest you speak to him."

Her lips parted with an expression of shock and a shadow of hurt she could not cover. "You tell me this after all I confessed to you? You know I cannot depend on him for answers."

"Then do not look for them from me." Justin yanked on his clothing with jerky motions. "Remember what you said to me tonight, Victoria. I wanted you to behave like a mistress, and you told me you wished me to treat you as one. If that is the case, then having long, probing conversations about our past is not appropriate."

Victoria's nostrils flared, and she got out of the bed in one smooth motion. The sheets dropped around her feet, but unlike before, she made no effort to cover herself. He stopped to stare. Dear God, she was temptation embodied. An erotic Eve, offering him all kinds of forbidden fruit.

"Damn you," she whispered, her voice husky with emotion. "You do delight in games. Tonight I thought . . ." She trailed off and shook her head. "This is my *life*. Marrying me didn't only involve you, you selfish boor. It changed everything in my world, and I think I have a right to know why. *Why,* when it is clear you could have had any woman?"

He stopped. If she wasn't involved in her father's schemes, then Victoria was correct. She *did* deserve the truth about why she had been forced to marry a man who had deserted her.

But if she was lying, then she was better than any actress he'd seen in all his years in London. She deserved an ovation for the way her eyes grew misty with angry tears, her fists trembled at her sides. The way her innocence and sensuality hung about her like a multicolored cloak.

If she was pretending all that, Justin had made his bargain with the wrong member of the Reed family. His own wife had far more cunning in one finger than her bastard of a father ever had.

He shook his head. "Mistresses don't ask questions," he finally said, his voice as icy as it had ever been, although he found it more and more difficult to dismiss her. "And protectors owe no answers. Now, I've had my pleasure, I've certainly given you yours."

A hardness entered Victoria's eyes. She nodded once. "I see."

"I suggest you spend the rest of your evening preparing to speak to Alyssa about Chloe."

For a long moment, Victoria simply stared at him. Then she ground out. "Is that all?"

He nodded. "Yes. It is."

"Then you will find the list you prepared for me awaiting you in the parlor where you began your little games tonight. I wrote my thoughts, as well as Marah's, in the margins. Good evening, my lord."

She turned her back and stalked, completely naked, into the adjoining dressing room. Justin watched her go with a strange sense of longing tightening his chest. How he hated wondering if Victoria was somehow involved in the blackmail that had brought them together. He *wanted* to trust her. He wanted to be able to ask her to trust him.

But it wasn't possible. And even if they had pretended for a while tonight, it never would be.

Chapter 14

Lesson 14: Be wary of who you trust.

"Do you remember how you are to approach Alyssa?" Justin said as his opulent carriage pulled up onto the drive of Lord Livingworth's London home.

Victoria tore her gaze away from the bright lights outside the window to glare at him. "I have not forgotten in the last five minutes, I assure you. I am your erotic plaything, not touched in the head, if you remember."

Justin pursed his lips at her tone and demeanor, but Victoria felt no pleasure at angering him. She had felt no pleasure at all since their parting the night before. There had been a time after they made love when she'd thought they'd had a true connection. Lying in his arms, talking about the past, wondering about what drove the future, she'd felt a peace that rarely touched her when Justin was near.

But when he used her own words against her, telling her to speak to her father when he *knew* she could not . . . that had left her feeling foolish and empty. Alone. It was a bitter reminder that he could not be trusted. Thank God she had shared no deeper secrets than the ones about her father's transformation.

The carriage pulled to a stop, but Justin made no move toward the door except to hold it shut when his groom came around. He stared at her, dark eyes glittering in the faint light.

"If you want to be angry with me, I won't argue with you," he said, his voice deceptively soft. "But the moment you step out of this carriage, you will play the part of my devoted lover, do you understand? You will dance with me, you will stare up at me with lust in your eyes, and you will behave like you want me more than any other man in the world. It is imperative to your safety."

Victoria looked away. In none of those things would she be forced to "play the part." Lust, desire . . . they had always come naturally. It was trust and honesty that were difficult.

"Of course," she said softly. "No matter my true feelings, I wouldn't do anything to reveal our ruse and endanger my friend."

He remained silent for a moment, and she felt his seeking stare on her, though she didn't dare look at him. Finally he pushed the carriage door open and stepped out.

Victoria followed, taking the groom's hand for assistance. She looked up at the towering home before her with a sigh. Yet another night of playing her role, an act that was wearing on her more with each failed attempt at finding information.

But at least this time she was not alone.

She stepped up to Justin. Dear God, he was handsome in his dark green frock coat and matching shirtwaist. His hair was slightly tousled by the breeze, which gave him a debauched appearance.

Drawing a harsh breath, she took his arm. Not with the proper, gentle touch of a lady, but with a familiar one. She curled her fingers around his bicep, leaning against him with her breasts as she stared up adoringly.

He jolted at the contact, and his gaze darted down. For a moment, heat flared between them, rising up to that place that Victoria knew could only end in his bed. But then a little distance entered his stare. Something troubled him.

He turned his face. "Yes, that will do nicely, Victoria. Let us enter the house, shall we?"

She followed his lead, moving beside him up the marble staircase and into a wide great hall where dozens of guests were already buzzing and milling about. Victoria scanned the crowd, searching for the men on Justin's list.

The first one she found was Alexander Wittingham. She couldn't help but think about his reaction to her mention of Chloe's name a few days before. And Alyssa had been so hesitant when Victoria asked to meet him.

She leaned up close to Justin's ear, hoping to look like she was cooing erotic secrets rather than conspiring with him.

"Wittingham is here," she whispered, stirring the hair above his ear with her breath. The scent of shaving lotion and sin assailed her nostrils and set her on edge.

Justin let out a strangled sound before he whispered, "Yes, I see him. I have never heard anything about the man except for his luck with ladies, but that doesn't mean he isn't capable of something vile. And Evenwise is also here tonight."

He motioned across the floor, and Victoria stiffened as she saw the other man talking with a few others. A faint fluttering of the nervousness she'd felt with Evenwise that night in the hallway returned. Was her unease a warning, or a silly reaction to a man who had made it no secret that he wanted her?

She swallowed back her fear. "Perhaps after I speak to Alyssa, I should approach one or both men. Even dance with them. They might reveal more to me if I—"

Justin turned on her with a harsh frown. "No," he said through clenched teeth. "You are to stay away from them. If either of them is responsible for the kidnapping, the mur—"

He cut himself off suddenly, but Victoria knew full well what he was going to say. He thought Chloe was dead. Killed by whomever she had written about.

Victoria looked away from her husband and stared straight ahead into the milling crowd, though she didn't see the people any longer. She struggled to keep tears at bay, fought to remain calm and sensual and flirtatious as a mistress should. It was almost impossible when her mind was creating horrible images of Chloe in pain, Chloe's life slipping away at the whim of some monster.

Justin's warm hand slipped into the small of her back, comforting, protective. It drew her away from the harsh images in her mind and brought her back to the present.

With a gasp, Victoria looked up at him.

"I'm sorry," he whispered, and his voice was suddenly kind. "We have no evidence that anything of that kind has happened to your friend. I am simply worried for your safety. Don't despair. We *will* find her."

Victoria nodded, shocked at the relief that

rushed through her. A few words, a gentle touch, and she was soothed. But that was the job of a husband, not a temporary lover.

"There is Alyssa," she whispered as she returned her attention to the crowd. She was glad for the distraction. Things between her and Justin were suddenly too intense. "I ought to approach her."

Justin nodded. "If you encounter any trouble, give me the signal. I shall be watching, even if it appears I am not."

Victoria gave him a surreptitious glance from the corner of her eye. How could a man so dangerous to her make her feel so . . . safe?

"Yes, I will."

She moved to leave his side, but Justin caught her arm. Drawing her against his chest, he whispered, "My mistress needs a kiss before she goes."

Victoria's eyes widened, but she didn't resist, even as he kissed her passionately, right there in front of several of the gentlemen of the Upper Ten Thousand. Her lips parted of their own accord, and she surrendered, briefly, to the seductive taste of his mouth, the feel of his tongue stroking over hers.

But there was more than passion to this kiss. There was . . . encouragement. Comfort.

Then he parted from her and smiled. "That should make my claiming of you clear, even to those who haven't heard the rumors."

Victoria blinked. Of course, the kiss was all part

of the show. It meant nothing. *None* of it meant anything, even if it sometimes felt like it did.

"I'll r-return in a while," she stammered, before she glided away on unsteady feet.

"You two are looking quite cozy." Alyssa laughed as she handed Victoria a flute of champagne.

Victoria took a long sip from the bubbly drink, letting the warmth spread through her chest. If only it would grant her calm.

"And here you said you didn't even want to be introduced to him," Alyssa continued. "But Justin always gets what Justin wants. That fact is well-known."

Victoria forced a smile. "Yes, I'm beginning to learn that."

The other woman tilted her head at Victoria's tone, and a little concern entered her bright blue eyes. "Are you quite well? He isn't . . . he isn't cruel to you, is he?"

"No!" Victoria held up her hands instantly. "Of course not. He is just—he's—"

"Overwhelming?" Alyssa suggested as she cast her gaze toward Justin.

Victoria all but choked on her drink. That was *exactly* what Justin was. Overwhelming to her body, to her senses, and, occasionally, to her emotions.

The courtesan seemed to take Victoria's silence as confirmation. She nodded. "Yes, I could see how he would be. But you are happy, yes?"

Victoria considered that question. Since her arrival in London, nothing had gone according to her careful plans. Justin had intruded and forced and controlled. He had proven himself capable of *taking* what she would not willingly share.

And yet there had been moments between them. Times when she was able to forget their troubled past, when she saw something deeper in the man she had married than she had ever dared anticipate. In those fleeting times, there had been warmth and pleasure . . . and she *had* been happy.

"Yes," she said with a sigh.

The other woman nodded with a brief expression of relief. "But if you were not, I hope you would come to me," Alyssa said quietly. "I do not only match gentlemen with companions, you know."

"No?" Victoria cocked her head.

"If need be, I can do more. And have in the past."

Victoria stared at the other woman in utter shock. Was Alyssa saying she would help "Ria" escape a dangerous situation if need be? Hope blossomed within her. If she was reading Alyssa's implication correctly, perhaps the courtesan had made the same offer to Chloe. If she had, that could very well mean her friend was alive.

"You have, er, assisted others?" Victoria asked, careful to keep her tone neutral before she took another sip of her champagne.

A hint of caution entered Alyssa's stare.

"Occasionally men can become . . . overly enamored of women of our station. And a few of these men"—she glanced around the room with a wave of her hand—"believe their money and position can buy them far more than they are owed. In that situation, I would be remiss if I didn't help a woman in need."

Victoria nodded slowly. She pushed at the hope that was building in her with every moment. She knew nothing yet; she couldn't get ahead of herself. Caution was her best weapon now.

"It seems you have influence and knowledge in all quarters," she said, staring off into the crowd with practiced indifference.

Alyssa shrugged. "I have been a mistress for ten years and warmed the beds of half a dozen powerful men. Over time, being exposed to that life gives you some authority yourself. And I make it my business to know what is happening in Society, both the pretty face of it and the life led behind closed doors. A woman never knows when she might need that kind of information."

Victoria looked at her companion again. She had no doubt Alyssa knew far more than most even suspected. Especially those who only saw her as a pretty face and lush body to hang on their arm.

The courtesan gave her a hawk-eyed stare. "Actually, that is a good fact for you to keep in mind."

"What do you mean?" Victoria asked, desperate for any additional information or clue.

Alyssa looked at Justin. He was standing off in the distance, talking to some other men. But Victoria was well aware that he was always watching her, even from the corner of his eye. Keeping ready for any signal that she was in trouble.

"All I am saying is to keep the door open for other men. Although he seems to look at you with more depth of feeling than any other woman I've ever seen, Justin has never been known to keep his lovers long. In fact, he hasn't had a true mistress under his protection for . . ." Alyssa hesitated as she thought. "It must be years now. Not since his marriage."

Victoria jolted. The other woman's eyes were completely clear and innocent. She had no idea that Justin's wife herself was standing before her.

A thousand questions swirled in Victoria's mind, ones she didn't dare share with Justin. She wanted to ask Alyssa why Justin hadn't taken a mistress since his marriage. She wanted to discover what Alyssa knew about his feelings for his wife.

But pressing those issues would only rouse suspicion and remove her from the subject of Chloe. Victoria couldn't let her own selfish desires interfere with her friend's safety.

And perhaps, on some deep and powerful level, she didn't want to face even more proof that Justin didn't care about her.

"Since you are acquainted with so many people, perhaps you can assist me," she began, ignoring the tempting subject of Justin and steering the conversation back to Chloe where it belonged.

Alyssa turned toward her with a smile. "Ah, so you already *are* thinking about your next protector, are you? Clever girl."

Victoria shook her head. "Oh no. It isn't that at all, although I will certainly take your advice to heart and not let myself become too close to Justin."

The courtesan tilted her head. "Then what is it?"

Drawing a calming breath, Victoria launched into the lies she had practiced. "When I arrived in London, I attempted to make contact with an old friend of mine, but I have not yet been able to find her. I thought perhaps you knew of her since she is a courtesan."

Brow furrowing, Alyssa nodded. "Of course. If I can be of assistance to you, I will gladly help."

"Her name is Chloe Hillsborough," Victoria began.

Alyssa blinked twice. It was her only reaction to the name, but Victoria noticed it.

"I'm sorry," the courtesan said. "I do not recognize the name. As connected as I am, I do not always know every young lady who moves about in these circles."

Victoria tilted her head. Alyssa's face was calm, but she continued to sense that the other woman was lying. Why?

She pondered what she should do. Push Alyssa? Demand the truth? Unmask herself?

Victoria shivered. No, none of those things was a prudent idea, not when she didn't know Alyssa's intent. Instead she shrugged. "Oh well. It makes little difference. She was an old acquaintance, but perhaps I was wrong about her coming here after all."

"Yes. This life is not for everyone. Perhaps your friend changed her mind." Alyssa shifted uncomfortably. "Now, if you will excuse me, I must find an acquaintance I promised to speak to this evening. It was very nice seeing you again, Ria."

Victoria bobbed out a little nod. "And you as well, Alyssa. Thank you for your assistance."

The other woman turned to leave her side, and Victoria watched her go. Her blond head weaved in and out of the crowd and then was gone in a sea of peacock feathers, satin, and lace.

Victoria turned to find Justin, but came up short when she realized he was already standing at her elbow.

"There you are, Ria," he said in a voice loud enough to be heard by a smattering of people around them. "I believe you owe me this dance."

She gave a sultry laugh befitting her role and took his hand, smiling for the benefit of those around them.

"I have much to share," she murmured beneath her breath.

"Then waltz with me, and tell me everything," Justin replied as he pulled her scandalously close and spun them into the first turns of the dance.

If Victoria was shocked by the music, which was slower than a normal waltz, or distracted by the couples around them, some of whom had a very interesting take on the sensual dance, she gave no indication. Justin cupped his wife's hip as he maneuvered her around one swaying couple and away from the ears of the other dancers.

"Alyssa may know something about Chloe," she whispered. "In fact, she may be involved in her disappearance."

Justin looked down at her in surprise. He had never suspected Alyssa of anything more than vast knowledge of most of the powerful men in his circle. "Tell me."

Quietly, Victoria relayed the particulars of their conversation. Justin moved them through the steps, being especially careful to concentrate on his wife's words, not the way her hips occasionally grazed his or how her breasts brushed the fabric of his coat when they came too close to another couple.

"There was something so strange to her demeanor," Victoria finally said with a sigh. "But if she assisted Chloe in escaping from an overzealous lover, why wouldn't she tell me?"

Justin shrugged. "If she is involved in the disappearance, it could be she feels she is in danger herself. Or she might not want to be the one to tell you bad news if she knows it."

Victoria's footsteps faltered, and Justin tightened his hold on her waist to keep her from falling. He winced at the forlorn look in her eyes. Every time she thought of her friend being hurt or worse, he could see how deeply it cut her. And he wanted so much to spare her from that pain.

But after so long with no word, and after seeing what kind of men Chloe had been involved with, Justin had little expectation that Victoria and Marah would leave London in anything but mourning. He could already see what that would do to his wife, and yet he would not be with her to comfort her.

"I caught Evenwise watching you with Alyssa,"

he said, changing the subject to spare her from her thoughts.

Of course, *his* thoughts when it came to Evenwise were of little comfort. He knew the man's reputation. The idea that he had turned his attentions to Victoria was stomach-turning.

Her gaze flitted up, a little fear making the green dark as a jungle. "I had such a feeling about him when we were alone," she mused with a little shiver.

He nodded. "He has a reputation for pain more than pleasure. And one mistress who has already disappeared without a trace."

Victoria jolted as the music came to an end. She stared up at him, lips parted. "What? Wh-why didn't you tell me?"

Justin bit back a curse. "We don't even know if your friend was acquainted with him, Vic"—he shut his eyes—"*Ria*. I didn't see any point to upsetting you. I spoke out of turn in telling you now."

Her nostrils flared delicately. "And what else are you withholding, Justin?"

He flinched at the accusation. "I could ask the same of you, my dear. All you are is secrets."

A shadow briefly crossed her face. Something unbearably sad that stirred Justin's heart in an unexpected way. What was she thinking of that could make her look so brokenhearted?

"Some secrets are better kept, but not ones that have to do with my friend," she hissed.

Justin clenched his fingers. "You are right."

She opened her mouth for what he could tell was going to be a harsh set-down, but then what he'd said seemed to sink in, and she stopped, eyes wide. "What did you say?"

He sighed. Apologies had never been his strong suit. "I said that you were right," he ground out through clenched teeth. "I should not have withheld information from you that had to do with your friend. I was trying to—"

He broke off.

She leaned in closer. "Trying to what, Justin?"

"Protect you," he said softly. "I was trying to keep you from suffering any more pain than you already are. I didn't want you to picture the worst."

Victoria's eyes softened, all her righteous anger gone, replaced by something so much deeper and more meaningful. His heart swelled at the sight of it.

"Justin—" she began, her voice trembling. But before she said anything more, she stopped. Her attention moved from his face to a spot behind him, and her eyes widened.

"Victoria?" he asked. "What is it?"

He began to turn around, to follow her stare, but she grasped his coat and held him in place. "Alyssa . . . she's talking to Alexander Wittingham."

Justin drew back. "I never knew they were close."

"She introduced me to him, but they didn't seem to be anything more than faint acquaintances. But now . . ." She darted her gaze to his face. "Justin, embrace me. Then move so you can see them without being obvious."

She didn't have to ask him more than once. Justin slipped his arms around Victoria's waist, drawing her against his chest with a little shudder. Even though what he was doing had an ulterior purpose, he couldn't ignore how good Victoria's body felt against his. How warm and filled with life she was. How her scent tormented him with sensual promise.

Slowly they shifted positions, and he reluctantly parted from her to look in the direction that had caught her eye. Sure enough, Alexander Wittingham and Alyssa Manning stood close together, their heads near enough to almost touch as they whispered. For a moment, Justin wondered if Alyssa was the man's lover, despite having her own protector floating around somewhere.

But their expressions weren't the ones of lovers. Or even friends. Both had a focused urgency, a serious intent. And then Wittingham looked at Victoria. Immediately Justin dropped his lips to his wife's in a passionate kiss. Through hooded lids, he watched as Wittingham motioned ever so subtly in her direction, then frowned.

Justin began to break the contact of their lips, but he felt Victoria's fingers curl around the back of his neck, holding him in place as her tongue traced the crease of his mouth. For a moment, everything else was forgotten, and Justin crushed her to him. Damn, but this woman was a drug. She could make him forget everything, everyone but her.

She could almost make him forget the past.

They broke apart, each breathless as they stared at each other for a long moment. Then Justin managed to tear his gaze away to search for Alyssa and Wittingham. To his disappointment, they were no longer standing within his view.

"Damn," he muttered.

Victoria shook her head, as if she were clearing away a fog. "Did you see them?"

He nodded silently. "Come, we need to find my brother and Shaw. I saw Caleb heading into the hallway a few moments ago."

She slipped her hand into his and followed without comment. Justin maneuvered them through the crowd, but with every step he wasn't thinking about his brother. He wasn't even thinking about Alyssa and Wittingham.

He was thinking about Victoria, and wondering how he would ever break the spell she had woven around him. And if he wanted to.

Chapter 15

Lesson 15: Never beg.

Victoria clung to Justin's hand as they entered yet another darkened hallway in the twisting corridors of the estate. She could feel the tension pulsing through him, but she realized it was for a far different reason than her own.

He was thinking about Alyssa, about Wittingham and Evenwise, about Chloe. About getting rid of Victoria.

She, on the other hand, couldn't rid her mind of thoughts of the intimate way he had held her while they danced. Of the warmth of his hand on her back that was comforting, as well as arousing. Of his unexpected apology for withholding information about Evenwise's history.

A shiver racked her. Little by little, she was getting in far too deep for her own good. But being aware of that fact and fighting it were two very different things.

"There is Caleb," Justin said, motioning down the hallway.

Indeed, his brother was there, leaning against the wall in the empty corridor, puffing on a cigar. When they approached, Caleb nodded in greeting.

Victoria looked at the younger man as they drew near. She'd never noticed how much and yet how little he resembled Justin. They had the same dark hair, the same cocky smile, but their eyes were very different. While Caleb's were a striking pale blue, filled with mischief and naughtiness, Justin's were so dark that they cloaked his emotions, even when they reflected his darkest desires. They were eyes she could lose herself in. Even to her detriment.

"Whatever are you doing here?" Justin asked, an edge to his voice that drew her from her thoughts. "And where is Shaw? We need to speak to you both."

Caleb motioned to the door beside him with a wordless grunt. Justin's brow wrinkled as he stepped forward and reached for the handle.

"You might not want to—" Caleb began on a harsh whisper.

But it was too late. The door swung open to

reveal Shaw sitting on a bench in front of a huge bed. A lady knelt between his legs and she was . . .

Victoria's lips parted, and she could not hold back a gasp as she stared at the scene before her. The other woman was pleasuring him with her mouth. Shaw leaned back, eyes shut, neck straining with pleasure as the young woman did her work with a lusty zeal that sent a strange pulsing throb between Victoria's own legs. She turned her face as Justin yanked the door shut silently and glared at his brother.

"You might have mentioned that," he hissed.

Caleb smiled as he took another puff of his cigar. "I did try. I was told to stand guard. Shaw is working very hard to get Ellie away from her latest protector. He didn't want any interruptions."

"Well, he didn't seem to notice any interruptions, at any rate." Justin tossed a quick glance at Victoria. "My apologies."

But he didn't look apologetic. He looked just as hungry as she felt. Even as Justin and his brother talked, Victoria thought of what she'd seen. Only instead of Shaw and the unknown woman, she put herself and Justin in their places. What would it feel like to take him into her mouth?

Her mind drifted to the night he had kissed her in a similar way. That kiss had been so intimate.

The feeling had been the most intense of her life. If her mouth could bring him even half as much pleasure—

"Victoria!"

She started from her erotic thoughts to find the two men staring at her. With a blush, she squeaked, "Yes?"

"Come," Justin said, his voice suddenly rough as he took her hand. "My brother will meet with us at home after he's fulfilled his 'duty.'"

Victoria blindly nodded, even as she cast one final glance behind her at the door where Caleb stood.

It had been fully ten minutes since Victoria had said a word. She sat across from Justin on the carriage seat, staring out the window into the dark night outside. Even though he was denied her stare, the tension that had been coursing between them all night remained heavy in the air.

Since leaving the party, it had only intensified. Victoria's cheeks had taken on a high, aroused color when she saw Shaw and his paramour, and that blush had never faded. Which meant she was recalling the erotic scene they had stumbled upon over and over.

For that matter, so was Justin. All he could think about was Victoria's lips closing around his length, her tongue laving him from head to base. Squeezing his eyes shut, he adjusted around a growing erection.

The carriage rumbled over uneven cobblestones, and Victoria bit back a gasp as she braced a hand on the wall beside her. Her gaze darted to him, and her cheeks colored even further.

Justin muttered a curse. Knowing she was thinking about what they'd witnessed didn't ease his arousal one bit.

"You did a very good job tonight," he said, trying desperately not to look at her mouth.

She kept her gaze averted as well. "Did I? I don't feel like I uncovered anything of use. We have no idea whether Alyssa or Wittingham or even Evenwise had a part in Chloe's disappearance."

Justin shifted to lean closer. "But through your actions, we witnessed their suspicious behavior. That helps enormously." He reached out, hesitating for a brief moment before he covered her hand with his own. "You are doing as much as you can, Victoria. No friend could do more."

She stared at his hand for a long moment before her gaze shifted to his face.

"Thank you," she whispered, her voice breaking.

He should draw his hand away, but he found it impossible to do so. He just wanted to *touch* her. Feel her warmth beneath his skin. Forget all the things between them and just have the moment.

"Justin," she whispered, her fingers clenching beneath his.

He saw desire in her eyes, and for the first time it disappointed him. It was no secret that Victoria was willing to surrender her body, but it seemed she would never give anything else.

And he was having a harder and harder time pretending he didn't want more.

With a sigh, she leaned forward and pressed her lips to his with a burning passion that was sweet with its innocence and scorching with its power. Justin's thoughts faded, his emotions clearing to leave only the overpowering need that she continually inspired. If this was the only way she would allow them to connect, then by God, he would make sure she never forgot it.

He pulled her forward until she tumbled into his arms. Their mouths collided without finesse, but the pleasure still bordered on unbearable.

She yanked at his cravat, tugged his shirt free from his pant waist.

"Why—why is this happening?" she moaned.

He shook his head, needing no explanation for what she meant by *this*.

"I don't know," he managed between kisses as his fingers slipped beneath her gown's scandalously low neckline and found her breast.

She clawed at his chest with a keening cry

before she panted, "Is it always like this for you?"

He stopped, pulling back to look down at her. She was wedged between his legs, black hair around her face, eyes shining with both lust and the powerful emotion she normally hid.

"No," he admitted with difficulty. "It has never been like this except with you."

Her lips parted in surprise. "Justin," she whispered as she leaned forward to press a hot kiss against his throat where his pulse was pounding wildly.

"Yes?"

"There was never any other lover," she murmured against his skin. "There was only you."

His breath stolen, Justin stared down at her. Since he had made love to her the first time in London, he had suspected she had been with no other man. Or at least that her last lover had been long ago. But hearing her *admit* that there had been no one but him sent a blast of pleasure through him that was as powerful as her kiss.

He was the only one. And he found he wanted to be the only one forever.

Victoria smiled softly, then her mouth feathered across his collarbone. Justin's eyes went wide as he watched her trail her lips down. Her tongue was hot against his skin, the path where she suckled him tingling. Lower and lower, she shimmied, sucking one nipple as he had done to her so many times. And just as she had, he dipped his head back with a low groan.

"You don't have to do this," he ground out. "Not because of what you saw."

She shook her head as her lips grazed his belly and her fingers went to work on freeing his cock from the confines of his trousers.

She pulled his erection from the opening she had created and stroked him once from base to head, which elicited another harsh moan.

"I want this," she murmured. "I want you."

Before he could reply, her mouth closed on him. Justin's head lolled back against the carriage seat as an enormous wave of pleasure crashed across his senses. Though Victoria's movements were unpracticed, she was a quick study. She tested the pace of her mouth, slowing when he strained up to meet her, quickening when his fingers clenched helplessly against the fine leather seat.

He tangled those same fingers in her hair, strands pulling loose from the complicated fashion to fall down around her face. She never hesitated, just continued to lick and stroke his length. She lightly nipped, she rolled her tongue around his girth, she sucked with just enough pressure to bring him up to the edge.

Justin wasn't even trying to hold back the sounds of pleasure now. He had experienced this act too many times to count, from lovers of all experience and proclivity. But never had he been so washed away. Never had it been more than a pleasant diversion designed to give him release.

With Victoria it felt like a gift.

One he didn't want to take selfishly. The end was coming. He felt his seed moving within him, rushing toward release. Before he could find it, he grasped her arms, pulling her up with such efficient speed that her eyes widened in shock.

He turned her around in one swift motion, lifting her skirts even as he settled her into his lap. When her wet, ready body naturally enveloped him as her mouth had, they let out a simultaneous groan that echoed in the quiet dimness of the vehicle.

Victoria didn't have to be told what he wanted. Immediately she stroked over him, her sheath gripping and releasing in perfect time. Justin buried his mouth against her shoulder, suckling the bare skin as he wrapped his hands around her to stroke and tease her breasts.

With every rocking motion of their bodies, of the carriage, they drove closer to home and release. Justin strained up, reveling in the stretch and clench of her body, the soft, needy moans that poured from her lips like an unending symphony.

The carriage began to slow as they eased around

the final corner onto the drive of the home where Justin had installed Victoria.

"Now," he growled against her ear. "Come for me."

Her body lurched with pleasure, grinding down over him with a reckless rocking that almost masked the final jolting movements of the carriage. Justin roared his pleasure with her, allowing her to milk his essence from his body until they were both weak.

Resting his head against her shoulder, Justin let out a shuddering breath. When he'd confessed that sex had never been like this with anyone but her, he hadn't been lying.

Nothing about Victoria was like any other woman he'd been with before. And that was dangerous.

Victoria smoothed her skirts another time, but she couldn't seem to erase the wrinkles. Just as she couldn't quite make her hair look right or draw the flush from her chest and cheeks. She had been trying to return to some pretense of normalcy ever since she and Justin had staggered from the carriage and up to the parlor. It was a losing battle.

Now they sat with Marah and Caleb, who looked at them with knowing or accusing eyes, depending upon which one Victoria dared look at. Her friend knew what she and Justin had done.

Everyone knew.

From the guests at tonight's party down to the scullery maids, anyone who came in contact with her and Justin seemed to have instantaneous knowledge that they could scarcely keep their clothing on when they were within ten paces of each other.

Everyone thought they were having a magnificent, passionate affair. But what no one could see was that there was a desperation that taunted her every time they touched. Making love to Justin was the only thing that seemed to satisfy the hungry fire that burned inside of her whenever they were near.

But it was a temporary satisfaction. Within moments of their bodies parting, she needed him again. And not just his body. Not just his touch.

"After what we witnessed tonight, I believe we should shift all our attention to Alexander Wittingham, Alyssa Manning, and Darius Evenwise," Justin said.

Victoria stared at him in disbelief. Though he was slightly disheveled from their powerful coupling in the carriage, his tone was completely calm. Did nothing move him? He wanted her, but it didn't seem to be the same all-consuming desire that haunted her constantly. Even if he admitted that no other lover drove him as she did, it didn't necessarily follow that she had become important to him outside of the bed they shared.

Caleb nodded. "I'm comfortable with that. Evenwise has a reputation when it comes to women. And you've already determined that Wittingham has some kind of connection to Chloe." He frowned. "I hate to think Alyssa would be mixed up in this kind of thing, though."

Marah turned to look at him sharply. "Why wouldn't she be?"

Victoria started at her friend's tone. From the flash of emotion in her eyes, it was clear Marah didn't like the idea that Caleb would defend the beautiful courtesan.

Caleb tilted his head and locked eyes with Marah. "You don't know Alyssa, Miss Marah."

Marah hesitated before she turned away with a sniff. "And I'm sure you do, Mr. Talbot."

"Alyssa has always seemed a decent woman," Justin said, ignoring their sniping. "She has no reputation for anything underhanded. But Victoria sensed that Alyssa knew something more about Chloe than she shared. And that is enough for me to believe she should be watched."

Victoria stared at her husband. He was saying he had faith in her instincts, even if it went against what he already knew. A warmth spread through her that couldn't be pretended away.

"So what should we do?" she asked softly.

It was strange, she had resisted their partnership in the beginning, but now she was happy for it. Justin had once said she could trust him in this, and she had started to realize he was right.

He turned to her. "Evenwise and Wittingham will both be at the opera tomorrow night. Evenwise never misses a show, and Wittingham's mother is in town and always insists he join her in her box. I say you and I go and see if we can determine something more about their relationships to Chloe."

Marah surged to her feet. "But the opera will contain mixed company. It won't be just randy gentlemen and their mistresses like the parties Victoria has attended thus far in her search. What if someone recognizes her?"

Justin looked at Victoria, his eyebrows lifting slightly. "Marah is correct. There is always a chance that your true identity will be uncovered. But I'll do everything in my power to protect you."

With a sigh, Victoria said, "I will be wearing seductive clothing, walking differently, talking differently. I don't know more than a handful of people in London. If I see them, I'll signal you, and we can move in the opposite direction." She looked at Marah. "If we could find Chloe, I think it will be worth the risk."

Marah pursed her lips, and Victoria could see

her friend wanted to argue. But how could she when it was Chloe's safety they were debating? Finally she nodded.

"Yes, you are correct. I just don't want to see you hurt in this."

Victoria sucked in her breath as she cast a surreptitious side glance at Justin.

"I won't be, Marah," she finally said softly. "I cannot allow myself to be."

Chapter 16

Lesson 16: Be careful how close you play to the fire. You might get burned.

"My God, you truly are stunning," Justin breathed as Victoria stepped into the foyer the next night.

She looked down at herself. Marah had helped her dress in a gorgeous spring green gown, embroidered with little yellow flowers along the sheer overlaid skirt. Her friend had complained all the while about Victoria's shockingly low neckline and fitted bodice until Victoria questioned herself about the propriety of such a garment.

But standing with Justin now, seeing his approving stare, she couldn't help but feel beautiful.

"Thank you," she said with a blush.

"Shall we go?" He motioned to the door.

She allowed him to settle a light wrap over her shoulders, and they set out into the warm summer night. As they approached the carriage, Victoria hesitated. Her thoughts turned traitorously to the last time they had shared the vehicle and the wanton behavior on her part that had led to a most passionate encounter.

From the smug grin on his face as he helped her in and then settled into the seat across from her, Justin was thinking about the same thing. Tension hung between them for a long moment before he smiled at her and broke the tide of desire.

"Are you nervous about tonight?" he asked.

She shrugged. "I think I would be a fool not to feel some anxiety. And Marah certainly didn't help with her constant reminders of all that could go horribly wrong."

Justin rolled his eyes. "Ignore her. The likelihood is that this evening will be utterly uneventful."

She smiled at his reassurance, although the idea was a bit troubling, considering their reasons for attending the opera. "I hope you are wrong. I hope we shall discover some key information that will eventually lead us to Chloe."

"Perhaps," he replied, though from his expression she could tell he held little faith in that outcome.

She sighed. There was no use getting too maudlin about the night. So instead of pressing the subject, she tilted her head. "I have never been to an opera before."

Justin's eyes widened. "Never?"

She shook her head with a blush at her inexperience. "They do not often perform such things in Baybary."

"B-but—" he stammered. "Surely when you visited London before—"

She looked out the window with a frown. "I was never given a Season, remember? My father arranged our marriage before I could experience any of the pleasures of the city."

At one time, she had longed for those things. Time and pain and the responsibility of her station had eventually driven those wants into hiding.

Justin let out his breath in a low whistle. "There is so much for you to see, to do."

Victoria shook her head. "This is not the trip for frivolity. Chloe is the most important thing to me now. And after we find her"—she ignored the painful voice that whispered that they might never find her friend—"after we find her, I somehow doubt I will return."

"Ah yes, you have important things to attend to in the country. I had forgotten," he said softly, returning his gaze to the city outside.

She stifled a sigh at the wall that had come between them once again. She, too, looked at the passing buildings, their lights glittering merrily.

If this was a trip for pleasure, she was certain there was much to be had here. And Justin loved the city so much. Under other circumstances, she had no doubt he would be a charming guide to all its diversions.

But she had long ago learned not to live on dreams of what might have been. Those thoughts invariably led to disappointment.

The carriage began to slow, and Victoria peeked out the window at the dazzling lights of the theater.

"My, it is lovely," she breathed, caught up in the moment, despite herself.

Justin scooted closer and leaned over to look out the window beside her. "Yes. And my box affords a perfect view of the stage, so at least you will be able to enjoy the show."

She looked at him from the corner of her eye. His mouth was drawn down and his expression far more serious than normal.

"I'm sure I will enjoy it," she said quietly. "Even if it is part of a charade."

He moved away from her as the carriage door swung open. "Then let the charade begin."

Justin tucked Victoria's hand into the crook of his arm as they swept from his private box and into the crowded hallway for intermission. He felt her fingers tighten around his bicep with a nervous flutter and set his hand on top of hers to offer her a little comfort.

He had to admit, he had been impressed by her conduct so far. She'd been flirtatious and amusing and absolutely lovely. Despite her concerns about being recognized, she had still looked those she met in the eye and acted as if she belonged there as much as any other mistress who had come to the show that night.

And, as he had predicted, not one person had shown any signs of suspicion of Victoria's true identity. They all saw exactly what they were being misled to see. He would wager if he brought her back to the opera in her normal garb a month later, the very same people she had been presented to tonight wouldn't even blink when she was introduced as Lady Baybary.

Perception was so rarely about reality.

After his box darkened, Justin had thought he would be plagued by erotic thoughts. And he had been, for it was impossible not to be when Victoria was close to him.

However, for the first time, he had been more distracted by watching her than by a driving need to touch her. She leaned forward, engrossed in every note, tracking every move of the actors. His mind kept turning to her confession in the carriage about her lack of experience in the world.

Watching her take so much pleasure in the opera

made him want to show her more of London and the Continent. He wanted to take her to Vauxhall Gardens and the British Museum. He wanted to watch her lips part in shocked pleasure when she saw Paris or Rome.

But as she said, once she found her friend, she would leave, perhaps never to return. And even though that was exactly what Justin had been saying he wanted, he felt no pleasure in the reality.

Victoria's fingers tightened again, shaking him from his thoughts. He glanced down to find her staring across the crowded hallway. He followed her gaze to find Darius Evenwise standing a few feet away, watching Justin's wife with more than a little interest gleaming in his stare.

Justin wanted to cross the room and grab the bastard by the neck. It took everything in him not to do just that.

"I must speak to him," Victoria whispered.

He stiffened. His instinctive reaction was to drag her as far away from the man as possible, but remembering where they were, he murmured, "No."

She turned toward him with a false, flirtatious smile that hit him directly in the gut.

"Justin, it is the only way. You know that. You will be no more than ten feet away, and you can watch me the entire time." She pressed her fingers against his arm with firm pressure. "Please."

Justin frowned. She was correct, of course. After

the harsh words he had exchanged with Evenwise the night he claimed Victoria as his mistress, there was no way the man wouldn't be guarded around him and his friends. But his interest in Victoria could provide a gateway for information.

He clenched his fists. "Very well. But don't approach him. When I step away to fetch us a drink, he will come to you."

She glanced up at him with a surprised expression. "How do you know?"

Justin stared at her for a moment, drinking in the bright beauty of her eyes, brought out more fully by the pale green gown that clung to her frame. Her dark hair curled around her face in tempting tendrils, framing her luscious skin to perfection. Not to mention the way her breasts were lifted high on display in her gown's plunging neckline.

"He would be a fool not to come to you," he murmured before he lifted her hand to his lips and brushed his mouth across her knuckles. "Any man would be a fool if he could resist you."

Her mouth parted, but he didn't allow her to respond. He simply backed away.

It was going to be a very long intermission, indeed.

* * *

Victoria stared at Justin as he moved away from her. His compliment warmed her from head to toe, and for the first time since they departed his plush carriage, her nervousness was a faint memory.

"Good evening, Ria."

She stiffened at the deep baritone that said her name at her elbow. She turned to find Justin's prediction was correct. Darius Evenwise stood at her side, smiling down at her with a predatory interest that pushed away any warmth her husband's presence had provided.

Somehow she managed to smile as she held out her hand. "Good evening, Mr. Evenwise. How good it is to see you again."

With a feral smile, he brushed a kiss across her glove. She fought the urge to shiver as she drew her hand away.

"As it is to see you, dear lady," Evenwise replied. His smile fell a fraction. "I have not seen you since the evening we walked together. I must admit, I was a bit disappointed to learn that all the while you were encouraging my advances, you had already accepted the protection of Lord Baybary."

Victoria swallowed hard. "I should apologize for my actions. I wasn't certain of Baybary's intentions. It was not my plan to mislead you."

"And yet often our best plans go awry."

Evenwise sipped the drink in his hand. Victoria studied his striking face, but couldn't determine if he was enraged, embarrassed, or simply indifferent.

"I'm certain your disappointment faded quickly enough," she ventured. "A gentleman of your appearance and status must not have trouble finding feminine companionship."

She held her breath as his gaze slowly came down and focused on her. He searched her face. Looking for . . . *something,* though he cloaked his intentions yet again.

Victoria wanted to turn away, but remained steady. Any tip of her hand could be as dangerous to herself as it might be to Chloe.

"Only two women have ever dared refuse me," he conceded finally. "You were one."

"And what other lady was foolish enough to deny you?" she whispered, voice cracking just a fraction.

Evenwise tilted his head and leaned closer. She felt his breath stroke over her skin, felt the implied strength in his superior size. Though he looked deceptively gentlemanly, he was certainly not weak. He could hurt her if he wanted to.

"Actually, it is ironic you ask that. I believe you know the lady."

Victoria's lips parted, and she couldn't hold back her gasp. He couldn't mean, he couldn't know her relationship to—

"Her name is Chloe Hillsborough," Evenwise said with a smug smile.

From his intent study of her face, Victoria knew

the man was testing her. Toying with her. Perhaps even using her reaction for an investigation of his own. But try as she might, she couldn't keep the blood from draining from her face, her hands from trembling.

"Who—who told you I knew Chloe?"

He smiled. "Don't you? I heard you were looking for her."

How did he know that? Outside the small circle of people who knew her true identity, she had told only Alyssa and Wittingham that she had a friendship with Chloe.

"I—I—"

She stopped. If she wanted to help her friend, she couldn't fall apart in the face of this unexpected turn of events.

"She was a passing acquaintance from many years ago, Mr. Evenwise," she said, pleased that her voice had finally regained some calm.

"Hmmm," he practically purred. "Well, if you do stumble upon her, I hope you will let me know. And now I see your protector approaching. We wouldn't want Baybary to become jealous again, would we?" He backed away. "Good evening, my dear."

"Good evening," Victoria repeated.

When Evenwise disappeared into the crowd, she drew a shuddering breath, almost at the exact moment Justin reached her side.

"You are pale. Did he threaten you?" he asked as he grasped her elbow and put a steadying hand around her waist.

She leaned against him, wishing she could turn and melt into his embrace. Sob into his neck. But this was not the time, or the place, to collapse.

"I don't know if that man took Chloe," she whispered. "But if he did, she is probably dead." She darted her gaze up over her shoulder to look at Justin, and he winced at the fear she couldn't keep from her stare.

"And I think he may want . . . he may want *me* next."

A haze of protective fury slammed over Justin, blocking out everything but its angry fist. The idea that Evenwise would threaten his wife—*his wife*—nearly broke his already severely tested self-control. It was only the terror in Victoria's eyes, the fear she was trying desperately to mask, that kept him from doing just that.

She needed him right now.

"I won't let him hurt you," he whispered close to her ear. "I wouldn't let anyone hurt you."

She turned to face him, looking up at him with tears shimmering in her eyes.

"Justin—" she began.

Then her eyes widened even further as something over his shoulder caught her attention. "Oh dear God, Justin. My—my father! It's my father, and he's coming toward us."

Justin froze as her words sank beneath his skin and tore away everything else. He darted his gaze down to her face. She looked just as horrified as he felt, as if she was shocked by her father's sudden appearance.

"Is he looking at you?" Justin hissed. She didn't answer, but continued to stare, her lips rapidly turning pale. He grasped her arms and whispered, "Victoria!"

She blinked. "N-no. He's looking at your back. I think you're blocking me with your shoulder."

"I'm going to turn around. And you slip away to my opera box if you can. I will meet you there when I'm through with him."

"But—" she began.

"Do it," he ordered. "I cannot allow him to have one more secret to hang over me."

Her eyes widened, and he winced. There was one confession he hadn't wanted to escape his lips. But she didn't question him, merely turned away and slipped through the crowd to leave him to deal with her father. Somehow that fact gave him a modicum of peace. If she wasn't present, she would have no chance to manipulate the encounter. Which perhaps meant she had no desire to do so.

He found himself hoping that was true.

"There you are, Baybary," Martin Reed grunted as his greeting.

Justin stared at the man whom he had hated for so long. Time had not been kind to him. He had grown fatter, his face reddened by excessive drink over three years. His hair, which had been thinning when they last spoke in the corridor outside Justin's bedchamber on his wedding night, was nearly gone. Except for his green eyes, which were dull and shiny, Justin saw nothing of Victoria in her father.

For which he was glad.

"What the hell are you doing here?" Justin asked, trying to sound bored rather than far too interested in his father-in-law's sudden appearance.

"Where is my daughter?" Reed asked, his voice slightly slurred and far too loud.

Justin grasped his arm and yanked the drunken man into a corner before he shouted his business to the entire room and inadvertently revealed Victoria's true identity.

"Shut your mouth, old man," Justin growled.

Reed's eyes lit up with a cruel glint. "You *should* wish for me to shut my mouth, boy. If I open it too far—"

Justin cut him off by grasping his throat and thrusting him back against the wall. He glanced around, but most of the patrons had already returned to their seats. The ones who did continue to mill about were shielded from view of his actions by a large plant.

"If you aren't careful, you won't have a mouth to shut," he said, leaning in so he could speak softly. "You do not want to trifle with me, not tonight of all nights. What are you doing in London?"

He released the pressure on Reed's throat to allow his answer. The other man wheezed as he filled his lungs with air and glared at Justin.

"I heard my daughter came to Town," he explained as he rubbed his red throat. "I also heard you have a new whore you're keeping in one of your homes. Beneath her very nose, Baybary, really."

Justin shook his head in disgust. "Spare me your concerned tones, Reed. I know for a fact you haven't spoken to Victoria in person since a few months after our marriage. That was the first and last time you ever visited her, so don't pretend to me that you care about her well-being."

Reed smirked. "That may be true. But I want to see her, nonetheless. Where is she?"

Justin shut his eyes with a shuddering sigh. Damn this man. Hatred boiled inside him at the mere sight of Martin Reed, but there would be no avoiding him. No ignoring him. He was like a bulldog. He wouldn't let go of the idea of seeing Victoria until the deed was done. And if Justin didn't allow him that request, Reed would only show up to harangue Justin until he did.

Which could put Victoria in great danger, both to her reputation and possibly to her life if her thoughts about Evenwise were true.

"Your daughter is at my home," Justin growled. "Probably in her bed, which is where you should be, you drunken sot."

His father-in-law folded his arms. "I want to see her. Victoria and I have business."

Justin stared, his mouth suddenly dry. "Business? What kind of business?"

Reed smiled, thin and brittle. "The kind you do not want to interfere with, if you know what is good for you."

Justin's jaw clenched. He couldn't tell if Reed was just tormenting him or if his implications about Victoria were true. Could it be possible that she had intended to meet with Reed, perhaps not tonight, but some other night, in secret?

"Well, you aren't seeing her now," he finally snapped. "Call tomorrow afternoon. If she wishes to endure your presence, I won't stop her."

Reed stepped away. "Very good."

Justin pushed the other man aside and stalked toward his opera box. Before he could reach it, though, Reed's voice stopped him.

"And you might want to think of taking a more respectful tone, Lord Baybary. After all, I wouldn't want anything to happen that would humiliate you . . . or your family."

Justin stopped, fists clenched at his sides, and stared at the wall in front of him with unseeing eyes. This man's manipulations had forced Justin into marriage, pained him with a bitter truth he wished he'd never known, and kept him paying a monthly stipend that tasted sour every time he saw the withdrawal in his ledgers.

It was a deal with the devil he had made. One that was inescapable.

He tossed a glare at Reed over his shoulder.

"Don't press your luck. Go home and sleep off your drunk. Victoria wouldn't want to see you like this."

He entered the box to find Victoria ignoring the opera below them. She was pacing the small space, and her face dropped when he stormed inside.

"What did he want?" she whispered, voice breaking.

Justin looked at her, just barely keeping his emotions in check. "Did you tell him you were here?"

She drew back at his fierce expression. "Of course not. Our correspondence is quite rare. I certainly don't inform him of my plans. We haven't gotten along since—" She stopped, and pain filled her gaze. "For a long time. Why?"

Justin searched her face for a lie, but found none. "Somehow he knows of your presence here. And he wants to see you."

She sucked in a breath. "Does he know of my masquerade?"

"He doesn't appear to." Justin ran a hand through his hair. "Damn it. He is coming to my home tomorrow to see you."

Her throat worked as she swallowed hard. "Why there?"

He tilted his head. "Would you prefer I have him meet you in the house I granted to my 'mistress'? He believes you have come to Town and are staying with me. That would make sense since you *are* my wife."

Victoria covered her pink cheeks with her gloved fingers and found her way to one of the seats in his box. Sinking down, she nodded.

"Yes, of course."

Justin sighed. "Tomorrow I will have a carriage bring you to my home. And we will play yet another game for your father."

"Games," she repeated, her dull voice shaking. "It seems all we play are games."

Justin nodded as he threw himself into a seat beside her to wait out the remainder of the opera. "Yes, my dear. Just as we always have."

Chapter 17

Lesson 17: No amount of money or security is worth your pride.

Victoria stared around the foyer of Justin's home, taking in every inch. His London estate was nothing like she had pictured. For so long she'd imagined the life he led in Town, and Chloe's letters before her disappearance had only increased Victoria's image of his libertine ways.

But this house was stylish, classic. Exactly the kind of place she had once dreamed of living in so many years ago. There was nothing garish or overt about anything she saw.

"His Lordship is in his office, Lady Baybary," the butler said as he took her wrap.

Victoria couldn't help but notice the way the kindly looking man kept stealing side glances at her. She ignored the urge to smooth her hands over her gown or check herself in the mirror beside the door. It wasn't her appearance that caused his curiosity, of that she was certain. Today she wasn't dressed like Justin's mistress, with her daring gowns and outrageous hairstyles. And she wasn't garbed like a starchy maiden aunt, either.

For the first time in weeks, she was simply herself in one of the few pretty day gowns she'd brought from home. Yet somehow she still felt out of place.

Perhaps because even though she was wearing her own clothing, the role she was playing was not one she was comfortable in.

Justin's wife.

From the corner of her eye, she caught the stare of a parlor maid who had paused, hand hovering over a banister in mid-shine. When she saw Victoria looking at her, she scurried away with a blush. Heat filled Victoria's cheeks with the knowledge that Justin's servants had such curiosity about the wife they had never met.

She shook off her feelings. She had a role to play and she would play it, by God.

"Thank you very much, er . . ."

She hesitated with a pointed glance that the servant seemed to understand without explanation.

"I apologize, my lady. I am Crenshaw. My wife is the housekeeper, Mrs. Crenshaw. If you would like, I'm happy to arrange for the servants to be presented to you." The butler tilted his head as he awaited her answer.

Victoria stiffened. So the staff wasn't aware that her visit would be a brief one. "Er, no, I don't think that will be required this afternoon, Crenshaw. Thank you for the offer, though."

He wrinkled his brow, but bowed at her answer and led her down the hallway to a closed door. All along the way, Victoria could have sworn she saw flashes of other people. Another maid who dove into a vacant parlor. A footman who stepped around a corner. Her blush darkened. The entire household was apparently mesmerized by her sudden appearance.

Crenshaw opened the door before them with a sweeping motion and announced, "Your wife, my lord."

From around the butler, Victoria saw her husband. Justin was sitting at a large oak desk, scribbling away in a ledger. For a moment, he didn't look up, merely finished what he was doing. He looked nothing like the master seducer who had been whittling away at her resolve for so many weeks. Today Justin looked like the lord of the manor.

Signing the papers in front of him with a flourish, Justin got to his feet.

"Thank you, Crenshaw. Would you be so kind

as to have Mrs. Crenshaw bring us tea in the Blue Room in a quarter of an hour? And we are expecting Lady Baybary's father, Mr. Reed, at around that time. He can be shown in immediately."

If Crenshaw was put off by Justin's short tone, his blank expression, or his flurry of orders, he made no indication, merely nodded his head before he exited the room. The moment the door shut behind him, Victoria stepped forward.

"What in the world did you tell your servants, Justin?"

He stepped around the desk with a frown. "What do you mean?"

She pursed her lips in frustration. "I mean, they all look at me like I am part of a sideshow at a country fair. I've never seen so many servants doing so much work and hiding so quickly in a hallway in my life."

The corner of Justin's lips quirked up in a smile. "Ah, well, my wife is a legend, you see. Someone my servants have heard exists, but have never seen evidence of. Having you here is like welcoming a witch or that creature rumored to live in the River Ness into the house."

Victoria glared at him for the comparison, and his smile grew wider. Blast him for being charming and attempting to distract her from her point. It was working far too well.

She folded her arms, refusing to smile along

with him. "Crenshaw wanted to know if I would like the servants presented for my review. Do they not know my visit is only to be for one afternoon?"

Justin was quiet for a long moment, staring at her face with an intensity that troubled her and set her off balance. "What do you think of my home?"

She tilted her head in surprise. Apparently he intended to ignore her question about the servants entirely.

"I . . ." She hesitated.

If she complimented his residence, would it reveal too much? Did admiring his home translate to liking him, admiring *him*?

"You . . ." he said, lifting his eyebrows in encouragement for her to finish her thought.

"From what little I have seen, it is lovely," she admitted.

"Would you like a tour?"

Again, Victoria hesitated. Did she really want to see the life she would never lead? The home she would never inhabit? The servants she would never be mistress to? If she did, wouldn't it only intensify the strange, growing ache to be more to Justin than what she was?

"Yes," she finally admitted on a whisper. "But my father—"

He offered her an arm. "Your father can wait."

Victoria stared at him before she slipped her hand into the crook of his elbow.

Leading her from the room, Justin took her from chamber to chamber, showing her a beautiful music room with a pianoforte in the center facing a green garden outside. She wondered at the beautiful parlors, each painted a different color and each more lovely than the next. She saw his formal dining room, as well as a cozy breakfast nook where she couldn't help but imagine taking her morning tea every day.

As they moved upstairs, her heart caught in her throat. With each room, she knew what was coming next. And when he hesitated at a final chamber, she realized the moment she had been anticipating had come.

"And this is my chamber," he said, slowly pushing the door open as he released her arm and motioned for her to go inside.

Victoria stared at the threshold. If she went in, she feared she wouldn't come out the same. Seeing Justin's bedroom, the one he would never share with her, felt like an altering experience. Fearful and frightening.

But it was also alluring, seductive, and her curiosity won out over prudence. She stepped inside and looked around.

Again, she was struck by how different the room was from the decadent darkness she had pictured. The curtains were drawn aside, bathing the chamber in a golden glow of afternoon sunlight. A wide expanse of it cascaded over the bed, and her eyes were naturally drawn there.

It was a large bed, big enough to fit three or four grown people, the idea of which had heat rushing to her cheeks even as she walked toward it as if she could no longer control her steps.

With a trembling hand, she touched the snowy white coverlet and found it soft and inviting. She could only imagine how alluring her husband would look, his tanned skin against the stark white. His muscled body drawing her . . . or some other woman . . . or a dozen other women . . . to join him in the sheets.

"Victoria?" he asked, his voice rough behind her.

She turned to face him and looked him up and down. "How many women have you shared this bed with?"

He started at the question, and his gaze moved to where she still clenched the counterpane in tight fingers.

"None," he finally said softly.

Victoria blinked at the obvious falsehood. "How foolish do you think me, Justin? Even if I hadn't heard firsthand accounts from Chloe about your activities before you left for the Continent, I never believed you to be a saint. Do you truly expect me to trust you haven't had a woman in this bed with you? Or ten? Or a hundred? I thought we were beyond petty little lies like that."

Justin stepped forward. "Chloe told you about me?"

Her blush darkened, and she turned her face so he wouldn't see any remnants of the foolish pain those reports had once brought. "Yes."

"Had I known, I would have—" He stopped and turned her face back to his. "Our marriage was never a true one, Victoria, but I would have been more discreet had I known you were receiving reports about my life."

She wrinkled her brow even as little twinges of heat pulsed within her when he stroked the back of his hand against her cheek. "Why?"

He hesitated. "Because I wouldn't have ever wanted to hurt you. And no matter what our relationship, I'm certain firsthand reports of your husband's . . ."

She met his gaze evenly. "Infidelities?"

He flinched. "Yes. It could not have been easy to bear." He shook his head. "The way I have treated you, I am not proud of it."

She drew in a harsh breath as she watched him with wide eyes. Never would she have imagined that he would admit shame for his ways, that he would *apologize* for hurting her.

But then, nothing about Justin was the flat

picture she had kept of him in her mind. He wasn't a sensual, yet callous devil. He was a man. Flawed, but no more than herself. After all, hadn't *she* lied? Kept painful secrets from him? And when she arrived and realized he was in London, she had taken actions with little regard to his feelings.

In fact, sometimes she had behaved in a way designed to hurt or anger him.

Judging from his admission the day before that her father did, indeed, have something to hold over his head, perhaps his behavior came from something deeper than she had ever granted him. Certainly since her arrival, she had grown to know him all the better. She'd come to respect his loyalty to his friends. To anticipate his playful wit and sharp intelligence. And to crave the touch that made her weak.

She'd begun to *like* him a great deal, despite her best intentions to keep a distance.

"As for this bed," he said, moving even closer. "I have never brought a woman here. And that is the truth."

"Wh-why?" she whispered.

He drew in the sharp breath now. "That bed was meant to be shared with my wife," he explained, voice rough. "It didn't seem right."

Her lips parted at the admission, but before she could formulate a reply, he leaned down and pressed his mouth to hers. The kiss was infinitely gentle, far different from any other they had shared. Slow and steady, he coaxed pleasure from her with just the slightest movements, the barest touch. She found herself melting against him, clinging to him as the world faded away and all that was left was him.

"I want you in that bed, Victoria," he whispered as he drew back and buried his lips against her neck. "You belong there."

She pulled back to cup his rough cheeks and stare at him. She searched his gaze and was shocked by what she found there in the dark brown depths.

For once, he wasn't playing a game with her. If she went to that bed with him, he would be claiming her as his wife in a way far different from any time they had made love before. For once, she would be a wife in more than name alone.

She would be *his*.

They stared at each other, their breath merging in pants. But a light knock on the chamber door interrupted them.

"My lord?" came Crenshaw's precise tones in the hallway. "Are you in your chamber?"

Justin shut his eyes with a quiet curse. "Yes, Crenshaw, what is it?"

There must have been something in Justin's tone, for the butler did not open the door. "Lady

Baybary's father has arrived and is awaiting you in the Blue Room."

"Thank you," Justin called as he released Victoria and drew back from her. She felt cold with the loss of his touch. "We should go to him."

She nodded. "Yes, he doesn't like to be kept waiting."

Turning away, Victoria felt the heat of a blush burn her cheeks. Something had happened between them, and now she wasn't certain how to behave. She was confused, trapped in by emotions she hadn't expected. A moment to compose herself would do her good.

"Justin, perhaps I should speak to him first alone. I haven't seen him since—"

She cut herself off, not sure how to explain how long it had been or why. Still not daring to break down one of the remaining walls between them.

He stared at her. "You want to see him alone?"

She started at the sharpness of his tone. "Yes. At least for a few moments."

He nodded slowly. "Of course. By all means, go to him."

Victoria stared at Justin, warned by his tone, but his face was utterly bland. Still, her body and soul were off-kilter from their encounter, too dizzy to fully analyze why his lips were pursed and his posture was suddenly angry.

Finally, she stepped toward the door and left him to join her father.

Justin paced his chamber, waging a war within himself. He didn't know why he'd brought Victoria up to his rooms, or why he had admitted no other woman had ever joined him in his bed. Mostly, he was shocked that he had admitted he wanted *her* to share that bed with him.

It wasn't that those things weren't true, they all were, it was more that he still wasn't certain he could trust her, and telling her had opened him up to a world of potential pain.

When she had told him she wanted to see her father alone, it had been a harsh reminder of that fact. For all he knew, the two of them were hatching some plot against him or planning to reveal her father's secret in a way that would do the most damage.

Justin stopped pacing and thought of his wife. It was far too easy to conjure an image of her lovely face. He could picture every detail about her lips, her hair, her sultry body.

But for the first time, he *couldn't* picture Victoria engaging in a deception meant to hurt him.

Since her arrival in London, she had proven herself to be brave, kind, decent—everything opposite of Martin Reed. Hell, she had chased after her missing friend, putting herself in danger just to find a woman who could very well be dead. That alone spoke of a loyalty Justin doubted her father could understand if it was explained to him for a lifetime.

Yet his questions lingered. His doubts niggled. Even though he was starting to wish that he could leave those feelings behind and simply put his trust in his wife.

He stared at the door where Victoria had left a few moments before. By now she was with her father. If Justin wanted to know the truth, all he had to do was go the room adjacent to the Blue Room and listen at the fireplace. As a boy, he had learned the tricks of this house. One of which was that voices carried clearly from one room to the next.

It was a petty act, but if Victoria was telling the truth, he would know it for once and for all. And if she was part of her father's schemes, then Justin could stop wasting his time wishing for . . . whatever it was he wished for when he looked into her eyes.

Either way, he could judge her character by her actions, not just what he believed her to be, hoped her to be, longed for her to be.

So with guilt pushing at him, Justin made his way downstairs and took his place to listen.

Chapter 18

Lesson 18: Lies and secrets have a way of coming out, so be prepared.

Victoria watched as her father guzzled tea and shoved a finger sandwich into his mouth. Sadness and anger gripped her in equal measure. Sadness to see how much further into madness and ruin her father had spiraled since they'd last met. He was even more of a stranger to her now.

But her anger was deeper. Her father had done things, said things, while in the depths of his drunken hazes that could never be undone. Seeing him was a painful reminder of all that. And it made her think of Justin's comment that her father had some kind of secret he had held over her husband's head for years.

"Why did you come here, Papa?" she asked softly.

"Does a father have to explain his desire to see his daughter?" he grunted without even sparing her a glance.

Victoria shook her head at the lie. "Considering that you never even took my hand when I entered the room, you were so busy eating my food, I somehow doubt you came here for a family reunion. You and I have not shared a closeness since Mama died."

Her father's head came up at the mention of his wife, and his face twisted in brief pain. She almost wished she could take back the reminder of his beloved wife. Her mother had been the lone thread that once bound them together.

"Very well," he said with a frown. "If you do not want polite platitudes, I *did* come with a purpose. I want your husband to increase my monthly payment, but he refuses to hear me regarding that matter. I came to Baybary to ask for your assistance, but found that you weren't there. They told me you had come to London."

Victoria's lips parted in surprise.

"Monthly payment?" she repeated, her heart sinking.

He stopped eating to stare at her, but his gaze never fully focused. It was then she realized he was drunk. Sadly, that was no longer a surprise to her. It had become his constant state years before.

However, his inebriation did not mean he was lying.

"You didn't know?" He chuckled. "Lord Baybary has been paying me to keep my mouth shut since you married. In fact, wedding you was part of our arrangement. I ensured you a very comfortable life with my bargaining, you should thank me."

Victoria's lips pursed. So finally her suspicions were fully proven. From the beginning, she'd guessed her father had brokered some kind of shady deal with Justin. Their heated words in the hallway on her wedding night had been her first indication, but there had been plenty of evidence over the years to verify her belief, even before Justin all but confirmed it the night before.

"You are despicable," she said softly. "To hang a secret over a man's head, force him to marry your kin when it was not his choice, threaten him for money. Great God, Papa, I hardly know you."

Her father wheeled on her, and she fought the urge to recoil. He'd only struck her a few times before her marriage, but she remembered the shock of every blow all too well.

"I wouldn't do that," she said, fighting to maintain calm. "If you leave a mark, I'll wager Justin won't like it."

Her father stopped advancing on her. "How would he know?" he sneered. "He only touched you that one night, didn't he?"

She folded her arms. "I'm here now, aren't I?"

Her father's eyes lit up with greed. "Yes, I suppose you are. Good girl, I knew I could depend upon you. You give that man an heir and he'll never be able to escape you. Even if he despises you in the future, he'll continue to provide a healthy income for his sons. One you can easily share with me. I recommend you get yourself with child again as soon as you can."

The blood began to drain from Victoria's face. "Papa!" she breathed as pain gripped her heart.

He shrugged. "We might as well speak plain. It's been three years since the other babe. And you handled that situation poorly. The money you could have gotten—"

"Stop it!" Victoria cried as she clenched her fists at her sides. "You have no right to speak to me about that subject! No right."

"And what about me?"

Victoria bit back a sob before she slowly turned to find Justin standing in the parlor doorway. His eyes were wild, his face pale, and he was staring at her with so much pain and betrayal that it took all of Victoria's strength not to run away from the raw emotion he had never revealed to her before.

"Do *I* have a right to speak to you about our child?" Justin asked, his tone cold and broken.

"Now Baybary—" her father began, stepping forward.

Justin turned on him with such quickness and anger that it made both Victoria and her father jump.

"I swear to the heavens, old man, if you do not get out of my house this instant, I will break every bone in your body and not be sorry for it, no matter whose father you are."

"Baybary—" her father said, but his eyes bulged. He reached into his pocket with trembling fingers and withdrew a few yellow letters. Holding them out, he said, "Don't forget what I know."

Justin's eyes had gone frighteningly fierce as he stared at the worn pages clutched in her father's fat fingers. Victoria leaned forward, but from the distance, she could not make out any words, only the even, crisp handwriting of a woman.

"You bastard," Justin said, deceptively low. "You brought those here? To my home?"

Her father shook the pages at him. "I wanted to remind you, to—"

Before he could finish, Justin lunged for him. He snatched the sheets away from her father's shaky hands, rending a few brittle pieces away to flutter to the floor.

"Your greed has been your undoing," he snapped as he strode to the fire and tossed the letters on the low flames. "You will *never* force me to do your will again."

The pages did not immediately burn, but slipped against the uneven wood. Her father ran forward with a harsh cry of "No!"

Justin didn't move as he watched her father get down on his hands and knees. At first he tried to pull the letters out by hand, but all he got for his troubles were burns. Then he grasped the fireplace poker and instead used it to drag away the sheets that had not been entirely devoured. They smoked on the fine Oriental carpet, their edges blackened, but some of their words intact.

"Papa!" Victoria gasped. "Stop this!"

Neither Justin nor her father seemed to even recognize she was in the room anymore. Her husband caught her father by the collar, lifting him away from the smoldering papers with enough force that the poker that still remained in his hand went flying across the room. It hit a mirror that was mounted above the poor boy and shattered glass along the wooden surface and the floor below.

"Get out!" Justin roared.

Victoria covered her mouth, helpless to do anything but watch. She had never seen Justin like this. Wild, out of control, completely emotional. He had reached some kind of breaking point.

One she had caused. Her family had caused.

He hauled her father to the door and shoved him into the hallway. "This is *over,* old man."

Her father had never had much sense, but even he could see that Justin had no ability to stop himself. And if he pushed, it could lead to far worse than a few shoves. Staggering, her father rushed from the house.

Victoria almost expected Justin to chase him, but instead he slammed the door and turned back. To her. His normally calm face was dark with emotions so raw that she had an urge to run away from them. But she couldn't. She was responsible, and now it was time to finally face what she had created.

Slowly, he moved on her. Step by step, as if he was taking all his control to meter his movements.

"You tell me, Victoria. Tell me the truth," he said, his voice quavering. There were no shouts for her, no rage like what he had given her father.

She would have almost preferred that outward anger to this. She drew in harsh breaths, fighting to keep the hot tears that burned her eyes from falling.

"Justin—" she whispered.

"Did you bear me a child? Do I have a son or

daughter who I do not know?" he roared, finally grasping her arms and hauling her against him. But still, there was no violence in his touch, just desperation.

She hated herself as tears began to flow down her cheeks freely. The last thing she wanted was for him to think she was attempting to manipulate him with her emotions.

"N-no, Justin," she stammered, choking on pain. "You have no child."

He let her go and staggered back, raking a hand through his hair. "Your father told you to get with child *again*, Victoria. He spoke of another baby. Was that child not mine, then?"

She flinched. "I told you there was never any other lover but you."

He tilted his head and laughed, but the sound was anything but pleasant. It was harsh and unforgiving in the silent room. "You have told me so many things, Victoria. You have lied so many times."

"I'm not lying!" she sobbed before she gathered her emotions.

This was a secret she had kept for three long years. And Justin deserved to know the truth. It was the only thing she could give him now, no matter how much it broke her heart to recount the worst experience she had ever endured.

"You and I shared one . . ." She hesitated. "It was

one wonderful night, at least for me. When you left, it shattered any dreams I had of finding new happiness. At first, I was so very unhappy. I didn't know how to run a household, all I could think about was how undesirable I must have been for you to practically sprint from our marriage bed and back to London and your lovers there."

"So you hid a child from me as punishment?" he hissed.

"No!" She sank into the deep cushions of the settee and picked absently at a loose thread on the seam. "After a month, I realized I had not had my monthly courses. I explained it away. But by the second month, when I began exhibiting other signs of breeding, I knew I couldn't pretend away the truth. I wanted to tell you, but how could I?"

He paced away from her with a sound of disgust. "You could have sent me a message. 'Justin, I am bearing your child.' Easy enough."

She shook her head. "It wasn't easy at all. You didn't want me. You had made that perfectly clear by walking out of my life without so much as a backward glance. So I had no idea how you would react to such news. I did write you over a dozen letters and burned them all. Weeks went by, and I tormented myself on how to tell you. And on how I would survive if you told me you didn't want me or the child we had created."

She shut her eyes and let the guilt wash over her. She deserved it. Her inability to tell Justin the truth had always been her greatest shame.

"Before I could tell you anything, something happened." She swallowed, forcing harsh, horrible memories away. She had to tell the story. She couldn't be stopped by the heartbreak that was welling within her. "I—I woke up bleeding and in terrible pain. A few servants had suspected my condition, and they called upon a local midwife to come to me. It was Marah's grandmother, and Marah came with her to attend me. That was how we met. But there was nothing that could be done. I lost the baby."

Justin made a little sound from the position he had taken, facing away from her at the window. It was a low, painful groan that touched a place deep inside her. God knew, she understood his pain.

"Why didn't you tell me then?" he asked. She had never heard that tone to his voice before. So . . . broken. "Why didn't you write me?"

She shook her head. "Unlike my father, I never wanted to ensnare you, Justin. Losing that child was the worst pain in my life. I didn't even fathom how much I wanted the baby until it was gone. I sank into a sadness so deep that I could hardly rise from my bed, let alone write a letter. It was so bad that Marah wrote to my father."

Justin turned to her. "*That* was the last time he visited you in Baybary."

She nodded. "He was horrible. He wanted me to use the child I'd lost to tempt you back. He talked to me about heirs and money just as he did today. And from my sadness came a great anger. I told him to go away and never come back." She shook her head. "I broke my final bond with my family, and I was all alone. But somehow that gave me strength. I began to work on issues of the estate. I made friends in the shire. I started to live again, without wishing for you. Without crying every day for the life I had lost, both the one that had grown inside me and the one I dreamed of as a girl."

"But you still never told me," he murmured.

She shook her head. There was no denying that fact. She could only hope he would come to understand her reasons once the shock wore off.

"I didn't know how. And the more time passed, the harder it became. Ultimately, I decided there was no good way to say what had happened without the words seeming trite or manipulative." She frowned. "So I never told you."

"I should have known."

"Yes, you should have." She held his accusing stare evenly. "Just as I should have known you were blackmailed into our marriage, forced into consummating our union."

His mouth twisted and his voice was ugly when he sneered, "Didn't you know? Are you saying your father didn't make you party to his disgusting machinations?"

She recoiled, his contempt like a slap. "Obviously you were listening to our conversation, did you not hear that part of our exchange?"

"Yes, I heard." Justin turned away and paced the room like a restless animal. "But now that I know what you kept from me, I wonder if I can trust *anything* you say. Or ever know everything you withhold."

Victoria flinched, but she did not retort. She deserved what he said. But she also deserved more.

"You should have been told the truth, but so should I. Let us end *all* the lies today, Justin. Tell me what my father knows. What was in those letters, since it clearly had to do with his blackmail?" She motioned to the still smoldering remains of the papers her father had foolishly brought today. "Perhaps I can help."

"Help me or help yourself?" Justin snapped.

"Help you!" she cried, stepping toward him.

She reached for him, but he stepped out of her way. Her hand shook as she lowered it to her side. That was the first time Justin had ever resisted her touch.

"This secret, it is obviously one that causes

you deep pain," she said softly. "One that was powerful enough to threaten you. I want no part in benefiting from that. But perhaps if I know, I can—"

He shook his head. "You can what? What can you do? What could you *possibly* do if I told you that my mother turned to at least one other man in the course of her marriage? Or that her indiscretion led to the birth of my brother? Would it *help* you if you heard that neither my father nor Caleb know the truth? Or that I have carried this secret like a weight in my soul since the moment your father laid it at my feet and told me he would destroy my world if I didn't marry you?"

The confession rang in the air around them like a gunshot. All Victoria could do was stare at Justin as the power of his words sank beneath her skin into her heart, her soul. In the years she'd tried to fathom what had led Justin to her, she had never imagined this. When she pictured blackmail, it was about something Justin had done. A lie he had told or a friend he had betrayed.

She'd never once imagined that he had lived this bitter lie in order to protect those he loved. That it was his honor that kept him bound, not his sins.

"And the proof was in those letters?" she whispered.

He looked at the few pages that had survived

his encounter with her father. "Yes. At one point your mother and mine were friends, long before the breach between our families. They were close enough that my mother confessed to yours about her affair and her fears about Caleb's parentage. Apparently your father found those letters after your mother's death."

Victoria shut her eyes with a pained, shuddering sigh. God, her father's madness, his break with the man she had known as a child, it really had been made complete by her mother's death.

And it made her sick.

"Justin," she whispered as she stepped forward, praying she would find some words to say, something to do to make him believe that she had no part in her father's schemes. That she was sorry for her own deceptions. "I—"

He stared down at her, eyes devoid of all the feeling they normally held. Once again, she was staring at a distant stranger, just as she had on their wedding night.

Only now she knew the man he was. In the past few weeks, she had grown to care for him in ways that were foolish and dangerous. So seeing him look at her as if he didn't know her, feeling as if she didn't know him, cut her as deeply as any pain she had ever endured.

She halted her forward movement. He didn't

want anything to do with her. Too much damage had been done.

"I am glad you told me," she finally said softly. "Perhaps the letters my father brought here today were the only evidence in his possession. But if they are not, I will do everything in my power to stop him from continuing this. I know you do not trust my promises at present, but I make this one to you, regardless."

Justin grunted out a sound of disbelief and moved to the fire to watch the flames. Victoria stared at his rigid back. Whatever fragile bond they had built, it had been broken in a span of mere minutes. The weight of too many lies, too many secrets, had been too much to bear. And now they were back where they started.

Distant.

Her entire body ached as if she had been in a fight, her heart felt swollen and crushed. All she wanted to do was run. She could no longer take being in the same room with Justin, knowing that he despised her for both what her father had done and for her own betrayals.

"I'm sorry, Justin," she whispered before she turned from the room. "I know that isn't enough. But it's all that I have."

For a long time after Victoria left and he heard her say good-bye to Crenshaw in the hallway,

Justin stood staring with unseeing eyes at the fire. Pages of his mother's letters were still strewn about the floor, their burned edges reminding him of his own life. The world he had so carefully built around himself was crashing down in ruin, and he could do nothing to stop it.

For years, he had wondered if Victoria was a liar like her father. Today she had proven it, yet it had hurt him more than he thought possible.

To know she had kept the secret of a child he would never know, had never been given the chance to mourn, that was like being shot in the back. And even though he understood her reasons in some dark place in his heart, he needed to think about what he had lost, and why he longed for it so keenly, before he spoke to her about it again.

And then he had told her the secret. The horrible thing that had hung over his head like a guillotine for so long. The words had come flowing from his lips, even though as he told her the truth, he had longed to take them back.

Yet the confession, for all its dangers, made him feel . . . better somehow. Even in the moments he accused her of colluding with her father, Justin had known that wasn't true. Everything she'd said when she wasn't aware of his presence made it perfectly clear that she had only been a victim of Reed's manipulations, not a conspirator. He knew in his very soul that Victoria would never repeat his secrets.

She would only keep her own, ones so bitter and painful that he could hardly think of them.

So he was caught between trusting her and losing faith. Caring for her in ways he'd never thought possible and wishing he had never seen her face.

"My lord?" His butler's voice came tentatively behind him from the area of the doorway.

Justin scrubbed a hand over his face. He wasn't up to facing his servants or anyone else at present. He felt too raw, raked over the coals.

"Not now, Crenshaw. I need a moment." Justin bent to gather up the evidence that still existed and finally destroy it all, but when he didn't hear his servant depart, he straightened up and stared at the man. "What is it?"

"I'm sorry, my lord. Normally I would not dream of disobeying your order, but you have a visitor—" The butler broke off to shift from foot to foot.

Justin looked around. The parlor was a wreck. Broken glass was scattered about the room, papers had flown everywhere, furniture was overturned. How would he explain those things to some unwanted caller?

Especially when he could hardly breathe, let alone think clearly.

"I am not in house," he said low. "Tell whoever it is to go away."

"Forgive me, sir," the butler said. "I, er, assumed you did not wish to see anyone and told the man as much, but he refuses to leave. He says—"

Before the servant could finish, Alexander Wittingham burst into the room, shoving the man aside without so much as a side glance.

"You bastard!"

Justin bit back a humorless laugh. This day was just getting better and better.

"Go, Crenshaw. I will deal with my *dear friend,* the viscount."

Crenshaw backed from the room with an expression of concern, and closed the door behind him.

"What?" Justin asked, in no mood to make polite conversation.

Wittingham advanced without so much as a look at the destruction around him. Justin's brow furrowed. As the viscount drew closer, he saw the other man was sweating and pale.

Wittingham caught Justin's arm and shook it. "Do you know what the hell you've done?"

Justin yanked free of the other man's grasp. His grip on control was quickly unraveling. "I've done so much lately, you'll need to be more specific."

"You have been making a search of London and the surrounding towns for Chloe Hillsborough."

Justin froze. For a moment, his own troubles faded. How did Wittingham know that?

"I—" he began.

"Don't bother to deny it, I know it is true," the other man hissed. "And thanks to your investigation, Chloe is in even more danger than before. And it has put your wife in peril as well."

Justin stared at Wittingham for a long moment before he straightened up to his full height.

"My wife?" he asked in a practiced bland tone.

Wittingham shook his head. "It took me a while to put the pieces together, but I know that the courtesan 'Ria' is really your long estranged wife, Victoria Talbot."

Justin folded his arms. "I resent that comment, Wittingham. Are you calling my wife a courtesan?"

Wittingham rolled his eyes. "We don't have time for this. I know your wife because Chloe used to speak with great warmth of her friends back in Baybary. Victoria Talbot was one of those friends. Now do you want to help me or not? At this very moment Evenwise could be making a move on Victoria or Chloe or both."

Justin's very blood froze as he thought of Evenwise's vicious reputation. Any anger he felt toward Victoria bled away as he pictured her the victim of the other man's wrath. If Wittingham was telling the truth, it wouldn't do to waste more time trying to protect Victoria's reputation. Not when her very life could be at stake.

Stepping forward, Justin said, "Tell me what the hell is going on, Wittingham. And tell me right now."

Chapter 19

Lesson 19: Do not confuse weakness with vulnerability. They are not the same.

"Chloe was my mistress," Wittingham said as he paced the room. His tone was quiet, pensive. "I was an idiot. Perhaps if I had been able to give her what she wanted, if I had been able to accept—"

"Stop rambling and tell me how this relates to Victoria!" Justin snapped.

Wittingham faced him with a twisted expression. He gave a nod. "I apologize. Let me give you a very brief explanation. Chloe loved me, but for various reasons I did not think I could offer her any more than my protection." He gave a pained wince. "So we ended our relationship."

Justin studied the other man's face. Though he

was talking about a young woman some might consider no more than a glorified lightskirt, Wittingham's emotions, his deep feelings for the woman he couldn't have, shone through. Justin found he could empathize with the pain he saw there. Since Victoria's return to his life, he'd often felt the same emotions, even though he did his best to tamp them down. Crush them.

"Chloe began to search for a new protector and caught the eye of Darius Evenwise. I believe Alyssa warned her of his proclivities, so she turned him down. He would not accept that. One night he arrived at her home. Things became"—Wittingham swallowed, rage lighting in his stare—"rough. But she managed to escape and came to me. I couldn't do anything to stop him. You know his money, his power."

Justin nodded. All peers were not created equal. His own elevated title and vast holdings gave him a wide range of influence, but Wittingham had a much less prestigious name and far more modest funds. Evenwise might not have a title, but his money and connections made him both powerful and feared.

Wittingham shook his head. "I spoke to Alyssa, and she offered to help me hide Chloe until Evenwise stopped looking for her. But he didn't. He was obsessed, driven to find her by any means possible. When 'Ria' arrived in Town,

I thought perhaps he would transfer his attentions to her."

Justin stepped forward with hands fisted at his sides. "And you were willing to sacrifice another woman?"

"For Chloe's life? Damned right. Perhaps that isn't noble, but it's true." Wittingham ran a hand through his hair. "But then Victoria started asking questions. It raised my suspicions, as I'm sure it did Evenwise's. When he began following her, I believe he realized she might be Victoria Talbot, your wife and Chloe's best friend."

Justin's eyes widened. "How many people know?"

"You can never be certain, but I think only Evenwise and myself." Wittingham shrugged. "No one else was so vested in Victoria's true identity. Even *I* didn't realize who she was until I took the chance to write to Chloe in her hiding place. She confirmed Victoria's appearance and her relationship to you. But before I could come to you and tell you that Chloe was unharmed, your damned brother and Shaw uncovered Chloe's hiding place."

Justin shook his head. "When? I've heard nothing of this."

Wittingham scowled. "It was only this morning. But it matters little, if Evenwise is aware of your search, their actions might have revealed the truth to him. And at the very least, if he knows Victoria's true identity—"

Justin was already making for the door, his heart throbbing. "Then he might use her to force a trade! Come on, you fool. Let's go."

Victoria swiped at her eyes before she took another drink of sherry from the tumbler in her hand. She stared at the fire dwindling in the twilight. The servants Justin had hired for "Ria" had offered to raise it up, warm the room, but she didn't want that. She just wanted to sit in the dark and think.

"Victoria?"

She shut her eyes. Marah wasn't going to allow her the peace she desired. She motioned her friend into the room with her free hand.

Marah came around to face her. When the dim light hit her just right, Victoria saw her friend's worried frown.

"Would you like to tell me what happened?"

Victoria flinched as her friend tossed a log on the fire. The light in the room lifted slowly as the low flames devoured the fuel. When Marah turned, she sucked in a breath.

"Oh, Victoria!"

Victoria turned her face, embarrassed that her tears had been seen. But she could no longer hold them back. They fell quietly, wetting her hands and dotting the knotted handkerchief she twisted in her trembling fingers.

"What did he do?" Marah asked, her mouth setting in a thin line as she held out a fresh handkerchief. "What did Justin do this time?"

Victoria shook her head. "No, Justin did nothing to cause this."

Marah folded her arms with a snort of disbelief. "You are not one to cry, Victoria. I have only seen you like this a few times, and each one was related to Justin Talbot."

"Truly, this is not his fault." Victoria dabbed her eyes and forced the tears to stop. She gathered her strength and whispered, "My father *did* blackmail him into the marriage, just as I always suspected."

"And I'm sure Justin gave him plenty of ammunition for such an act," her friend snapped.

Victoria dipped her chin in shame. "I thought that as well. Tonight I learned the truth. It wasn't something Justin did at all. In fact, he was trying to protect someone he loved, to be honorable."

"Honor," Marah scoffed. "That man knows nothing of honor."

Victoria stiffened. "You are so wrong. Justin could have gone back on his word so many times since we came to London. He could have found a way to get rid of me without finding Chloe. But he didn't." She sucked in a harsh breath. "And now he knows the truth about—about the baby I lost. And I fear he will never be able to forgive me for keeping that secret."

Marah stood in stunned silence for a long moment, then she wrapped her arms around Victoria and hugged her hard. All the emotions, all the pain, all the loss she had experienced that day crashed around her. Clinging to Marah, she finally allowed herself to lose control. For a long time, all she could do was cry.

"Oh, Victoria," Marah said when her tears had finally subsided. "Why did you tell him about the baby?"

Victoria pulled away in horror. "He had every right to know. That was his child. Keeping the truth from him was *never* proper."

Marah shook her head. "I assume he did not take the news well."

Victoria shut her eyes, but couldn't block out images of Justin's broken, horrified expression as he realized he had sired a child that had not survived to see its birth.

"Oh, Marah, you should have seen Justin's eyes when I confessed to him. Even when I tried to explain the position I was in, they were so filled with disbelief. So cold. If he had begun to care for me, even the slightest bit, I killed that today. I killed it, and perhaps I don't deserve it."

Marah shook her head. "Do not speak in such

a way. You deserve everything you've always dreamed of. But perhaps it is better this way. You know Justin will never give you what you need. Once we find Chloe, we can go home and you can forget about him."

"I love him," Victoria admitted, her voice dull.

There, now it had been said out loud. The thing she had been trying to deny, the emotion she had been fighting against since she first saw Justin in the ballroom, she had finally admitted it. It didn't even seem shocking to her, just a matter of life as normal as breathing.

Only breathing wasn't a foolish exercise that could only bring her pain.

Marah's words died on her lips, and she shoved to her feet. "No. Oh, Victoria, no. You cannot mean that. Don't mistake pleasure for love."

Victoria's gaze darted up to snare her disbelieving friend's. Marah seemed so very young at present. She had never felt desire or passion or love for a man that burned so hot and bright that it threatened to consume everything around it.

"I am not making that mistake. What I feel is sadly real." Victoria shook her head as she fought for a way to explain her heart. "Since my arrival in London, there has been much more than mere pleasure between us. For years, I built this image of the man my husband was. But it was wooden, hazy. I made Justin so big in my mind. In my thoughts, he was the quintessential rake, the lusty lover, the cold lord of the manor who could dismiss me like a servant. But when I came here, I realized he is so much more."

"He left you, he hurt you," Marah pointed out with a frown.

Victoria nodded. "Yes. He did. But after hearing what my father did to him, I have begun to understand why Justin rebelled against our marriage. I cannot say that I wouldn't have done the same if I had been in his place."

"You could never have been so cruel as he was," Marah objected.

Victoria paced the room, thinking back to all her encounters with Justin since they'd first met. "But he was never as cruel as he could have been. The night of our wedding, he was gentle with me when he could have vented his anger on my body as some kind of vengeance. And when I arrived here, he seduced me, but he never hurt me. In fact, he offered me protection, assistance. The more time I have spent with him, the more I have realized that Justin Talbot is far more than his reputation led me to believe."

With a sad shake of her head, Victoria whispered, "And I love him."

These feelings were what she had been trying so desperately to avoid, then to quash. Justin had never wanted her to begin with, and after hearing about her secret and knowing the lies that separated them, he probably never would.

Loving him was no gift. It was a wound that would never heal.

Marah stared at her, pity in her eyes. Even her disapproving friend knew that this emotion was no pleasure to her.

"What will you do?" Marah asked softly.

Victoria shrugged. She had been wondering that all the way home from the house where she was an absent mistress. Where her life had once seemed ordered and bearable, now it was confused. The idea of going back to Baybary and pretending that none of this had happened left her empty.

But what choice did she have?

"I feel in my heart that we are close to finding out what happened to Chloe. And Justin may be many things, but he wouldn't—" She broke off as she thought of the proud anger on his face when he admitted his family's secret. "He wouldn't abandon that search. He is too honorable a man."

Marah snorted her derision, but said nothing.

"So we will do our best to find her, and then . . ." Victoria sighed. "Then you and I will go home, hopefully with Chloe by our side. As difficult as it will be, I shall return to my duties on our estate. There are certainly more than enough of them to keep me busy. Justin will return to the life he led before I intruded upon him. And I will . . . try to forget my feelings."

The two women met gazes. Victoria could see her friend didn't believe that was possible, nor did she. Now that her heart had been opened, her life changed, she couldn't go back to the way things were, when Justin was no more than a distant fantasy. She would hold the brief time they had shared in her heart forever. And it would color her views on the world until the day she died.

The door behind them opened, and Victoria got to her feet, almost happy for the interruption that would distract her from her musings. But when she turned to face what she thought would be a servant, she staggered back in shock. There, framing the door with his big body, was Darius Evenwise.

"Mr. Evenwise," she gasped as she maneuvered herself in front of Marah without even thinking. She felt her friend grasp her skirt in fear at the mention of the gentleman's name.

"Good evening, Ria," he drawled as he stepped into the parlor and shut the door behind him. "Or should I call you Victoria?"

Victoria stepped back, bumping into Marah's frozen form as the blood drained from her face. Her friend's free hand clamped around Victoria's upper arm, and her fingers dug in to an almost painful degree.

Evenwise smiled. "But then, perhaps you prefer Lady Baybary, after all. Though I feel we know each other so well that the formality isn't appropriate."

Victoria swallowed and fought to find her composure. "I am sure I don't know what you are talking about. Although I am sharing Justin's bed, I certainly have not been elevated to the position of Lady Baybary. You must have me confused with someone else." She glanced at the door behind him. "How did you get into this room without being announced?"

Evenwise's eyebrow arched. "One of the advantages of having holdings in the shipping yards is that I always know a crew of men willing to help me for a price. For a big enough price, they don't even ask questions."

Marah bit back a gasp and retreated one staggering step, but Victoria moved forward, her hands shaking. "What have you done to my servants?"

He laughed. "Don't worry, my dear, I promise you none of them will have permanent injuries. Only the butler had to be handled so the others wouldn't be alerted. But he'll have little more than a headache when he wakes. The others are being restrained in the lower kitchen."

"Restrained?" Victoria breathed. "Why in the world would you need to restrain my staff?"

"Because I don't want to be interrupted, Victoria," he drawled.

She flinched as he used her real name a second time. "I have no idea why you insist upon calling me that."

"Let's not play games." He tilted his head and gave her a smile as if she were a child. "You have left so many clues in your wake. Anyone paying any kind of attention could make the connection you've fought so hard to deny. And, my dear, I have paid attention to you since the first moment I saw you." His gaze turned heated, feral. "I couldn't take my eyes off you."

Victoria forced herself to continue staring at him, even though she wanted to turn away from him and the blatant sexual overtones of his words. In the safety of a ballroom or garden, she could pretend they were not a threat. But here . . . well, he could do anything he liked, and she would have little recourse.

She analyzed her next move. Evenwise was too certain in his tone to refute his claims about her identity. And he was far too large for her to attempt a physical attack, especially if he had a crew of men assisting him. She would be stopped before she could get out the door, and that could result in injury to Marah or her servants, not to mention herself.

It was too great a risk. She needed her senses if

she was to escape, so her only option was to keep talking, keep Evenwise distracted . . . and pray someone would arrive who could help them.

And she knew one subject, at least, that would capture his interest.

"Where is Chloe?" she whispered, her harsh voice cutting through the distance between them.

She heard Marah's gasp behind her, and Evenwise smiled. He shoved off the door where he had been leaning and crossed the room in a few long strides. His dark eyes sparkled with anger and lust as he caught her arms and gave her a none-too-gentle shake.

"My dear, *that* is exactly why I'm here."

She struggled in his grasp to no avail. "Take me to her, you brute," she snapped, all her emotion from the entire trying day bubbling to the surface.

He shoved her aside with a long sigh, and she staggered to maintain balance. "If only I could."

She rubbed her arms where he had held her. She would have bruises, he had crushed her so tightly.

"Don't pretend you don't know where she is. I know you took her."

He smiled, but there was no amusement in his blank stare. "I *wanted* to take her. I wanted to keep her with me, but she wouldn't allow that. Whatever you think, I am not the one responsible for her disappearance. Someone has hidden Chloe from me."

A rush of hope washed over Victoria. Evenwise was so angry, so tense, that she tended to believe his statement that Chloe was not in his custody.

She thought once again of Alyssa and her comments on saving women in bad situations. Chloe *could* be alive. Unharmed.

Evenwise glared at her. "I think your husband and his friends may have discovered her in their search. So you will come with me, and we will all make a friendly trade."

He stepped forward, and this time Victoria couldn't help but back away. His brittle smile fell as she maneuvered in front of Marah again. Her friend had not moved, and her normally sharp tongue had been silent long enough that even without looking at her, Victoria knew Marah was utterly terrified.

"You do not have to be injured if you simply show me the respect I have earned and cause me no trouble." Evenwise's gaze flickered over her. "But fight me, and I will be certain you feel the power of my anger."

"You are mad if you think I shall go with you," Victoria said with a humorless laugh. "I would never be a part of allowing Chloe to fall under your influence."

Evenwise pivoted and caught up a crystal vase on the table closest to him. With a growl, he hurtled it across the room. It shattered against the door, sending shards spraying every way. Victoria staggered back, lifting her hand to protect her face as glass skittered across the floor. Marah grabbed at her with a truncated scream.

"Do not toy with me," he said, his tone suddenly soft, but not remotely kind. "I have ways of convincing you to do my bidding."

Victoria lifted her chin in silent defiance.

Evenwise tilted his head. "I can see you are a fighter and think you can endure whatever punishment I have in store for you. But what of your friend there who is trembling like a kitten? She would not look so very pretty after some of that lot in the hallway were through with her."

Marah sucked in a heaving breath behind her, and Victoria reached back to reassure her friend. So much for her hopes to remain in the house. Perhaps it was for the best. No one was coming. That was a fool's hope. Justin was too angry to make any attempt at contact for at least a few days.

According to their discussions, his brother was meant to be watching the house, but since Caleb hadn't come storming to their rescue, she had to assume he was either injured or no longer at his post.

If no one was coming, the best she could do

was leave with Evenwise and give Marah every chance at escape to alert Justin.

"Very well," she whispered, squeezing Marah's icy fingers before she began to walk toward Evenwise.

Marah caught her hand. "No! No! Don't be foolish!"

Victoria turned on her, pulling her hand free. Marah's face was streaked with tears, her lips pale and trembling. She'd never seen her strong friend look so frightened, and she attempted a weak smile of reassurance, though all it served to do was make Marah let out a broken sob.

"My maid is very attached," she explained without looking at Evenwise.

She kept her stare trained on Marah with the hopes that through her fear, her friend would be able to read the message in her stare. If Evenwise thought Marah was more than a servant, he might take her, too.

She faced their attacker again. "But she will not fight you, and neither will I. If you leave *all* my servants here, unharmed, I will come with you without making it difficult for you and your men. Just keep my staff out of your plans."

Evenwise looked her up and down, his narrowed gaze taking in everything about her. He was reading her, trying to determine if she was lying or playing him for a fool. Finally he nodded.

"I see no reason why I would need anyone but you," he conceded. "You are the one Baybary loves."

She flinched at that assessment. But if the lie kept her safe, kept her servants and Marah from harm, she would not argue the point.

"Now just let me get my men, and we will make the final preparations for our departure."

Evenwise motioned to the door with an almost courtly bow, as if he were taking her on a carriage ride in Hyde Park. She shivered at his quick shift in mood. This was a dangerous man, in more ways than one.

And all she could hope was that she could escape him before she became his victim.

Chapter 20

Lesson 20: Your body is your greatest commodity. Protect it.

Justin was off his horse before it even came to a stop and was halfway up the stairs to the home where Victoria had been staying, Wittingham at his heels, when Shaw's carriage came rushing into the drive.

He didn't wait for his friend, but kicked the door in and burst into the quiet halls. When no servant came to check on the commotion, when there was no call of voices ringing through the silence, his heart sank.

"Victoria!" he called into the emptiness, trying desperately to check his panic. "Victoria!"

Wittingham pushed passed him. "I'll check upstairs."

Shaw ran up to him from outside, confusion lining his face. "What the hell is going on?" he asked. "The servant you sent for me was most vague."

Justin shot his friend a glance. "The servant didn't know any more than what he told you. Victoria may have been taken by Evenwise."

Saying the words out loud made his stomach turn and bile rise into his throat.

"What?" his friend repeated in shock.

"I'll explain everything later. Just help me search."

If Shaw wanted more information, he didn't ask for it. He simply clasped a hand on his friend's shoulder and headed for the back rooms. Justin flung open a few doors in the front hallway, glancing into the various dining rooms, libraries, and parlors. In some of the chambers, he found tipped over furniture in broken pieces, but no human presence to greet him.

His frustration, laced with fear, was almost at its peak when he heard a muffled sound from the back parlor. Heart racing, he hurried to the room and flung the door open. What he saw inside brought him up short.

Marah Farnsworth was sitting in a chair in the middle of the room. She had been bound with her hands behind her back, and a piece of cloth was tied around her mouth to muffle her cries for help.

Her blue eyes met his, and she let out a muted scream.

Shaking off his shock, Justin rushed to her. He pulled the gag away from her lips.

"It's all right. Where is Victoria?" he asked as he pulled a knife from his boot and cut the bonds at her wrists and around her body.

Marah didn't answer, just stared at him, shaking like a newborn. With a growl, Justin caught her arms. "Where the hell is my wife, Marah?"

"Why don't you tie her back up to the chair and beat it out of her, you lout?" came a voice from behind him.

Justin got up and spun around to find his brother in the doorway. Caleb's hair was spiked from running his fingers through the thick locks, and his eyes were just slightly glassy from at least a few drinks.

Justin stared at him, rage bubbling up in him. "Caleb? Why weren't you at your post watching the house? And what is wrong with you?"

His brother refused to meet his gaze. "Look at her."

He motioned to Marah as he came into the room. Justin followed the gesture and looked at Marah again. But this time he saw past his own terror and really *saw* her. A frightened young woman, trembling as she shied away from him, her wrists cut deeply from the ties that had bound her.

Caleb pushed past him and got to his knees in front of her.

"Marah," he whispered, his voice strangely gentle. Justin had never seen that kind of care in his brother before.

She looked up at him, tears filling her eyes. "Hello, Caleb."

His brother smiled as he reached up to push a lock of hair away from the corner of her lip. She flinched, but then relaxed.

"Sweetheart, do you know what happened to Victoria? Where is Victoria?" Caleb asked.

She shook her head. "E-Evenwise," she choked out. "He came here. He t-tied up the servants. He said you knew where Chloe was and he was going to take Victoria to make a trade."

"Where?" Justin cried.

Panic overwhelmed him as his worst fears came true. Dear God, if Evenwise would tie Marah so cruelly that she would bleed, what the hell would he do to Victoria once he had her alone?

Marah flinched, and his brother glared at him over his shoulder.

"Did he give you any clue as to where he might take her?" Caleb asked as he pulled a handkerchief from his pocket and used it to wipe away a few tears from Marah's face.

Marah shook her head. "No. He brought men—"

Her breath caught. "He said they would hurt me if she didn't go with him. She tried to protect me b-by saying I was her maid."

Caleb touched her hand gently, but didn't interrupt.

She looked up at Justin. "He didn't say where they would take her. I'm sorry."

"Don't apologize," Caleb whispered.

Justin turned to find Alexander Wittingham and Russell Shaw already waiting for him. A small collection of terrified servants were gathered behind them. From their tattered looks, some had fought the intruders.

Wittingham looked past him at Marah. "I found the staff locked in a back room. Is the girl unharmed?"

Justin nodded. "Frightened, and the bastard tied her wrists so tightly that he cut her, but she's not hurt otherwise. What do you think of what she said? You know Evenwise better. Where would he take my wife?"

Wittingham nodded. "He owns two warehouses. The men with him could have worked on his docks. We should begin our search there."

Shaw nodded. "I agree. May I bring my brother in on this? The War Department could be of help."

"I'll take any help we can get to find Victoria, go get your brother," Justin said with a sense of relief. The more people on the search, the better chance they had to find his wife.

Shaw was already heading down the hallway to the broken door and his waiting carriage.

"Wittingham, there is a pistol in the master chamber," Justin said. "In the side table. Fetch it. We may need extra firepower."

The other man turned and hurried away.

Justin turned back to Caleb. "Come on."

Caleb hadn't moved from his spot in front of Marah. "No."

Justin's lips parted in surprise. "But I—"

"I was at your home. That's why I wasn't here at my post."

Justin froze at the strange, strained tone of his brother's voice. "What are you talking about? We can discuss your reasons for not being here later. Please, I need your help."

Caleb got to his feet, and slowly he turned. Pain was slashed across his face like a knife wound. It brightened his blue eyes.

"*You* should have burned your correspondence more fully."

"Correspondence?" Justin repeated in confusion.

"Or should I say, *Mother's* correspondence?"

Staggering back, Justin stared. His stomach turned. He had been ready to destroy the last remnants of his mother's letters when Wittingham intruded. Once he realized Victoria was in danger, he hadn't thought about the evidence again.

But if his brother had come to the house and seen the destruction in the parlor, of course he would have entered. Of course he would have picked up burned letters, if only out of concern for Justin's well-being.

"Caleb," Justin began. He held up his hands in mute entreaty, for he could think of nothing to say. No way to explain himself or the truth about his brother's life.

"Come on," Wittingham said from the hallway as he passed by on his way to the front door. "We have no time to waste."

Suddenly the pain Caleb had shown so clearly was wiped away. He straightened his shoulders.

"Right now your priority should be Victoria." He turned his attention back to Marah. "And mine is here. Someone must stay in case Evenwise sends men back."

At that, Marah shivered from head to toe. Justin pursed his lips. Caleb was correct. He couldn't leave the household unprotected until they were certain Evenwise wasn't able to hurt anyone again.

But the idea of abandoning his brother now . . .

"Caleb," Justin said softly.

His brother looked over his shoulder, and the two men locked eyes. Justin searched his brother's face, hoping to find some indication of how he felt. But there was nothing.

"Go find your wife," Caleb said quietly before he returned his attention to Marah and her raw wrists. "You and I will talk about everything when you return."

Justin nodded. That would have to be good enough. Victoria's safety was more important than anything else at present. He just hoped that he would return with her unharmed. And that his relationship with his younger brother would somehow overcome the secret he had kept.

The room smelled of musty crates and unwashed bodies. Victoria shifted from her uncomfortable position on the hard, uneven floor, but her bound hands kept her from removing the blindfold over her eyes.

She growled out her frustration and discomfort. One of Evenwise's hired men had tied her. At least he'd had the decency to look apologetic, unlike Evenwise, who had seemed to take perverse pleasure in hurting Marah while he bound her. Victoria winced as she thought of her friend's muffled sounds of pain as he tightened the ropes. She could only hope Marah would be found quickly and helped.

As for herself . . .

She strained to hear anything that would aid in

her escape. She'd been in this place for over half an hour, and without her sight, her other senses were slowly becoming clearer. The room was big, she had been able to tell that from the echoing voices of her captors when she was brought inside. It was mostly empty, too. They hadn't been forced to maneuver her around many items.

She pursed her lips in frustration. If she couldn't even determine her location, how in the world would Justin find her? He didn't even know she was missing. It could be a day or more before anyone came searching. By then, God only knew what Evenwise would do.

Her heart throbbed at the thought, but she tamped her fear down. No. Evenwise claimed he wanted her for a trade. He would keep her alive at least until he made contact with Justin and demanded Chloe.

Once he did that, someone would come for her. She had to believe that.

Until then, she would take care of herself.

She refocused on her surroundings. In the distance, she heard men's voices calling to one another in strong, crude accents. There was a banging of wood and metal and the occasional slap of water.

The docks. She was likely on one of the docks that dotted the Thames. From the sounds of the footsteps, there were quite a few men outside. That meant she would have to be careful if she managed an escape. The last thing she wanted to do was run headlong into the arms of a man with just as sinister an intent as Evenwise's.

The sound of a door opening to her right echoed through her head like a gunshot. Scrambling, she turned to face the intruder though she couldn't see whoever it was.

"You look terrified," came a voice she instantly recognized as Evenwise's. He chuckled, and it sent a chill through her. "Don't worry, my dear. Tonight your husband will receive a note from me, detailing how he can get you back. Assuming he doesn't act a fool, by tomorrow afternoon you will be safely in your 'mistress' quarters, only slightly rat-bitten."

Victoria shuddered at the thought, unable to hold back a little cry of displeasure. Now that Evenwise had mentioned rats, the hairs on her neck and arms stood up and her skin itched.

"And what if Justin refuses?" she hissed. "What if he doesn't know where Chloe is? Or he won't bring her to you?"

Evenwise's boots shuffled as he moved toward her. She felt his breath on her cheek when he crouched down in front of her. "Then you will still be returned eventually, only it will be slightly worse for wear. As punishment."

His sudden touch on her cheek made her recoil, skirting back only to find she was pinned against the wall. His second chuckle vibrated up her spine as he braced one hand on either side of her head. He leaned in, blowing a steady stream of air against her face that she turned away from as best she could.

He was toying with her.

"You know, you are almost lovelier than Chloe," he mused. "Perhaps I can arrange a way to keep you both."

"You are a bastard," she bit out.

His fingers traced her cheekbone, and she gasped at the touch of his skin on hers. How she hated her hands being bound, her sight removed. She had no way to dodge, no way to fight. Nowhere to run.

And he knew it.

"The way Baybary looks at you from across a room, you must be something to behold in bed," Evenwise continued, stroking his thumb lower to her jawline. "And he would know, wouldn't he? He's certainly had more than his fair share of women. Yes, perhaps I'll just keep you both. Once Baybary arrives with Chloe—"

"He won't," she spat, yanking away from his touch yet again.

"Oh, he will," he breathed, this time next to her ear. "He loves you. He would trade his own mother for you if I told him you would suffer for his refusal."

She shook her head. That wasn't true, but it could very well be the only thing keeping her alive and untouched beyond this torture of the graze of Evenwise's fingertips.

"Thanks to your foolish ruse as Baybary's mistress, no one knows who you really are. Since you have lived in the countryside for so long, it could take months before anyone realized you were missing. Your staff could be easily silenced through the proper methods."

"And what about Justin?" she asked, her stomach turning as his breath washed over her lips.

"There is nothing that says he couldn't meet with a tragic accident when he comes to make the exchange. If his body washed up on the shores of the Thames, I would wager people would chalk it up to years of living dangerously. No one would care much if one more spoiled rake left this world."

Victoria's eyes went wide beneath her blindfold. Evenwise wasn't just tormenting her anymore. He meant it. He had every intention of killing Justin if he got a chance. Rage pulled its veil over her, pure anger at the idea that this disgusting excuse for a man would harm her husband. Use her as a pawn in his twisted game.

Before she could say anything, Evenwise's mouth clamped over hers. His tongue pressed past her lips to assault her with a painful force that stole her breath.

She thought of Chloe, she thought of Marah. But mostly she thought of her husband. Of Justin falling into the cold river. Of his lifeless body washing up on shore.

She bit down until she tasted blood.

Evenwise yanked back with a roar of anguish.

"You little bitch," he cried, and then his fist made contact with her cheek.

Victoria's mind went fuzzy as an explosion of pain took away all her ability to think or react. Through her fog, she felt Evenwise grasp her upper arms as she slipped sideways. He slammed her against the wall, and another burst of pain rocked through her cloudy mind. He slammed her back a second time, and then there was only darkness.

Chapter 21

Lesson 21: Never fall in love.

Justin had long moved past the point of pretending panic wasn't taking over every part of him. It clawed at him and blurred his vision.

It had been well over an hour since they'd discovered Marah alone in Victoria's house. He and Wittingham had arrived at the docks where Evenwise had his holdings shortly afterward and had separated to save time. Since then they had been joined by Shaw and his brother's friends from the War Department.

But it had been a frustrating hour of searching to no avail. Every moment they found no clues, Justin feared for Victoria's life. Images were beginning to creep into his brain. Horrible pictures of Victoria afraid, hurt, even . . .

No.

He shook them away. He refused to think of his wife, so full of life, as anything but fine. He would find her.

He had to.

"You, boy!" he called out to a child of about eleven who had just slipped away from the part of the dock that contained one of Evenwise's warehouses.

The child flinched and eyed him suspiciously. He was filthy to the bone, his clothes little more than rags around his slender shoulders.

"What you want?" he grunted, slouching over and giving a glare that Justin could only assume was meant to be tough. Instead it came off as sad and jaded.

"Have you seen a woman around here?" Justin asked.

The boy coughed out a laugh that was far too wise for his years. "'Undreds of 'em, guv. What kind do you like?"

Justin pursed his lips. "Not a lightskirt, boy. A lady. And she wouldn't have been coming of her own volition."

The child's brow wrinkled in confusion. "Vo-li-"

Justin shook his head. "She would have been fighting."

The little boy's face went passive, and he stared at Justin evenly. "Wa's it worth to you?"

He looked the child up and down. "Twenty pounds."

The boy staggered back. "Lor'. Yeah, I know the bird."

Justin's heart leapt into his chest as he leaned in closer. He wanted to rail and demand, but he remembered Caleb's calm behavior with Marah and tried to rein in his emotions.

"What's your name?"

"Why you want to know?" the child asked suspiciously.

Justin tilted his head and speared the boy with a stern look.

He shrugged. "Tom. Can I have me money?"

"Half now," Justin said as he dug in his pocket for the blunt. "Half after I find her."

Tom seemed to consider that for a moment, then shrugged. "It's a fair bargain."

He took the money Justin held out and stuffed it into his worn boot with an apprehensive look around him.

"Tell me what you know," Justin said.

"Me cousin works for Evenwise," Tom said, motioning behind them toward the warehouse. "I came down to bring him somethin' from me ma, and he told me Evenwise paid him a pretty penny to break into some fancy lady's house and take her. He felt real bad about it, too."

Justin clenched his fists at the thought of Victoria being touched by some wretched thug. He could make the man feel so much worse.

"Where did he take the fancy lady?" he asked, measuring his tone.

"Dunno." Tom shrugged. "'E had to go back to work afore he could tell me."

Justin ground his teeth. "Can you show me which man is your cousin?"

The child eyed him, his mistrust renewed. "You ain't gonna kill 'im or nothin', are ya?"

Justin drew back in surprise at the serious tone of the child's voice. It was the sound of someone who had seen plenty of death. "No."

"Swear," the boy pressed. "Wren's the only one workin' since Ma got sick. If he dies, she won't get her medicine. Swear."

Justin sighed. "I swear I won't hurt him, Tom. In fact, if I get my fancy lady back, I promise that you and your ma won't ever have to worry again about where she's getting her medicine. Is *that* a fair bargain?"

The boy's eyes went as wide as saucers, but still he hesitated. "You promise?"

Justin held out his hand. "I give you my word as a gentleman."

Tom seemed to consider that for a moment before he held out a greasy hand in return.

"It's a bargain. Come on!" he shouted before he darted off toward the warehouse.

Justin lengthened his stride to keep up with the scamp and crouched down beside some crates as the boy indicated a tall, gangly youth in the distance. He was loading crates, but even from far away, Justin could see the mournful expression on the lad's face.

"That's Wren," Tom whispered.

Justin reached out to tousle the boy's dirty hair. "Good lad. Now here, take the other ten." He tossed the boy the rest of the blunt and held out one of his cards. "And come to this address tomorrow. We'll work out how to make sure your ma gets what she needs. Do you know how to read?"

"No. But old lady Quincy at the pub does. Hope you find your fancy lady, guv!" The boy shoved the card and the money into his other boot and was already off into the crowd.

Justin pushed to his feet and strode into the dock slowly. The men who were working hardly paid him any heed as he approached the young man called Wren.

"What you want, mister?" he asked sullenly when Justin reached his side.

"How much did Evenwise pay you to take my wife?" Justin asked low.

The man's eyes jolted up, and a dark flush colored his pale cheeks. "I—I—" he stammered, backing away.

Justin caught his arm and held him in place.

His anger faded as he felt the frail boniness. With his terrified expression, the young man looked hardly more than a child himself. And if he was supporting a family, Evenwise's blunt might have made too tempting a draw to refuse.

With a sigh, Justin thought of his promise to Tom.

"Tell these boys I'll triple his payment, whatever it was, if they help me instead."

Justin looked around at the small group of men beside the warehouse doors. Wittingham and Shaw were at the front of the pack, along with a handful of War Department gentlemen. But mixed in were half a dozen dockworkers who had taken his offer for blunt. The ones who hadn't had already run for their skins when they saw the dark, angry purpose in Justin's expression.

"Now listen, you lot," Justin growled quietly. "There is only one rule. No one is to let any harm come to Victoria. I swear to heaven itself, if one hair on the head of the woman I love is touched by any of you, I will make the wrath of God look tame. Understood?"

Nods in the crowd reassured him, even though he didn't understand why Shaw was staring at him like he had snakes growing out of his skull.

Turning, Justin threw all his weight into the door and broke it down.

A rush of men came screaming into the warehouse with Justin at their forefront.

"Victoria!" he cried as they scattered into the wide space.

He stepped around a line of boxes and found what he was looking for. Victoria leaned halfway against the back wall of the warehouse. She was blindfolded, her hands twisted behind her back, and even though Justin couldn't see her eyes, he could tell from her limp form that she was unconscious . . . or worse.

"There's the bastard! Trying to go out the side window!" someone called, and a group of men rushed off in the direction he had indicated. But Justin no longer cared.

He ran to Victoria's side, yanking the blindfold from her face and tossing it away as he gathered her into his arms. Her head lolled back, cheek bruised and eyes shut in unnatural slumber.

A vise wrapped around his heart as he leaned down to see if she was still breathing, and he had never been so relieved as when the soft brush of her breath tickled his ear.

"Victoria," he murmured, holding her closer. His cheek pressed against her unbruised one, and he rubbed the satiny skin gently. "Victoria, wake up."

She didn't stir. Justin tried not to think of all the horrors he had heard about injuries to the head.

"Listen to me," he whispered close to her ear. "You promised to obey me when we said our vows three years ago. And I am telling you to wake up. I am telling you to hear me. I'm *asking* you to let me love you, Victoria."

He drew back to look at her face, and he realized what he had just said. *That* was why Shaw had stared at him so strangely. He had admitted not once, but twice, that he loved her.

Before he could let that truly sink in, her eyes came open, dark green and unfocused. She looked at him with a foggy smile.

"You came for me," she whispered. "I didn't think you'd come for me."

Justin smiled at her even though her words cut him deeper than any knife could have. *That* was his legacy to her. Her belief that he would always abandon her. But no more. He would never again let her think that.

"I will *always* come for you," he whispered, his voice catching.

"Good," she said. But then she shut her eyes again.

Victoria nodded at the doctor who was droning on and on as she lay on the big bed in Justin's home. Hours had passed since she'd woken up here, her head pounding and her mind ringing with foggy fantasies that Justin had told her he loved her.

She pushed that aside when the doctor finally left with a few stern admonishments. As he exited, two women entered, and Victoria could hardly contain herself.

"Chloe," she cried, as a beautiful blond woman with dark brown eyes launched herself onto the bed with a laughing sob. For a long moment, the two women hung on to each other, too emotional to be coherent.

Victoria opened her eyes to see Marah standing aside at the door. Though she was smiling, there was a strange expression on her face. Something stiff and distant.

"Come over here, Marah," she said as Chloe extracted herself from Victoria's arms and sat on the bed at her feet. "You belong in this hug as well."

Marah laughed. "I have been hugging her since Wittingham brought her here an hour ago. But I have not allowed her to tell me the story. I thought after all we've been through . . ." She hesitated. "All we sacrificed, that we deserved to hear her tale together."

"Yes, tell," Victoria said with a laugh.

Chloe fiddled with her hem as she quietly told her tale of falling in love with Wittingham, being stalked by Evenwise, and finally going into hiding with Wittingham and Alyssa's assistance.

"I told Alex that you would be worried, but he

didn't want to risk my making contact with you while Evenwise was still searching. I never in the world thought you would come looking for me," she said, and her voice caught. "I am so sorry I put you in danger, Victoria. So very, very sorry."

Victoria leaned down and caught her friend's hand, tangling their fingers and squeezing gently. "I would do it all again if it meant bringing you home safely. I don't regret a thing."

She smiled. She meant that. Being in such danger had made everything clear in her mind. Perhaps Justin would never return her love, but it no longer hurt her to love him. It was far more than some people ever got in life.

"What happened to Evenwise?" she finally whispered, shivering as she thought of his brutal attack and the final moments when she believed she would die.

Marah smiled. "Justin, Shaw, and Wittingham took care of *that* issue."

Victoria gasped. "He's dead?"

"No," Chloe said, touching her hand for reassurance. "But he's already gone on the last ship out of London bound for the Orient." She smiled. "Justin made certain he won't be back."

"Justin," Victoria said with a sigh. The fact that he hadn't come to her when she awoke spoke volumes. "And where is my husband?"

"Pacing outside the door like a tiger with his

friend Shaw and that very handsome brother of his." Chloe laughed.

Marah flinched visibly, and Victoria looked at her with a wrinkled brow. But before she could question her friend's reaction, Chloe added, "Marah says you believe yourself in love with him."

Victoria spun her attention on her other friend. "You two didn't discuss this in his presence, did you?"

"Of course not." Chloe smiled sadly. "I understand, Victoria. I, too, love someone who I cannot have. Wittingham already refused my love once."

Victoria sighed as the two women locked eyes, forging a new bond over men with whom they could not have the future they desired.

Marah stepped toward the door, "Should I have him come in?"

Victoria shook her head. "I need a moment more before I face him."

Because when she did, she didn't want him to see her heart in her eyes. If all he could give her in return was lust and pity, she couldn't share her feelings with him. It wasn't fair to either one of them.

Chapter 22

Lesson 22: If you break the rules, do it with all your heart.

Justin stared at his brother, the silence between them like a wall. Caleb leaned against the door across from Justin's chamber, a cheroot hanging lazily from his mouth. Every affectation said he was as calm as ever, but Justin could see the pain in his brother's eyes.

Pain that both Justin's lies and his recent stammering of the truth had helped put there.

"I should have told you," he said abruptly. "But when Reed proved to me that his claims were true with the letters you found, it ripped me apart. I was too cowardly to do the same, to do worse, to you."

"This was what changed your relationship with Mother and—" His brother broke off abruptly.

Justin nodded. "Yes. Neither of them knows the secret. It was too hard to face them. And I hated lying to you. I hope you know that."

Caleb was silent for a long moment. "I suppose I should appreciate your protection. But I can't at the moment. All I can think about is that you knew something so powerful about me for over three years. And you never told me. Even though you are my best friend."

Justin dipped his chin in shame. "Yes. And what will you do with the information now?"

His brother barked out a humorless laugh. "Are you asking if I'll confront Mother, confess to Father? No. I'll join you in this tangled web of lies. But what about Martin Reed? How can you be certain *he'll* remain silent?"

Justin shook his head. "In the commotion after Victoria was taken, one of the servants notified her father. While the doctor was examining her, I had a long conversation with Reed. He confessed that those letters were all the physical evidence he had of Mother's betrayal."

"So the drunken sot was so thick as to bring them to you?" Caleb shook his head. "Stupid, stupid *bastard*."

Justin winced at Caleb's emphasis on the last word. "He may be that, but in some twisted way he does love his daughter. The fact that I saved her life seems to have softened his view of me. I think as long as I continue to provide him the small stipend I pay each month, he'll keep silent."

"Hmmm."

Justin watched his brother carefully. He could see that Caleb was still processing everything he'd heard. It would probably be a long time before he truly felt and understood it all.

Caleb looked down the hallway to where Wittingham sat at the top of the stairs out of earshot. "And why is *he* still here?"

Justin fisted his hands at his sides. There was so much more he longed to say to his brother, but it wasn't the time. Only Caleb could determine when he would forgive. Justin could not make him recover from the shock any faster by pushing him.

"I believe Wittingham is going to ask Chloe to be his wife," Justin said. "It seems it was a day for changes of heart."

Caleb turned his seeing gaze back on Justin. "What about your heart? Before he left to take care of the Evenwise problem, Shaw said you confessed being in love with Victoria."

Justin shuffled restlessly. For so many years it had been he and Shaw and Caleb, carousing around London, doing as they pleased. But in a few short weeks, everything had changed. His brother no longer looked at him with openness.

And he had fallen in love with the wife he never

wanted. His life had been altered. But could they truly overcome a past filled with blackmail and lies?

"Is love enough?" he mused out loud. "I married her based upon a falsehood and tormented her for years with the knowledge of my infidelity. She kept a bitter secret from me that I should have known. Is there room there for love? For a future?"

Caleb pushed off the door and took a step toward him. "Why not? The past is unchangeable, but the future is unwritten. You can fill it with empty encounters with women you don't even remember the next day. Or you can wipe away what has happened before and love the woman in that room. It's your choice."

His brother reached out to briefly clasp his upper arm, then let go and turned away to depart.

Justin watched him for a few steps before he called out, "Will you be all right?"

His brother hesitated, his shoulders rolling forward in a slump.

"Yes," he said softly. "Just not today."

Justin remained silent as he watched Caleb disappear down the stairs. It was going to take a long time to repair the relationship with his brother. But he believed they would one day be as close as they had once been. And if that was true, why couldn't it also be true that he could build a future with Victoria? If he only tried.

Drawing a deep breath, he entered her chamber.

Victoria's laughter faded as Justin slipped into the master bedroom.

"Ladies," he drawled, his deep voice sending a little twinge of longing through her. "I would like a moment with my wife."

Chloe and Marah gave her a glance, but didn't argue. As Chloe passed by Justin, he murmured, "I believe Lord Wittingham is waiting for you."

Her friend paled, then hurried into the hallway.

As the door shut, leaving her alone with her husband, Victoria sat up. Her head spun, but she blinked away the dizziness and stared at Justin.

Although they had shared every intimacy imaginable since she had come to London, she was suddenly at a loss for words. Shy as she had been the night of their wedding.

But Justin seemed to be at no such loss. He crossed the room in a few long strides and sat down on the bed beside her. He cupped her bruised cheek with infinite tenderness, and then his mouth was on hers. She clung to him with the realization that these moments would soon come to an end. He pulled back with a low groan.

She turned her face with a blush and picked at the soft white coverlet.

"Wh-why is Wittingham still here?" she asked, filling the silence with an empty question.

"He's going to ask Chloe to marry him."

Her gaze darted up in shock. From just the few moments she had spent speaking to Chloe, she knew that her friend was deeply in love with the young viscount. And while she should have been happy for Chloe's good fortune, she found that her overriding emotion was jealousy.

Chloe would receive the happy ending she desired.

And Victoria would go home to an empty estate.

"I'm glad for her," she whispered. "She deserves love."

He nodded. "Yes."

A long silence stretched between them, until Justin reached out to touch her hand. The gesture was featherlight.

"Victoria, when I saw you lying on that warehouse floor, when I thought you might be dead—" He cut himself off, and his breath shuddered. "It was the worst moment of my life."

She smiled as she reached out to trace the line of his jaw with a finger. "But I am unharmed. And we have had success in finding Chloe. Everything we hoped for has come to pass. And now I can—I can leave."

He hesitated. "And what if I asked you to stay?"

Victoria swallowed hard as she stared at him. "We have shared so much, Justin. And you tempt me more than you could ever know. But I couldn't stay here as your lover or your mistress. It isn't practical. Even if it was—"

She broke off. Did she really want to share her heart so openly with a man who didn't love her in return? Did she really want to take that risk?

"Even if it was, what?" Justin asked, his tone serious and his face more focused than she had ever seen it.

She turned away. If she was going to make a humiliating confession, at least she didn't want to see his pity or his discomfort.

"Even if it was, I don't think I could live with just being your lover." She shook her head. "I want—I want more than that. But you are free, Justin. You always have been. In time, you would be bored of me and turn to someone else. And that is one thing to realize from Baybary, where it is a distant reality. But if I were here . . . I think it would break my heart."

He made no response and was quiet for so long that she forced herself to look at him. His face was pensive, dark, but there was no pity.

"Do you know why I never took a mistress after we married?" he finally asked.

Victoria shook her head. That was the one question that had haunted her. "No."

He hesitated, as if admitting this was painful to him. "Because whether I wanted to believe it or not, you ruined every other woman for me. I compared them all to you . . . and no one lived up to you."

Victoria swallowed hard. "No?"

He ran a hand through his hair. "No. But since you came back into my life, it is like a piece of myself has returned. Something I never acknowledged was missing." He touched her chin, tilting her face until she looked into his dark eyes. "But now I do not think I could live without it. That is why I am not asking you to be my lover. I am asking you to be my wife."

She blinked. "Justin, we are already married."

He shook his head. "I am not asking you to marry me, Victoria. I am asking you to *be my wife*. Not in name alone. Not only in my bed. In my life. With no one else ever between us."

Her lips parted. She was still unconscious. That was the only explanation for his words. In a moment she would wake, and this lovely dream would be over.

"Victoria?" he asked, brow wrinkling. "Do you intend to answer?"

She pinched herself, but nothing happened.

"Justin, you cannot m-mean what you're asking," she finally stammered.

"I am certain I do," he said with a little smile

that melted her heart. "I don't want to lose you. The past, it is tangled. There is no denying there has been pain, there have been lies. We have each made mistakes. But I am in love with you."

She snatched her hands away from his with a little cry. Covering her mouth, she stared at him.

He continued without awaiting her response. "That may not be something that is easy to accept. Or even an emotion you feel in return after all these years of separation and pain. But if you stay with me, I will prove to you that I can be trusted. I can be true to you. I can make you happy." He stared at her, and there was so much emotion in his eyes that it brought her to tears. "I want to make you happy, Victoria."

She lowered her fingers from her lips. "Oh, Justin. I have tried so hard to fight my own heart. I told myself that I could leave you when this was over. Forget you. But the more time we spent together, the more I realized that forgetting you was impossible. I realized that if I returned home alone, that I would take my love for you with me. Even if I only had my memories of our time together in London as comfort."

His face softened in relief. "Then you are saying you love me as well?"

She nodded. "I do."

His face brightened, and hope like she had never seen before lit there.